THE DESIGNATED ONES

From Jerusalem to Ethiopia

BROWN REFLECTIONS

THE DESIGNATED ONES
From Jerusalem to Ethiopia

Copyright © 2019 by Karen Sloan-Brown

All rights reserved.
No part of this work may be reproduced or transmitted in any form or by any means, electronic or mechanical, including photocopying and recording, or by any information storage or retrieval system, except as may be expressly permitted by the 1976 Copyright Act or in writing from the publisher. Requests for permission should be addressed to Brown Reflections, Brown Reflectons, PO Box 281892, Nashville, Tennessee 37228. Brown-Reflections.com.

ISBN:
97819444401455

Library of Congress Cataloging-in-Publication Data on file.

MANUFACTURED IN THE UNITED STATES OF AMERICA

THE DESIGNATED ONES

From Jerusalem to Ethiopia

KAREN SLOAN-BROWN

This book is dedicated to my dear uncle, James Edward Frierson. It was at his funeral that a priest stood up and said to our family, "I believe you all are the lost tribe of Levi." That statement stuck in my head; and through some casual research, I learned of the Lemba tribe. Geneticists have found their DNA to be related to the descendants of Aaron, the priestly tribe of Levi. I was intrigued, and the concept for this book was realized.

Table of Contents

Introduction

"And the Lord *will scatter you among all peoples, from one end of the earth to the other, and there you shall serve other gods of wood and stone, which neither you nor your fathers have known." Deuteronomy 28:64*

That which is lost never loses the essence of its roots. Transplanted into foreign surroundings, the nature of its origin remains intact, even as a lion, snatched out of the jungle and placed in captivity, is no less fierce or aware of its instincts. As natural as a duck takes to water at birth, having the ability to swim coded into the fiber of its being, so are human characteristics passed on to their descendants, not by happenstance but divinely designated.

Some of us would like to believe we have authority, that our course is not already chosen, as written in the poem *Invictus*: "I am the master of my fate: I am the captain of my soul," but those of faith know that God has predetermined our lot; He controls our existence. Still, the better part of our lives is clouded in mystery without knowing the absolute path that leads to our destiny.

This awesome journey is not straightforward. It twists, turns, races ahead, and sometimes reverses. Much is lost or left behind on this trek as the essential provisions are cumbersome. For those who have lost their history, there is no way of knowing when they will collide head-on into their past. In some instances, the past and destiny are one and the same.

Prologue

I wanted to get on my feet and shout, rock this plane with praises. Instead I whispered, "Thank you, Lord," as I read Ephesians 4:8: "Just think! Though I did nothing to deserve it, and though I am the most useless Christian there is, yet I was the one chosen for this special joy of telling the Gentiles the glad news of the endless treasures available to them in Christ."

The revival was over, all said and done, and I still couldn't grasp the idea of it. I took off my glasses and leaned back against the cool leather of the headrest and closed my eyes. I could still envision the mass of people filling the expansive room and feel their rising anticipation of hearing me bring the Word. It buoyed me to the stage, and I rode it like a wave.

There I was, standing behind the podium, preaching from the Book of Joshua, trying to be a source of encouragement to this great gathering, and my own faith was renewed. If only Daddy could have been there to see it, to experience it all with me, I know it would have made a difference. My thoughts flashed back to the day he had had his first stroke.

"It's God's way, not ours," he told me in slurred words.

"Times have changed, Daddy. We're almost through the 20th century. Women can preach God's Word as well as any man."

Daddy grabbed the straps of his suspenders as if they held him up instead of his pants. "I only know what my father and

his father before him and his father before him and as far back
as we can recollect have been told. God ordained the men in
our family to be caretakers of His Word. I can't change the
Word or His ordinances just because the times have changed."

My jaws tightened. Why did he have to be so stubborn,
so stuck in his old-timey ways? "My call is real. Nobody
can tell me otherwise," I replied with conviction, trying to
control my emotions.

"In our teachings, it's not in God's plan for a woman to be
a steward of His Word," Daddy answered slowly, straining to
form each syllable, "Her responsibilities to her family are too
demanding for her to minister to the people."

He would repeat that to me on more than one occasion,
sometimes pensively, other times in protest. It was plain that
I couldn't convince him with my words. I would have to prove
it to him with my actions. Even now, I can't believe that it has
been 19 years since we had that first conversation. So, still after
preaching at the Christian Conference in Toronto before 30,000
people as the keynote speaker, I wondered if he'd approve of me.

I was about to put my glasses back on and continue reading
my Bible when the plane wobbled like a car rushing over a
speed bump. I shot a questioning glance toward James, who
was sitting in the aisle seat, one over from me. He closed the
magazine he was browsing through, but he didn't look up.
I could see his brow was furrowed and he was wearing the
expression he wore whenever he was unsure about something.

Timothy, our son, who was seated directly across the
aisle, turned toward us with wide worried eyes. "What was
that, Mama?"

"I don't know, sweetheart," I answered, trying to sound

confident. "I guess it was some turbulence. We may have run into that storm they were talking about."

James remained quiet. The chattering of the choir members seated behind us had gone eerily silent. Then we heard something that sounded like pieces of metal spinning around in a blender. The murmurs in the rear started again and were getting louder with each passing second.

"Pastor Priscilla, lead us in prayer!" Kenny, our choir director, called up to me earnestly.

I'd heard him say those words so many times, but tonight, they made my heart skip a beat. I stood up to face them and was interrupted.

"Ladies and gentlemen, please fasten your seatbelts!" the flight attendant at the front said urgently, speaking through the intercom, even though the plane was small enough for us to hear her without using it. "We're passing through some rough weather."

She was attempting to remain composed, but I detected a tremor in her voice. That let me know that we were in trouble, serious trouble. I clenched my hands into a fist to keep them from shaking, ignoring the pain of my nails digging into my skin. *This can't be happening*, I thought. My head rushed with regrets. This is my fault. Why did I charter this flight? We could have waited and flown on a commercial airline. It was my vanity and anxiousness to get back home to let Daddy know about how well things had gone.

The plane rocked and dipped.

"Help us, Lord!" somebody in the back shrieked.

Then I heard voices crying in harmony. My distress shifted into panic.

"James, I'm scared," I said only loud enough for him to hear.

"Pray, Princess, that's all we can do. It's in God's hands."

I should have listened to James's protests. We'd argued about me not wanting to wait. There had been warnings of a blizzard on the Canadian news. The forecast stated that much of the Northeast was getting clobbered with snow and freezing rain. Dozens of flights had been canceled. Instead, I insisted that we try to schedule a flight that evening and beat the storm.

The engine sputtered, and the plane shook. Then abruptly it turned sideways, and we were in freefall. All that I saw through the window were flashes of white mixed in the darkness. It could have been clouds or snow. I didn't know which. Screams echoed through the plane, first one, then many others.

"Put on your oxygen masks, and brace yourselves!" the flight attendant shouted. "We're going to have a hard landing!"

"Mama!" Timothy shrieked, his terrified voice muffled by the mask.

I lifted my mask up to speak. "I'm here, baby, it'll be all right." The words were for me as much as they were for him.

In a quick move, James threw his mask to the side, unfastened his seatbelt, and struggled to get into the seat next to our son. I squeezed my eyes tightly. My mind was reeling like the plane.

Is this how it ends? Will I feel any pain before I die? I thought about Daddy and Mama, imagining the sorrow they would feel when they received the call. Suddenly, the lights on the plane went dark. Pleading and praying, I reached for James's hand, but it wasn't there. I bowed my head in my lap and screamed, with my screeches hidden among those of others. Then I heard what sounded like a bomb exploding, throwing my seat through the air like a carnival ride.

Then everything went black.

I woke up, choking on the fumes and smoke from the burning fuel that enveloped the carnage around me like a thick fog. I was either numb or cold. In a daze, I couldn't distinguish whether a terrible thing had happened or whether I'd been caught in a horrible vivid dream. Not wanting to know, I shut my eyes and my mind from the possibility.

Chapter One
The Stranger

T his generational flashback began on September 29, 2014, the day I decided to end my unbearable suffering. The bottle of Petrus 1982 from my trip to Paris was perfect for the occasion. I've always been partial to the sensuous texture of Bordeaux.

Comfortably stretched out on my favorite chaise on the patio and wearing white silk pajamas, I poured myself a generous glass. I swirled the deep red blend and breathed in the bouquet before I took a sip. I held it in my mouth and savored its earthy essence. There was no need to rush the moment, especially with a $1,000 bottle of wine. I was in control of time. Finally, it was in my hands—or at least in the small bottle of pills beside me on the table that would ultimately erase the pain.

I was all alone in every sense of the word. There was no one to stop me. And why should they? It wasn't as if I was taking my own life. I had died more than a month ago in a plane crash.

I took another large sip of the wine, inhaled deeply, and stared out in the darkness. It was a beautiful night. The sky was peppered with countless stars and brightened by a full incandescent moon. The intermittent evening breeze soothed me, even though it had a slight coolness to it. I pulled my chenille blanket up over my shoulders. All around me, I could feel the transition in the air. Soon the earth would yield that from which summer seeds were sown. It seemed fitting for this occasion. Autumn is the season for relinquishing.

Halfway through my second glass of wine, I relaxed my eyelids to enjoy the aroma and to heighten my sense of taste. Within a few moments, I sensed a presence near me and opened my eyes to find standing over me a tall, middle-aged man wearing a tan caftan of rough woven fabric. Startled, I sat up so quickly, I spilled a bit of wine on the blanket.

The man had bushy silver hair, with a few remnants of black at the top, gray eyes, and skin that made me think of a brown fallen leaf that had once been green and full of life.

"Is this how you give thanks for the blessings you have received?" he asked in a chastising tone of familiarity.

"Who are you, and how did you get into my house?" I snapped with agitation, angrier about the interruption of my thoughts than afraid of what he would do.

"It doesn't matter who I am. I came here on my own volition."

I was completely confounded by his audacity. "I'm going to call the police if you don't get out of here!" I threatened, sliding my feet to ground and well aware that I had purposely left my cell phone in the kitchen on my way out.

"You have no reason to fear me," he replied, holding his palms open toward me. "I'm not here to hurt you." It was then that I saw a white aura emanating from him like the glow around a lightbulb. *He's a ghost or possibly a figment of my imagination*, I deduced, feeling mellowed by the wine. I didn't detect any signs of danger, so I exhaled, put my feet up, and relaxed my back against the chaise.

"Why are you here then, Mister?" I asked impatiently.

"Are you not grateful for God's favor?" he asked, staring at me.

"First of all," I said, crossing my ankles, "you have a lot of nerve trespassing on my property and questioning me. I don't know you, and I'm pretty sure you don't know me."

"Oh, but I do know you, Priscilla, I know you very well."

That made me mad all over again. He was much too presumptuous. I swung my legs to the side of the chaise again, ready to stand. "Look, whoever you are, I don't know how you know my name, but I'm trying to have a quiet and very private evening!"

"I know what you're trying to do, beloved, and I want you to tell me what's so agonizing in your life that you must surrender."

I was absolutely taken aback. "I don't see how that is any of your business!"

"Beloved, your plans are premature."

"Uh, uh, that's where you're wrong. Actually, my plans are long overdue. I've already stayed in the storm too long. Now I need peace."

"That's just it. You don't recognize peace unless you have suffered."

"I have suffered. I've fought, battled, and bled. Now I'm tired and want to die in peace."

He shook his head. "That's because you still don't recognize your victory. Yes, you've been tested, chastised, and allowed to suffer, but you are not alone in that. When you don't know where you've come from, you are ungrateful for where you are."

I glared up at him, his eyes shining like glass in the dark. He met my gaze as if looking through me. I didn't need this hassle right now.

"That's enough!" I said, putting my feet up and leaning back again. "You're trespassing, and I want you to leave."

"If you allow me to tell you a story first, then I'll leave."

"A story about what?" I asked, frowning with irritation. Why was this stranger or apparition ruining my planned evening?

"It's a story of the human experience: birth, knowledge, blessings, defeat, oppression, deliverance, sins, redemption, and victory."

I dropped my head back hard against the chaise, rolled my eyes, and looked back up into the sky in frustration.

"What if I don't want to hear your story?"

"It's not my story, Priscilla, it's your story."

I took a deep breath and stared into the abyss that were his eyes. "What could you possibly know about my story? I've never even seen you before."

"Your story is a lengthy one," he said, unperturbed. "You come from a people who never relented or retreated. It goes back thousands of years, beginning with Abraham, father of many nations, father to Isaac, grandfather to Jacob, and great-grandfather to the 12 tribes of Israel. The story crosses numerous generations."

I raised my hand to stop him. "Spare me, old man, I'm a preacher's daughter. I know that story. Besides, you've got the wrong address, Mister. I'm not Jewish."

"That's not what I'm saying to you. What you are is a descendant of the Hebrew people, specifically the Levites, the God-anointed priests."

I smirked and gave him a side-glance. "That's a bit of a stretch, don't you think?"

"Not at all, my dear, that's just the beginning. There's so much more to tell."

It was time to bring this unwanted visit to an end. "I'm sure that is an interesting tale, but I've got other plans this evening."

"I know you've lost your faith. That is why I'm here. You were about to do a disservice to yourself and to your ancestors."

"That's where you're wrong again!" I said, pointing up to his face, "I did that a long time ago. I broke my daddy's heart when I was born. I wasn't a son. So I failed him at birth, and there's nothing I can do about it."

"That burden doesn't rest on your shoulders. Your father loved you."

"Is that so?" I asked, my words drenched in sarcasm. "Well, he certainly had a strange way of showing it."

"It wasn't from a lack of love, dear daughter. He was flawed, as we all are. Your father did not intend it, but he passed the belief of his failure down to you. If you listen to the story I came to tell, it will change all that you believe to be true."

"What I believe is that you are probably crazier than I am, that is, if you are even real."

"Before you rush to your end, you must know the whole story."

I sighed, acquiesced, reached for the bottle of wine, refilled my glass, and adjusted the blanket.

"All right, Mister, since you won't let it go, tell me the story."

He took a deep breath, squared his shoulders, and folded his arms. "In the story you say you know, Jacob's sons became the 12 tribes of Israel. Because of jealousy, the elder ten brothers betrayed their younger brother Joseph and sold him to traders. The traders sold Joseph to an officer of Pharaoh, the king of Egypt."

I raised my hand again. I had to stop him. "Yes, I know all that, and as a result of Joseph's interpretation of dreams, Pharaoh gave him charge over all the land. Then during a time of drought in Canaan, Joseph's brothers were sent to Egypt for grain; and they were reunited with Joseph, who brought them all to live in Egypt. What does that have to do with me? I can't understand why you're here bothering me with Sunday school lessons?"

The man continued as if I said nothing. "The brothers—Rueben, Simeon, Levi, Judah, Issachar, Zebulun, Benjamin, Dan, Naphtali, Gad, and Asher—all died; but their children, the 12 tribes, multiplied in Egypt. Their numbers grew so large that they stirred fear inside the new pharaoh. To maintain control of Jacob's people, the Israelites, he made slaves of them. They suffered for many generations, enduring hard labor in the building of the great pyramids that stand in Giza, a city on the outskirts of Cairo in Egypt."

"Excuse me," I said, interrupting again, "but I thought you were going to tell me my story."

"The Hebrews' numbers continued to multiply," he said, ignoring my comment. "So much so that Pharaoh ordered all the sons born to be killed. One mother, a descendant of the tribe of Levi, hid her newborn son in the reeds along the side of the Nile River. He was found by one of Pharaoh's daughters, who took him for her son and named him Moses."

"Look," I fussed, sitting up again, "I know the story of the Ten Commandments, and I've seen the movie more times than

I can count. I even have a facsimile of the tablet in the vestibule of my church."

He lifted the bottle of wine from the table. "Let me fill your glass, Priscilla. Indulge me just a little longer."

I watched him as he filled my glass with wine. Something was amiss. The bottle that was nearly empty continued to pour. It was a fascinating trick. Was it an attempt to poison me? Why bother? It didn't make me any difference whether my demise came from the wine or the pills. He handed me the glass, and I leaned back against the chaise.

"OK, I'll listen for a while longer if we can skip the plagues and the parting of the Red Sea. It's not that I don't appreciate a good miracle, but why don't you tell me something I don't know?"

"All right, I'll skip ahead to when the Israelites were led out of bondage by Moses. It was in the year 1280 BC. They had traveled for three months when they set up camp at the base of Mount Sinai. The close living quarters without constructive work to occupy their hands and thoughts led to stealing from one another, adultery, and violent confrontations that occasionally ended in murder. It was there that the Lord called Moses to the top of the mountain and spoke to him, giving him the laws that would govern the Hebrew people, and presenting him the commandments written in stone.

"Moses was up on the mountain for 40 days and 40 nights. During that time, he was also given the construction specifications for building the Tabernacle and the ark of the covenant that would hold the Ten Commandments and the instructions for worship and sacrifice."

"Wait a minute. Let me guess," I said, jumping in. "Then the people became restless in all that time and demanded that

Moses' brother, Aaron, make them a god. He melted all their jewelry and made them a golden calf as an idol. When Moses came down from the mountain, he saw that Aaron had made the people a golden idol."

"Exactly. Now may I continue?" he asked, unflustered.

"I hate to tell you this, but my daddy had his second stroke in the pulpit, preaching about the unfaithfulness of the Israelites. I remember it word for word."

"You'll be happy to know that this is the part when your legacy began."

I held my hand up again. "Now you've lost me."

"When Moses came down from the mountain and saw the people reveling in their sin, he said, 'Who is on the lord's side? Let him come unto me. And all the sons of Levi, gathered themselves unto him,'" having not contributed gold to create the idol and after seeing their display of faithfulness, the Levites were designated by the Lord to oversee the worship of the entire nation of Israel and were responsible for the Tabernacle and the ark."

Puzzled, I shook my head. "I still don't see the connection."

He paused. "Daughter, you are a descendant of that tribe of Levi. You have a heritage stronger than you are, stronger than you have to be. All you have to do is stand on it."

"Look, I don't know what you're talking about. You've got me mixed up with somebody else. If you want to know my story, I'll tell it to you. I was born in Richmond, Virginia. My daddy, William Edward Freeman III, is the bishop of the Church of God in Christ on Thompson Boulevard, as his father was before him. My mother is Goldie Davis Freeman. I am my parents' only child."

He held up his hand. "There's so much more to your story, my dear," he said, cutting me off. "The Israelites wandered for 40 years. Tonight, you are lost. You can find you way. I want to be your guide."

"This is so ridiculous!" I said to myself, throwing my head back and rolling my eyes. "I'm hallucinating. Just my luck. I splurge on a high-priced bottle of wine, and it turns out to be tainted."

The man moved closer and reached his arm toward me. "Daughter of Levi, touch me and know that I am real."

Hesitating at first, I reached out my hand and touched his hand. It was calloused. I moved my hand up the length of his arm, where his skin was loose and warm.

"So you're flesh and blood. But, look, I don't have all night. Can you hurry up and say what you have to say and be done with it?"

"Your legacy began with Aaron—the brother of Moses, a Levite—who God called, with his sons, to be his high priest. The Levites were to minister to God from generation to generation, from son to son. They were responsible for the ark of the covenant, the sacrifices, and the offerings of the people."

"This is a great story, but it's not a revelation. Besides, I don't see how this has anything to do with me. That was like a gazillion years ago."

"I'm here to tell your whole story, and it is a revelation. You'll find your direction when you see where your ancestors have traveled."

"It's late, too late. I've already made my decision."

"As a woman of the Word, I don't have to remind you of the great prophets. Think of me as a prophet here to bring you a message, a vision of your past, a record of the high priests."

At that moment, I accepted that this man probably wasn't going to leave until I had heard what he had to say. The sooner I let him speak his peace, the sooner I could get on with my plans. I sighed in resignation; the insulation from the wine was wearing off.

"You have my undivided attention," I said, holding up my glass to be refilled.

The man poured wine from the empty bottle and said, "Aaron was the first high priest."

Chapter Two

Aaron

Streams of water rolled down upon his head, through his hair, down his back, around his neck, and then flowed along his long beard onto his chest and into the washtub. Aaron felt vulnerable and embarrassed with the multitude of eyes focused on him. The whole nation of Israel was watching. He was intensely thankful for the blinding glare from the morning sun that shone down in front of the meeting tent, sparing him the full sight of the people.

"I'm a grown man, Moses. I don't need you to wash me," Aaron complained, bothered by this part of the ceremony. "I can wash myself."

"I know you can, my brother. That isn't what this is about," Moses answered slowly as he drenched him with water. "This is about submission and surrender to God and His instructions for you as high priest. I'm just an instrument to do His will. Only He can wash away your sins."

Troubled and uncertain, Aaron bowed his head. "I'm not worthy to deliver God's word," he said in a muffled voice. "I broke His law just to pacify the people. I should have stood strong in front of them and not given in to their demands. I was as wrong as they were, even more, as I made the golden calf. I deserve to be punished."

"God has elevated you, Aaron," Moses said firmly, pouring more water over his brother in the washtub. "In spite of your sins against Him, He has chosen you and your descendants to serve as His high priests. Your sons and their sons shall forever be priests."

"Why not you, Moses?" Aaron asked, incredulous. "You were the one He chose to deliver our people out of bondage. You're a better man than I am."

Moses nodded and continued to bathe him. "When the Lord first spoke to me from that burning bush, telling me that I was to deliver our people out of Egypt, I wasn't the man you think I am. I didn't feel I was up to the task, and I made excuses. Even after Jehovah assured me that He would be there with me, that He would give me the words to say, I was still reluctant. I was certain that the job He offered was too big for me. Even after God performed a miracle to show me His power, my faith remained weak. I pleaded with Him to send someone else, that I couldn't even speak properly. That's why I was relieved when He told me that you would speak for me."

Aaron grabbed Moses' arm and held it tightly. "I don't understand. Why would you do that?"

"You're my older brother, Aaron; I thought it best that you would be the leader."

"You talk foolish! You know Pharaoh better than any of us. I was happy for you, overjoyed, when I heard God had chosen you to lead our people."

Moses nodded. "And that's why you will be the high priest. God said, 'That same heart that rejoiced in the greatness of his brother will have the precious stones of the priestly breastplate set upon it.' Now, I'm happy for you, Aaron, overjoyed. It's time for you to take your place as the elder brother. It's God's will."

"The people know that I have sinned," Aaron said, still feeling ashamed and uneasy. "How can I stand before them?"

"I've told you, brother, that is the purpose of this ceremony. It's my job to consecrate you. You'll stand before them washed clean as the Lord instructed. You've never hesitated to do what God asked of you. This day is not the time to start."

Aaron climbed out of the washtub; Moses dried him and held the underclothes for him to step into. Aaron tensed his body to still the shivers in the cool morning air, as he stood at the entrance to the meeting tent behind the wooden altar for sacrifice and burnt offerings. In front of the altar, four men held a young bull and two rams without any flaws or imperfections for sacrifice. Beside them was a basket of bread made without yeast.

Out the side of his eye, Aaron watched as Moses proceeded to wash Aaron's four sons one by one—first, Nadab, then Abihu, Eleazar, and Ithamar. Closing his eyes to the endless mass of people fixed on them, his mind drifted back to the conversation that he'd had the day before with his wife, Elisheba, outside of their tent while she was busy preparing bread to bake in the common makeshift oven.

"Don't do this, Aaron," she begged, her tears dropping into the dough. "Rising higher only makes you easier to attack."

He watched her knead the dough into the proper texture. It was the same back in Egypt. She had spent most of her time making bread. If nothing else changed, with this calling from Jehovah, at least someone else would have the chore of preparing the bread for her. As his wife, Elisheba wouldn't have to work her fingers to the bone for the rest of her days.

Aaron squeezed her shoulders to soothe her and spoke softly, "Elisheba, it's God's calling. I can't disobey Him. You should know that."

"What I know, husband, is that He ordered the Levites to kill, and they killed their own family without hesitation. I don't want you to be part of that. Why can't we just get to this place we're searching for, then go on and live our own lives?"

"Sweet wife, serving as high priest is an honor. It's a privilege to guard and deliver God's word. He's been good to us. There will be peace, and you'll be able to rest when we reach the Promised Land."

Elisheba shook her head, unconvinced. "What happens when you do something He doesn't like again?" she argued, her voice trembling in fear. "I've seen how powerful God is. That power can be turned against you. Anything can happen. At least back in Egypt, we knew what to expect."

"You must stop all this useless fretting. Jehovah brought us out of Egypt for our good. He has saved us and our sons. You mustn't worry. Trust me, and I'll trust God."

"The people will turn on you just like they did Moses," she said, looking at him with fresh tears in her eyes.

"I can handle the people," he said sternly. "God's grace is upon us."

"What makes you think you can handle a people that have turned away from their God? You don't have that power. You're not a god; you're a man. You yielded to them once. It could happen again, and then what? Maybe we should just go back to Goshen. I'm afraid. What will I do if something happens to you?" she sobbed.

Aaron pulled Elisheba up from the ground, brought her close to his chest, and wrapped her in his arms. "God will fulfill His promises," he whispered into her ear. "He's brought us this far, hasn't he?"

"I see that I can't change your mind," she said, going limp in his arms. "Go ahead with it, but remember this: If Jehovah doesn't kill you, the people will."

It was Moses' firm hand on his shoulder that brought Aaron back from his musings. He looked out among the many faces, searching for Elisheba, but did he not find her. He wanted so much to let her know that he shared her misgivings, but there was no turning back from this appointment.

"Children of Israel," Moses called out, addressing the crowd curiously looking on. "This is what the Lord commanded to be done. The Tabernacle has been constructed to the detailed instructions from the Lord. The ark containing the Ten Commandments has been placed inside, with the lamps, the table, and the utensils. I have sprinkled the anointing oil throughout the Tabernacle to consecrate everything that is inside.

"My brother, Aaron, standing here before you, is the first high priest appointed by Jehovah. Before he can enter the Tabernacle, the Lord ordered that he must be consecrated. God also ordered that the children of Israel be present at the Tent of Meeting for this consecration, a public ordination for all of you to see."

Then he whispered so only Aaron could hear, "You are to be humbled in front of Him and in front of the people."

"Then why give me such splendid garments?" Aaron asked in an equally low voice, gazing at the carefully crafted clothing before him.

"These clothes are, first, to show God's glory and, second, the dignity and beauty of the priesthood," Moses told him. "They are to be worn for seven days before you can minister in the Tabernacle and the Holy Place."

Aaron was self-conscious. The countless numbers of eyes pierced his body like a thousand tiny needles, and he ached to cover himself. Then Moses began to dress him, first, in the blue sleeveless robe without seams, and then he placed the checkered woven tunic over his head. The fabric was light on his back, but the responsibility of his position weighed heavily on his shoulders.

Moses then girded Aaron with a sash of finely twined linen embroidered with blue, purple, and scarlet threads and strands of gold. Then he took the ephod, a sleeveless garment engraved with blue, purple, and scarlet threads on the bottom, and put it over Aaron's head, and the pure gold bells attached to its hem tinkled. The two onyx stones in gold settings with the names of six tribes engraved on them rested on his shoulders.

The breastplate was the Lord's oracle, made with the same embroidered cloth as the sash and ephod and folded to make a pouch. Four gold rings had been sewn onto the corners to secure the breastplate. Attached to the front of the chest piece were 12 precious stones, four rows of three, each one representing a tribe of Israel. The Urim and the Thummim, the two mysterious stones by which the will of God would be determined, were placed inside the pocket of the breastplate. Moses fastened the breastplate to the onyx stones of the ephod with twisted cords made of pure gold. Aaron's heartbeat rushed beneath it.

With each piece of the sacred clothing Aaron was dressed in, the weight of the charge became heavier. The last garment was the turban, the holy crown. Moses placed it upon Aaron's head and tied a golden plate that read "Consecrated to Jehovah" around it with blue ribbon. Then Moses poured olive oil on Aaron's head to sanctify him.

Aaron peered again out of the side of his eye as his sons were dressed in similar white linen robes, sashes, and turbans to give them honor and respect. His sober expression belied the pride that filled him at the sight of them beaming in the linen garb. He hid his emotions while Moses anointed their heads with oil, sanctifying them as well.

Moses turned to the people and spoke. "These men have been dedicated as God's priests and the ministers of His word."

Aaron appeared steady, but inside he shuddered while Moses relayed to the people God's specific instructions for the priests to perform their duties. Elisheba was right about one thing. The people would not make his commission easy. There would be no room for error.

"Now we make the sacrifice as Jehovah commanded," Moses said to the people.

The bull, struggling to free himself at the altar, was for the sin offering. Aaron and his sons laid their hands on the animal's back while Moses sliced its throat. Their sins symbolically transferred to the bull as it bled to death. The first ram was burned on the altar as a burnt offering. The second ram was for consecration and was sacrificed in the same manner as the bull. The priests laid hands on it while Moses killed it.

Moses put the blood of the ram on the tips of the priests' right ears, the thumbs of their right hands, and on the big toes of their right feet—consecrating their hearing, the work of their hands, and their walk with the Lord. Then he mixed the blood with the anointing oil and sprinkled it on the priests' garments.

"Now you shall boil and eat the meat with the unleavened bread," Moses told Aaron and his sons after it was presented to God.

Elisheba's reservations were quieted as she watched the consecration ceremony. The tight fist of her right hand relaxed, releasing the knot of her veil she had held like a lifeline. There was no doubt that the people looked upon her husband and her sons with reverence. Seeing them set apart, she realized that the Lord had blessed them. To complete the consecration, they would have to remain at the Tent of the Meeting for seven days before they could enter the Tabernacle.

***

On the eighth day, while Aaron was out with two of his sons searching the herds for a bull calf without any defects for the sin offering, his older sons, Nadab and Abihu, were behind the Tent of Meeting drinking, wine to celebrate the completion of their consecration. They were weary of the seclusion the process demanded of them. They were eager for the end of the ceremony when they could finally leave the Tabernacle and have time to enjoy themselves.

The two priests were still drinking and lost track of time when the people began to gather outside the Tent of Meeting. Their censers, the vessels to present the incense, had not been prepared.

"It's time, priests," they heard Moses call out, summoning them all to take their places in front of the veil for the sacrifices.

Still woozy, Nadab panicked. "What are we going to do?" he asked his brother nervously, rising to his feet. "The people have already assembled. We don't have the coals from the altar."

"We can use those from the fire," Abihu answered, stuffing his censer with incense.

Quickly, they snatched up coals from their fire, put them in the censers, and rushed to join their father and brothers in front of the veil.

Outside the entrance of the Tabernacle, Elisheba pushed her way through the throng of people who had gathered to get to the front where she could see her husband. She breathed a sigh of relief when Aaron and her eldest sons followed Moses out to the altar. She had spent the whole week worrying about them.

"God is pleased with the offerings," Moses said to the people, standing behind the altar piled high with meat.

Before Moses could utter another word, a gust of fire flashed in the air, swooped down, and spread over the altar. The intensity of the flames seemed to vaporize the offerings on the altar. What would have taken all night to burn was gone in an instant. The people were shocked and aghast at what they saw. Some screamed at the sight, and then a hush came over them as their mouths hung open. Many dropped to their knees in the dirt and fell on their faces at the display of God's awesome power.

"This fire was sent from Jehovah," Moses said, turning toward Aaron. "It is your sons' duty to see that this flame never dies."

Aaron performed the consecration just as Moses had done the week prior. He offered a young bull for the sin offering, a ram for burnt offering, and another ram for sin offering, burnt offering, and meat offering. When Aaron finished with the peace offering, he lifted his arms, faced the people, and blessed them, saying,

> May the LORD bless you and keep you;
> The LORD make His face to shine upon you and be

gracious unto you.
The LORD lift up His countenance upon you and give
peace.

Now it was time to burn sweet incense before the Lord on
the golden altar. Nadab and Abihu moved toward the golden
altar next to the veil, censers in hand. But they had barely taken
two steps forward, when fire again burst from above them and
poured down on them until they were covered with flames. The
people gasped in horror, and Nadab and Abihu let out blood-
curdling screams, along with those who witnessed the burning.

Elisheba stood at the head of the crowd, her mouth
stretched wide, ready to scream, but she had no breath to
release it. The terror of the moment had snatched it from
her. Seeing her agony, Aaron wanted to comfort her, but he
had none to give. She took two steps forward and fell down
unconscious a few yards from her sons. Then all the people fell
on the ground in reverence to the Lord.

"I'm sorry for you, brother," Moses said in a staid voice.
"This is what the Lord spoke of when he said, 'Among those
who approach Me I will be proved holy; in the sight of all the
people I will be honored.'"

Aaron had no words. There were none that could express
his sorrow. The sight of the charred bodies of his sons was
worse than any nightmare he could have imagined. But
stopping to grieve or mourn was not an option. As the high
priest, he had to suffer in silence and continue the consecration
ceremony of the Tabernacle in obedience to the Lord.

To ease the terrible scene, Moses called upon the two
sons of Aaron's uncle, Uzziel, standing nearby. "Mishael and
Elzaphan, come and carry your cousins outside of the camp."

The young men carried the bodies away from the front of

the tent by the cloth of their tunics, which miraculously had not burned. Solemnly, Eleazar and Ithamar stared as their brothers were carted off, and then with blank faces, they took their places beside their father.

"Do not let your hair become unkempt, and do not tear your clothes, or you will die and the LORD will be angry with the whole community," Moses told them. "But your relatives, all the Israelites, may mourn for those the LORD has destroyed by fire. Do not leave the entrance to the tent of meeting, or you will die, because the LORD's anointing oil is on you."

Aaron and his sons asked no questions, out of reverence and fear. Before Moses left, he said to them, "You are to eat the unleavened bread and the food remains presented to LORD behind the veil because it is holy."

With the smell of their brothers' burnt flesh still in their nostrils, neither Eleazar nor Ithamar could bear to touch the food. They just sat there looking petrified, scared to move, scared to speak, and even scared to think. Aaron turned away from them, lest he lose control and his grief overtake him and bring more ire on his family and the people.

While they were there in the sanctuary, the Lord spoke to Aaron and told him that neither he nor his sons nor any of their future generations were allowed to drink wine or strong drink inside the Tabernacle. Their duty was to speak for the people, teach them what is holy and what is ordinary, and to teach them the laws of Jehovah.

***

All through the night, the horror of the day repeated over and over in Aaron's thoughts. *If I hadn't been chosen to be high priest, my sons would still be alive. I cannot even look Elisheba in the eyes. She begged me to step back from this post. I promised her that everything was going to be all right, but two of my sons are dead. That was an awfully steep price paid for this honor.*

Sometime later, when Moses returned to the sanctuary to check on Aaron and his nephews, he discovered that the goat sacrificed had burned up on the fire.

"Why haven't you and your sons eaten the sin offering as I told you?" Moses asked angrily. "It was given to you to erase the guilt of the people by making atonement for them before the Lord. It was holy; you should have eaten it in the sanctuary."

"Yes, the people sacrificed sin and burnt offerings before the Lord today," Aaron responded, "But how would it have pleased the Lord for me to have eaten the sin offering after what happened to me and my family?"

Moses felt for his brother and the pain he'd suffered and was quieted.

With every sacrifice, Aaron stared into the eyes of the animals that were unaware of their fate. Nadab and Abihu had been like those animals. Before it was over, he was sick of the smell of blood and death. The tribes had given much to be sacrificed, causing him to wonder if they had given out of obedience or sympathy.

***

Aaron dreaded coming home to his tent after he had been consecrated. There would be no warm welcome for him. He had taken off his priestly garments, but there was still blood under his fingernails. People dispersed to the left and to the right as he passed through the yard. Women who had been tending to Elisheba hurried out when he entered his tent. His wife was lying on the bed, thrashing from one side to the other, as if her whole body were wracked with pain. Aaron lay beside her to try and soothe her anguish, but she was inconsolable.

"I warned you that this would happen!" she shrieked between her sobs. "Why did you agree to do this, to put our family in danger?"

"I had no choice. We were chosen by God. If I would have disobeyed Him, we all would have been killed. Nadab and Abihu were punished because they used unauthorized fire and incense."

"They made a mistake!" she shouted, tears streaming down her face. "So why was the punishment so harsh?"

"You know how the people have behaved. The Lord had to show them He would not tolerate their disobedience. His laws must be adhered to."

"How can you ask me to worship a God who killed my sons over a mistake? Where was His mercy and forgiveness for them?"

"For the position the Lord has placed us in as His high priests, there is no room for mistakes. My heart is broken today, but we must be faithful. We still have two sons here with us, so God has blessed us."

Elisheba continued to weep. Aaron's words were of no comfort to her. They only reminded her that she still had two others that could be lost.

*****

The Cloud above the Tabernacle lifted on the 20th day of the second month of the second year, after the people of Israel had left Egypt. It was their signal from Jehovah that it was time to leave Sinai. By then, there was no vegetation left around them—not a single plant or even a few blades of grass. The earth beneath the camp had been overwhelmed with the weight and waste of the mass of people, the herds of cattle, flocks of sheep, and other animals. Impatience had risen with the stench, tempers flared from the strong, and grumbling came from the weak.

Aaron and his sons went into the Tabernacle to prepare for the move. They took down the veil and covered the ark of the covenant with it. They covered the veil with goatskin and covered the goatskin with blue cloth. Then they inserted the poles in the rings of the ark. They covered all the dishes and utensils with blue cloth, which was then covered by a scarlet cloth. Then they covered that with goatskin. They packed up the curtains, the frame, the tables, the lamps, the golden altar, and the rest of the sanctuary in a similar manner.

As the children of Israel continued on their journey, Eleazar was responsible for carrying the oil for the menorah, the sweet incense, the daily grain offering, and the anointing oil. He supervised transportation of the ark of the covenant, the altar, and the tables by the Kohathites. The men of the Levite tribe, carrying the Tabernacle on their shoulders, were third in line of the Israelites as they marched out of their camp. The Kohathites, carrying the inner sanctuary, were seventh in line.

They had only followed the cloud for three days when the people, especially those of Egyptian heritage, began to complain about having to eat manna all the time. Manna was the substance God provided each day that the people then formed like bread and cooked on heated stones. After so long, the people were tired of eating manna. They craved meat, fish, fresh fruit, and vegetables, which they couldn't get in the wilderness.

Elisheba began to worry. When they stopped, she searched for Aaron so she could prepare him for the people's whining and complaints.

"The people haven't changed," she said, warning him. "They have short memories. Their griping and bellyaching are going to get us all killed."

"They are just tired," he said, making excuses for them.

"That's true, but those at the head will bear the brunt of their protests."

Aaron put on a good face for Elisheba to calm her dissatisfaction, but he too was tired of the people's whining. They hadn't suffered what he had, yet criticism constantly spilled from their lips. Moses ignored it and kept pushing on.

Even so, the people's incessant complaining angered the Lord, and He had had enough. In anger, He poured down fire that burned and engulfed those bringing up the rear of the march. The people were terrified with fear and crazy with anguish.

Moses fell on his knees. "Please, Lord, I beg you, have mercy on your people! We are your children, though unruly and ill-mannered, we mean no disrespect to You. Forgive us for our impudence, almighty God."

Jehovah heeded his desperate prayer and stopped the consuming fire, but He vowed to address the people's complaints—in more ways than they could have ever imagined. God sent the dissatisfied people more meat than they could eat.

He rained so much quail down on them that they became sick of the taste and the sight of the birds.

Annoyed with the conditions around them having gone from bad to worse, Miriam vented her irritation and disparaged Moses to Aaron.

"Moses isn't the only one God speaks to," she complained. "How can he think he's so great? He married a Cushite woman!"

"God speaks to us as well, sister," Aaron added smugly, feeding on her frustration. "After all, I'm the high priest."

God heard them criticizing their brother and summoned the siblings, and Moses, to the Tabernacle. Aaron was alarmed, fearing the worst, so before going to the Tent of Meeting, he hurried back to his own tent to speak with his wife. He wanted to caution her before he went to the meeting place. He found her outside cleaning ashes out of the makeshift oven they'd dug into the ground.

He spoke anxiously. "Elisheba, God has summoned Miriam and me to the Tabernacle."

"Why? What's happened?" she asked, worried.

"We were talking about Moses, just blowing off steam."

"What were you thinking? Now you'll be punished!" she said, dread rising inside of her.

He bowed his head. "Possibly, but I wanted to see you first."

She rubbed the dust from her hands and embraced him. He held her close in silence, and then he left without another word.

Aaron walked quickly to the Tabernacle where Moses already stood with Miriam. God commanded that he and Miriam step forward. Then He spoke to them.

"You know the relationship that I have with Moses. It is above that of a prophet. We speak face to face. Knowing this, where did you find the courage to deride him?"

They stood silent. Angry, the cloud of the Lord moved away from the Tabernacle, and Miriam turned white as a sheet with leprosy. Aaron was filled with fear; he fell to his knees in front of Moses.

"Please, brother, forgive us! We were stupid to speak ill of you." Aaron pleaded frantically, "Please don't punish our sister this way! Don't leave her as one dead."

"I beg of You," Moses cried out in urgency to the Lord, "O God, please heal my sister!"

Once again, the Lord responded mercifully to Moses' prayer, telling them her condition was temporary. Miriam would be excluded from the camp for seven days, and then she could return, healed from the skin disease.

***

The people of Israel finally arrived at Canaan, the land that God had promised them. Camped on the fringes, Jehovah advised them to send spies into the country, one from each of the tribes. Their assignment was to report on the people living there, whether they were many or few, and whether they were weak or strong. They were to report on the land, whether it was fertile or dry, and how many trees grew there. Finally, they were to determine if the cities and villages were fortified.

Forty days later, the spies returned to the camp with the report. They spoke to Moses, Aaron, and the people, telling them that Canaan was indeed the land of milk and honey. But the cities were fortified, and the people were powerful—some of them were giants! Only Caleb and Joshua thought they had a chance to conquer them.

The people of Israel cried and criticized, carrying on all night. They threw blame and insults at Moses and Aaron. "We would have been better off in Egypt. We'll be slaves again! Why couldn't we have died in the wilderness? We need a new leader to take us back."

"They are charlatans. God doesn't speak to them!" another hollered. "We have been fooled."

Then another yelled, "They've led us here to be slaves of a new master!"

There were more shouts to incite the people, and Aaron knew they had to calm them down soon or they would kill him and Moses and then one another. He and Moses fell facedown on the ground. But some of the people were so irate and up in arms, they wanted to stone them where they lay in prayer.

The Lord spoke to Moses, utterly disgusted and disappointed with the people. He thought of destroying them, but Moses pleaded yet again for their lives, begging the Lord to be merciful and forgiving.

At Moses' request, the Lord pardoned the people but vowed that none who had rejected Him after seeing all the miracles and blessings on their behalf would enter into the land promised to them.

"You have a job to do, brother," Moses told Aaron. "You are the intercessor for the people. They want to hear from you."

Aaron felt like a failure. "What can I tell them? I'm no better than they are. I, too, have fallen short of Jehovah's expectations."

"They know that, and they've seen the Lord lift you up."

"I can't argue against that, but I have suffered," Aaron said, thinking of Nadab and Abihu. "If not for Jehovah's forgiveness, I would be dead. The only thing I can give them is hope, the only thing that pulls me to my feet each morning."

"Then ready yourself for the Sabbath," Moses told him and strode away.

Aaron dragged his feet on his walk back to his tent. The burden was extra heavy now. He had wanted better for his family, for his sons. How arrogant he had been to think they could lead such an army of people. He was jarred from his thoughts by the rushing of footsteps toward him. His eyes squinted in the darkness straining to see.

"Father, it's me, Eleazar. I wanted to walk with you."

Aaron put his arm around his young son, and it lightened the load he carried. It reminded him of the time so long ago when he himself was a young man. In his youth, he was just as fearless and bold, but he had been changed by this task given to him. Now, he was withdrawn most of the time and lived in fear of God. His blessing of being lifted had been a curse as well.

"I'm glad you came, son. There is so much I need to tell you. I expected that our lives would change when we left Egypt, but this is not the life I imagined for us. I envisioned a land where we could farm and raise sheep, a place where my sons would raise their families all around me on generous portions of land."

"We'll still be together," Eleazar said cheerfully, "except you won't have to work so hard. Jehovah has instructed the people to provide for us through their sacrifices."

"Son, I'm used to sweat and back-breaking work. I've always worked for whatever I have gotten and every bite of food on my table. I'm not accustomed to accepting tithes and offerings for something I would do without reward."

Eleazar didn't understand his father's brooding. "Father, the work we have been assigned, this spiritual work, seems more important than any physical work we could do. We have to keep our people close to God."

Aaron nodded. "Important work but doomed to fail."

Eleazar responded with strong conviction. "I have faith in God and in our people as well. I refuse to fail."

"That is youth talking," Aaron said in dismay. "I have seen His miracles and witnessed His ire; His awesome power is to be feared."

Filled with exuberance, Eleazar was not discouraged in his response. "More than His retribution, I see His love for us, for the children of Israel, and that is what marvels me most."

"Then I'm happy for you, my son. You will be a fitting high priest when the time comes. My old soul yearns for calm."

***

Aaron stared out at the despondent people who stood before him. He could feel their need for encouragement. Having tried to enter Canaan without the Lord on their side had proven futile. Battered physically and emotionally, they needed to hear words of comfort, assurances that the journey would be short and that the place they sought would someday soon belong to them. Aaron knew their pain, anxiety, fatigue, and latent fears. He felt all of it. What words could he offer them? He raised his arms and began to speak.

"Shalom, children of Israel. We have come a long way. We have been through days of sun and dark hours. So as we stand here today at another dark moment, we can be assured that there will be more days of sun ahead of us. We must understand that it was our unfaithfulness that kept us from entering Canaan. We were disobedient. We have disappointed Jehovah again. The good news is that we worship a merciful and forgiving God, and He keeps His word. Did not Jehovah fulfill His promise to our father, Abraham, that he would have descendants as numerous as the stars? We are living proof of that. He also promised Abraham a land that was designated for His people, and He will again keep His word. He has shown His faithfulness to us, and now it is time for us to demonstrate our faithfulness to Him. It will test us, and it will take time. With God's help, we will find our place of peace."

Then Aaron and his sons took their places for the morning sacrifices.

***

There was mutiny and rebellion on more than one occurrence from the people who challenged the authority of Moses and Aaron. On many occasions, the Lord destroyed them, but Moses and Aaron continued to intervene on their behalf, begging for patience and forgiveness. As a consequence, the people of Israel would wander in the wilderness until those who had been ungrateful had died. For their stubbornness, the people were contained in Kadesh for 38 years. This was time enough for all the males over 20 years old when they journeyed out of Egypt to die, for the Lord had declared they would not enter the Promised Land because of their insolence. Only Caleb and Joshua, who had been obedient and faithful, would enter.

While they were camped out in the Desert of Zin, Miriam died. It was during her burial that Aaron realized just how much time had passed as they wandered in the wilderness. Miriam was an old woman, and he and Moses were old men. He looked around at the people gathered there. Many faces that began the journey were missing, having been buried years ago. Other faces were timeworn and wrinkled. Some he had known as children were now adults with families of their own.

This wasn't the life Aaron had hoped for when they left Egypt decades ago. He thought he would have long since tasted the milk and honey that flowed in the Promised Land. They were close, practically at its door—maybe a day's walk at most—but Jehovah had kept them from crossing the threshold.

Over the years, the people had grown petulant and tired of their circumstances. The cloud had dispersed, and God had not seen fit to speak to them or to demonstrate any miracles for them to witness. To make matters worse, there was not enough water or food for the people or for their animals.

Aaron lay half asleep in bed, exhausted and dehydrated. His eyes were dry and tired. This trek should have only taken them 11 days. Instead, it had been 40 years.

"Wake up! Wake up!" Elisheba said, shaking Aaron vigorously. "The people are going mad without water, and there's a mob marching up to the Tabernacle, threatening to tear it down."

"Oh, Lord, how much more?" Aaron muttered, as he pulled himself to his feet.

He could hear the protests as he walked out of his tent. He pushed his way through the crowd to where Moses was standing, as the people hurled insults at his back.

"We should never have listened to you!" someone yelled. "You brought us out here to die!"

"Why did you lead us to this awful place? There's no water here!"

"You tricked us!"

Another hollered to Moses. "God doesn't even speak to you anymore!"

"Where is this wonderful place you told us about?"

"Where are all the figs and grapevines? I don't see them!"

"I would rather have died in Egypt than in this godforsaken desert."

Moses turned away. "Come with me, brother," he said, walking toward the Tent of Meeting. Aaron followed. When they got to the entrance of the Tabernacle, they fell prostrate before the Lord.

God said to Moses, "Get Aaron's rod, and call all the people to come. I want you to speak to that rock over there and tell it to pour out water, enough for the people and their cattle."

Aaron slowly rose to his feet and went back to the people. "Come, and bring all your families with you," Aaron said to the angry mob. "Everyone is to come and stand before the Lord."

When all the people had gathered before the rock, Moses shouted, "Listen, you rowdy agitators, must we bring you water from this rock?" Then he struck the rock twice with the rod, and water gushed out of it. The people and their livestock drank their fill.

Jehovah spoke to Moses and Aaron again, this time with anger and displeasure. "You did not do as you were told. I commanded you to speak to the rock, not strike it. You did not trust in me. You did not sanctify me in the eyes of the people of

Israel. For this, you will not bring the people into the Promised Land."

***

The irony of his predicament confounded Aaron as he trudged along the rough and uneven terrain, but he was at peace with it. His aching body constantly reminded him that he was an old man and that there was not a new life waiting for him in Canaan. How could he bemoan his punishment from Jehovah? He knew that he should have been struck down for his trespasses many years ago; his former sins were much greater. It was the main reason he could never become accustomed to receiving the sacrifices from the people. His biggest regret was the loss of his sons. If only he had counseled them better, they would have all entered the Promised Land together. And then there was Elisheba, still at his side after all these years.

"Wife, I'm very sorry," he said, gently squeezing her hand. "You've never left me through all of the struggles of this journey, and I'm grateful to you. I wish I could have been a better man for you and our sons."

"I don't see fault in you, Aaron. I only see good," she said, gazing up at him. "So much was asked of you and Moses, but you have served the people well."

Aaron turned his head and looked away, ashamed for disappointing her again. "Even though I can't be there with you, I want you to taste all the sweetness that Canaan has to offer. You deserve that."

"I'm not going there without you," she told him, guiding his face toward her with her free hand. "We started our journey together, and if it doesn't lead to the land promised, so be it. My place is with you."

"No, Elisheba, I need you to watch over our family."

"They have each other. I only have you," she said, gripping his hand tighter.

Aaron looked ahead, his eyes unfocused, feeling helpless. It had never been in his power to spare her pain, and it never would be.

They walked hand in hand for miles that day. That evening, all the people stood at the edge of Edom, the land between them and Canaan. Moses sent messengers ahead to ask permission to pass through. The king of Edom said no, threatening to attack them with an army if they moved forward. Moses retreated, and they all traveled to Mount Hor.

It was there the Lord spoke to Moses again. "It's time for Aaron to die. Take him up to the top of the mountain."

Moses looked at his brother with sadness in his eyes. There was no prayer or lament that could change his fate. His own day of reckoning was growing closer. Aaron tugged his hand from Elisheba's as she tried to hold onto him.

When he was loosed, she fell to her knees, pleading and crying. "Please, God! Moses speak to Him. We are old now. Can't we die in peace?"

Ithamar kneeled beside her and pulled her to his chest. "I'm with you, Mother."

Aaron moved forward. He couldn't look back at her without breaking down.

The people were bewildered as they watched Aaron march up the mountain with Moses and Eleazar trailing close behind. On the top of the mountain, with tears rolling down his face, Moses took off the priestly clothes with which he had so carefully dressed Aaron on the day of his consecration. With each piece removed, Aaron was humiliated for his shortcomings. He had tried to be the spiritual leader that God had appointed him to be; but time after time, instead of fearing the Lord and his retribution, the rebels rose up in defiance. Now he stood before them naked, stripped of all his clothes and his honor.

Aaron watched as Moses dressed Eleazar in his clothes. He trembled as each piece of the holy garments were placed on his son's back. He trembled not from a chill due to his nakedness but from the anguish mixed with pride that overwhelmed him. He knew the awesome task his son was receiving and the burden that came with it. Yet he was proud of his son and the anointing the Lord had bestowed on him and his generations to follow. Once Eleazar was completely dressed in his father's garment as high priest, Aaron collapsed and died at his feet. He was 123 years old.

Chapter Three
Eleazar

Eleazar's wife, Amira, was waiting for him at the base of the mountain with their son Phinehas beside her. His brother, Ithamar, stood near them, trying to comfort their mother, who was inconsolable. His nose burned as the people tore their clothes, wailing and weeping loudly for his father. Some of them rolled in the dirt, as if they were in agony, and put dust on their heads.

Eleazar steeled himself, silent, concealing his emotions as Aaron had done when his brothers Nadab and Abihu were destroyed. Watching them, he thought of the last conversation he'd had with his father, when he told him they were doomed to fail. These people before him who were mourning his father with so much vigor had turned on Aaron so many times before. For the first time, Eleazar wondered if they would be his undoing as they had been for his father.

Elisheba was overcome, exhausted in her heart and body, and had to be carried to her tent. Mourners, friends, and family paraded by to pay their respects and filled the tent for 30 days. During that time of mourning, no one did any work and there were no celebrations. Eleazar spent most of those days in prayer, beseeching the Lord for strength, wisdom, and patience for the people. Once his spirit was lifted, he was assured it was time to move on.

"It's time to pack up the Tabernacle," Eleazar announced after eating supper and rising to his feet. "This long journey is coming to an end." Amira and Phinehas sat wide-eyed, startled to hear the sound of his voice. Since Aaron's death, they had only heard soft murmurs from him while he prayed. "Son, it is also time for you to take your place at the Lord's altar. You must be consecrated. I will clean you and dress you in the priest's garments."

"I'm ready," Phinehas said without fear or hesitation. "Nothing and no one will keep us from the land Jehovah promised."

Eleazar smiled and nodded at his son's youth-inspired enthusiasm and innocence. He had spoken the same way only a brief time ago. Phinehas, inexperienced and naïve, knew nothing about their lives back in Egypt, neither the suffering nor the poverty. As the son of a priest, he had been well taken care of; and now that they had inherited Aaron's property. They were wealthy indeed.

Amira clapped her hands happily. "At last, we can get out of this cracked desert! I'm eager to live my life a little before I die. I have waited a long time to live in a beautiful home and get rid of this ragged tent."

"We must remain humble," Eleazar told her. "We benefit from the hard work of the people. It's their tithes that has kept food on our table."

"Where is it written that I can't live well if we can afford it?" she retorted, brushing and smoothing her tunic. "You were chosen to receive the Lord's blessings."

Eleazar hung his head. Few knew the price that came with that blessing, not even his wife. Amira wasn't the first woman he loved. The one he would have chosen to marry was a widow, a sweet young woman whose husband had been killed.

When he looked into his beloved's eyes, he saw softness and vulnerability, and he wanted to take care of her. But the rules would not allow it. A high priest must marry a virgin, not a woman widowed or divorced.

"My son and I must tread lightly in our service to the Lord or suffer his ire," Eleazar said in a scolding tone. "You married a man of God, not a man of business."

Amira was not fazed at all. "No, sir, I married a leader of the people. And as a leader, you have privileges. Besides, Moses is getting older. He can't live forever."

Now Eleazar was angry. "Hush, wife, for it was the tongues of our people that have caused us so much strife! If not for their complaining, my father would still be alive next to my mother." He stomped out, and Phinehas followed close behind him.

Amira grunted and rose to clean up the dishes from their supper. She knew better than to argue with a man. She would get her house in the Promised Land, and there would be no more baking bread and eating on the floor. Elisheba would move in with them, and Eleazar would certainly want his mother to be comfortable.

***

Without consent to get to Canaan through Edom, Moses decided they would turn back and take the long route around Edom. But even on that route, because of their immense numbers, the people were denied permission to travel through the cities on their path. Time and time again, they were denied passage through towns as they traveled because rulers feared that the multitude would devour their cities like locusts. Wherever they turned, there was always a barrier in front of them—the river, rugged terrain, or the borders of a sovereign city. Even more trying were the unforeseen attacks on them by a number of kings along the way, but God blessed them as they conquered country after country.

Unsurprisingly, the people grew frustrated at their lack of progress while being so close to their destination. At one point, they were camped on the plains of Moab beside the Jordan River and across from Jericho, waiting for word from the king to grant them permission to pass through. While they were there, Moabite girls invited the Israelite men to socialize with them at raucous and risqué parties. The men were beguiled and seduced by the women and eventually began making sacrifices to their gods and worshiping with them. It wasn't long before all the people of Israel were worshiping Baal, the god of Moab.

"My father told me this would happen," Eleazar said to Moses sadly. "I have fared no better than he did. The people are ignoring the commandments."

Moses shook his head in dismay. "God fought with us and destroyed our enemies, but we are our worst enemy. Now God has ordered all the tribal leaders to be killed."

"More death for our trespasses," Eleazar said, kicking the dirt. "We never learn."

"You are right. But not only them," Moses told him, "but anyone who worshiped Baal will be executed."

In God's judgment for the people's idol worship, countless lives were lost. Terrified of further retribution, the people became desperate. They gathered outside the entrance to the Tabernacle with Moses, Eleazar, Phinehas, and the other priests who were pleading for forgiveness and weeping for those that had already been killed. While they were there wailing, Zimri, the son of a tribal leader, came into the camp with a Midianite woman on his arm and shamelessly strolled past the gathering to his tent.

"How can he think he can insult Jehovah like that?" Phinehas asked angrily, untying his sash and pulling off his holy robe and turban. "It won't be tolerated!"

Shocked, Eleazar's eyes followed his son as he jumped up from the ground, grabbed a spear lying nearby, and rushed off in the direction of the man's tent. Phinehas stormed in on the couple having sex. Enraged, he plunged the spear into the man's back with such fervor that it went straight through him into the woman's belly.

Eleazar and Moses, followed by a small crowd, hurried to the tent to find the couple lying dead and Phinehas standing over them. Then the Lord spoke to Moses: "Phinehas has appeased my anger, for he was as angry as I was, concerning my honor, therefore I will no longer destroy Israel as I had intended. Because of his defense of me, because of his zeal for God, because of his atonement for the people of Israel for what he did—I promise that he and his descendants shall be priests forever."

Moses was relieved. "God is pleased with you!" he exclaimed to Phinehas. "You acted on his behalf, and you have saved your people from destruction. The plague against them will end. Your children and their children will always be priests."

Eleazar pulled his son to his chest and spoke in his ear. "You are a better man than I am and better than my father was. We both allowed the people to do wrong without punishing them. You stood up for God's laws. I'm proud of you!"

"Thank you, Father, but Grandfather Aaron was the tree, you are the limb, and I am just a branch. Without you both, I wouldn't exist."

Eleazar kissed Phinehas's head. "It is my honor to be your father."

"It's our honor to serve our heavenly Father," Phinehas said jubilantly.

"Amen!" Eleazar replied.

***

With the journey coming to an end, Eleazar helped Moses take a census of the people as Jehovah requested to determine the number of young men able to fight in war. The count would also help them get settled, as the land was to be divided among the tribes proportionately. When they were finished, Moses sat down to discuss the future plans with Eleazar.

"This has been a marathon for the Israelites," Moses said, staring down at his wrinkled hands. "The next step will be to enter the land that Jehovah promised us so many years ago."

Eleazar lifted his arms in the air in victory, and his face beamed with happiness. He had wondered how much longer he could maintain his authority under their current circumstances. Lately, he found himself holding his breath from stress and worry. There was always an unfortunate incident at every turn.

He inhaled deeply. "That is wonderful and long-awaited news."

"Yes, it is for the people of Israel," Moses added, subdued. "However, I must tell you that I will not be allowed to enter the land for the same reason that my brother, your father, was denied. I will die as he died."

Eleazar's smile fell in an instant, and he cried out in grief. "No, Uncle, the people need you. You are our leader. I need you to help me guide them. I can't do it without you."

"The judgment has been made by Jehovah, and it won't be changed. I have asked God to appoint a new leader," Moses told him soberly, "a man who will be a shepherd to them."

Eleazar's alarm ceased. Now he was insulted. "Are you saying that you don't think I can lead the people?"

"You are the high priest, Eleazar, our spiritual leader. The people need a man who can lead them into battle, protect, and provide for them. For that, God has chosen Joshua. You and I will stand together and dedicate him to his responsibilities in front of the people."

Eleazar's head filled with thoughts of his father, how he was humbled before the people more than once. Now he would have to bear his share of humiliation. They would know he had been passed over, that he wasn't strong enough to lead.

"If that is what Jehovah has deemed, I won't question it," Eleazar said in submission.

On the way to his tent, Eleazar forced a smile and politely greeted people he passed. He wondered what they would think of him when they found out he was rejected as the leader of the people.

Then Eleazar realized, truthfully, that it wasn't that important to him. He didn't want to be the leader. He had seen the Lord's retribution when He was dissatisfied. He had seen his brothers, Nadab and Abihu, burned and his father, Aaron, struck down. So he was quite relieved that he wouldn't have to be the main target of the Lord's displeasure or the people's ire.

But the person who would take this the hardest would

be Amira. She was the ambitious one in the family. If only Phinehas were older, he could have certainly been the leader of the people over Joshua. It was no secret that he would much rather fight with the army than officiate over sacrifices.

When he arrived at his tent, Eleazar said, "Come inside, Phinehas," as he patted his son on the back. "I have important news to share with the family."

Inside, Elisheba sat on the floor, nodding as Amira finished preparing the evening meal. She had never fully recovered from Aaron's death. Eleazar sat down on the floor between his wife and his mother and kissed his mother on her forehead. He squeezed his wife's shoulders as she stirred the soup.

"Sit down with us," he said motioning to Phinehas. "That can wait," he told Amira, pointing at the pot. There was an unusual tone to his voice that made her stop immediately. "I've just left Moses at the meeting tent," he said with a sigh. "Jehovah has spoken to him about our next move." He paused and looked down at the ground. "He won't be leading us into the Promised Land. He is to die as my father did." Phinehas looked down toward the spot his father's eye seemed to be focused on while Amira covered her mouth to hold in her response. Eleazar continued, "He wants all the people to assemble at the Tabernacle for the new leader to be installed."

Amira's eyes flashed with excitement as she dropped the spoon. "I knew it! You'll finally be the leader!"

Eleazar shook his head. "No, you're wrong, Amira. Joshua will be our leader."

She frowned. "Joshua? Why?" she asked, indignantly. "He has no standing."

"You know as well as I do that we were all slaves. None

of us had any authority. What we have now is God-given. If Jehovah wants Joshua to lead, then that is as it shall be. We have many more battles to fight, and I'm not a warrior."

"Moses didn't lead the army," Amira argued. "How can they pass over you?"

"It doesn't matter. We have enough to be content," he said, weary of her fussing. "My father's wealth is now mine. You won't want for anything."

Still riled up but knowing it would do no good, Amira picked up the spoon and went back to stirring the pot.

"Father, I'm ready to fight," Phinehas said eagerly.

Eleazar shook his head. "No, we have plenty of men to fight. Your job is to be a spiritual leader. Your fight is to save the people from sin."

Phineas stood up. "I can do both."

"Maybe you can, but now is the time for us to bathe. I'm going to dress you in your holy clothes before we dedicate Joshua."

Elisheba just kept nodding.

***

"Good evening, children of Israel," Moses said, standing before the huge flock of people that stretched farther than he could see. "I've asked you all to gather here because there are important things I must tell you. So much has happened to me and all of you since that day Jehovah spoke to me in front of a burning bush. It was then He told me that I was to lead my people out of Egypt and journey with them to a land that He promised."

Moses took a deep breath and looked out among them, remembering so many faces that no longer looked back at him.

Then he continued, "We have traveled a lot longer than I thought we would. We have been through many trials and tribulations. Our faith has been tested time and time again, and the Lord has been merciful unto us. I needed to meet with you this evening because we are near the gate of the city the Lord said He would give to us. As much as I would like to go through that gate with you, I won't be able to cross the Jordan River."

Groans, protests, and murmurs rose from the people as Moses' words were relayed through the massive crowd. They were fearful of what would happen in his absence. He had rescued them from certain death so many times. Some cried out, "No! We won't go without you!" They were afraid to move without the man who spoke with God.

"Listen to me!" he said, raising his hands to quiet their protests, "Don't be afraid. God has chosen a new leader for you." He motioned for Joshua to come and stand beside him, and then he laid his hands on him. "Joshua is the man who will lead you from now on. I pass on all my authority to him. I want you to obey him as you would me. He will get his instructions from Eleazar. The Lord will be speaking to Eleazar through the Urim, and he will relay those directions to Joshua."

The people looked on as Eleazar blessed Joshua. "May God bless you and guard you. May God shine His countenance upon you and be gracious to you. May God turn his countenance toward you and grant you peace."

Then Moses shouted, "Be strong, Joshua! Be courageous! The Lord will not forsake you."

Eleazar prayed, "May God give you wisdom and strength beyond all those who come against you. May our enemies fall at your feet. Amen."

Afterward, Moses raised his right arm and said, "Before we leave this place, the Lord has commanded us to destroy the Midianites because they persuaded His people to worship idols. Each tribe is to send 1,000 men to fight."

"This is my chance to fight," Phinehas said to Eleazar.

"We've talked about this before," his father said. "That is not your place. Your battle is to keep them obedient and faithful to God and to His word."

"You can't expect me to abandon the men who fight for Jehovah," Phinehas said, dashing away to join the soldiers.

Aaron and Eleazar had lived in fear of God. Phinehas lived in love.

****

Phinehas, carrying the ark of the covenant, led the people of Israel into battle to wage Jehovah's war. His position was as priest to the army. He marched at the front of the fighting Levites, blowing his trumpet along with the other priests whose bugles were blaring. All five kings of Midian were killed, and every Midian man was killed. All the cities and towns in their path were burned. The women, children, livestock, and anything of value were brought back to Moses and Eleazar.

Moses was totally enraged when he saw them. "Have you brains to think?" he asked. "Why didn't you destroy these women? They are the very reason that you began worshiping Baal. If it were not for them, we wouldn't have suffered the plagues and deaths in God's punishment. I cannot believe how foolish you all are! Kill all of them except for the virgin girls." Exasperated, he turned and walked away.

"Heed the word of God given to Moses," Eleazar added, stepping forward. "All of the men who have fought in the battle must stay outside of the camp for seven days. All the spoils you have brought must be purified. Items that can stand heat are to be purified by fire; things that cannot stand heat are to be purified by water. Then you must purify yourselves before you can return to the camp."

A portion of the booty was given to Eleazar as a wave offering, and the rest was divided among the men who fought in the battle and the people of Israel as the Lord instructed. Moses, who had been occupied with writing all the laws that God had given him in a scroll, came to talk with Eleazar.

"These laws are to be placed inside the ark of the covenant with the tablets of stone," he said, handing them to Eleazar. "At the end of every seven years, during the Festival of Tabernacles, read them to the people, for they must learn to fear the Lord in Canaan. For generations to come, the Levites must keep them safe."

"We will, Moses."

"The people have rebelled against the Lord while I live. When I die, I'm sure it will be worse. Disaster will come to the people when they arouse the Lord's anger with sin and evil."

Eleazar held the scrolls, feeling the weight of them and the awesome responsibility that came with them. His eyes rested on Moses' back as he slowly walked away, and he prayed that he would not fail.

***

The people stood at the bank of the Jordan River without Moses. Three days before, Joshua had stood there with them and had given them instructions to complete in preparation to cross the river. The people had gone before Eleazar, and with him they went through the purification ceremony in anticipation of the miracle that would be performed by the Lord on their behalf.

"Take up the ark," Joshua commanded to the priests. They looked over at Eleazar, and when he nodded to confirm, they picked up the poles of the ark of the covenant and set them on their shoulders. "Now lead us across the river."

The priests, with Eleazar leading them, moved toward the edge of the swollen river that was overflowing its bank. Eleazar lifted his foot high to take a large step into the river. When he brought it down and touched the wet surface, the water drew back. The water didn't just recede, but it drew back to a great height, as if it were being pushed against a colossal wall. The water beyond that point rushed toward the Dead Sea until the riverbed was dry.

Eleazar, with Phinehas behind him, walked to the middle of the river, with the priests carrying the ark following them. There, he and Phinehas stood with the priests for hours while the horde of people, the whole nation of Israel, passed by them to the other side of the Jordan to an area close to Jericho. When all the tribes and their animals had passed, the priests came out from the riverbed, and the water began to pour down until it overflowed its banks.

At last! The people of Israel had crossed into the land God had promised them. They camped outside the gates of Jericho until the Lord told Joshua that the king and his city had already been defeated. He adhered to the specific instructions that were given to him by a soldier of the Lord.

Before the battle of Jericho, seven priests walked ahead of the ark and blew trumpets as they trailed the procession of the army as it marched around the city once a day for six days. On the seventh day, after marching around the city seven times, the priests blew one long blast. Joshua told the people to shout, "The Lord has given us the city!" Their united voices boomed like thunder, and the walls of Jericho tumbled down. The Israelites entered the city and burned it to the ground.

There were many battles left to fight to take possession of the land. Before each battle, Eleazar charged the men, saying, "Listen to me, all you men of Israel! Don't be afraid as you go out to fight today! For the Lord your God is going with you! He will fight for you against your enemies, and He will give you the victory!"

It took seven years to take possession of the land. Thirty-one cities and their kings were overthrown. Afterward, Joshua and Eleazar divided the land. The Levites were not given a portion in the division. Instead, they were given land from the other tribes. In all, they were given 48 cities, and the Tabernacle was set up in the city of Shiloh.

After Joshua died, the people of Israel continued in cycles of rebellion against God, His punishment of them, and their cries for forgiveness. Their troubles stemmed from their disobedience in not destroying the cities and the people within them completely as God had instructed. Instead, they intermarried with them and began to worship their gods. As punishment, God stopped delivering them and giving them victories.

Eleazar began to suffer with insomnia. He lay awake in the night, muttering to himself between incoherent prayers. Guidance from his father and Moses was gone, the leadership from Joshua was gone, and the people ignored his preaching and warnings.

"Why are you so troubled?" Amir asked him in the early hours before sunrise. "You're going to make yourself sick with worry."

"I tried, wife, I tried to serve the Lord the best I could. I tried to love you the best I could. I have missed the mark on both. I don't have the time or the strength to make either right."

"You were weak," Amir chastised. "You followed in Aaron's place as high priest, but you wasted your position. The people want a strong hand over them."

"Forgive me, Amira, I know I have not provided you with the life you expected."

"Why are you surrendering before the fight?" she fussed. "I'm tired of your self-pity!"

"Our son is a better man than I am. He is stronger. He'll take care of you. I'm tired of being a disappointment to God, to you, and to the people."

The next morning, despondent at his failure and afraid of what the consequences would be, Eleazar bathed in the Jordan River and dressed himself in his holy garments. Outside of the Tabernacle, he took off his shoes, washed his hands and feet, and walked inside the veil to light incense on the flame. He prayed and prayed, but the Lord didn't answer him. He died waiting for a word from Jehovah.

Chapter Four

Phinehas

Gibeah was one of the cities assigned to Aaron's descendants from the tribe of Ephraim. Phinehas buried his father, Eleazar, on a secluded hill on the portion allotted to him. He felt bonded to the land and chose to live there. It was near the ark of the covenant located in Bethel, the place between the land of Ephraim and Benjamin. Bethel was the "house of God" and where Phinehas served as high priest and ministered to the Israelites.

It was a time of discord for the children of Israel, with the tribes fighting among themselves for many years. The conflict began when a concubine belonging to one of the men of Levi was gang-raped by a group of men from the tribe of Benjamin. In a quest to seek justice for the affront, 400,000 men of the other tribes gathered and went to Mizpah, a city assigned to the tribe of Benjamin. When they got there, they were turned away. The men came back and sought counsel from Phinehas at the sanctuary, asking for the Lord's direction and guidance on their plan to seek vengeance and fight against the Benjamites. Phinehas relayed to them that the men of Judah should go first in the battle.

On the first day, they lost the battle and 22,000 of the men of Judah were killed. The tribes returned to Phinehas, who told them to go back and fight again. On the second day, 18,000 more were killed. The whole army retreated back to

Bethel, weeping and wailing with grief before the Lord. They fasted and offered burnt offerings and fellowship offerings to the Lord. For the third time, they asked Phineas, "Shall we go out once more to battle against our brothers, the people of Benjamin, or shall we cease?"

Phinehas looked out among them before he answered. "The Lord said, 'Go up, for tomorrow I will give them into your hand.'"

Twenty-five thousand Benjamites were killed that day. They conceded defeat, and the remaining men fled into the wilderness.

After the war against the tribe of Benjamin, the children of Israel went back to Bethel and sat before God in sadness and mourning. Grieving for the loss they had suffered as a people and knowing they had the blood of their own people on their hands, they wondered how they had fallen to this level. Why did evil keep weighing on them so heavily? Phinehas, with the help of his son, Abishua, built an altar and offered burnt offering and peace offerings to the Lord.

Phinehas was a man of war. He never hesitated when the time came to draw his sword, but all those lives lost in the Battle of Gibeah seemed senseless to him. Time had turned him into his father and grandfather. He had failed to impart God's word to the people. The will to fight dried up inside him. He served as high priest for 19 years. When Phinehas died, Abishua, buried him on the Mount of Ephraim next to Eleazar. Abishua became the fourth high priest at Bethel.

***

A few years later, the children of Israel had not yet taken full possession of the land of Canaan. Seven tribes still had not received their allotment of land. The unpossessed land was divided among them in Shiloh, and it was there that the first permanent Tabernacle and the first altar were set up. At that time, there was no king or central government to keep the tribes united. Priests who were also judges settled their disputes. However, the infighting among the tribes caused a division in the nation of Israel and led them to worship apart.

Over time, their worship became less centralized. Abishua held worship at the altar built in Bethel, but his cousin Eli became the priest at Shiloh.

The ark of the covenant was now in Shiloh; and Eli, grandson of Ithamar, served as the high priest while Samuel served as judge. The two of them were dedicated to the Lord, but Eli's sons were evil idol worshipers who refused to follow God. His fat sons stole the meat from animals brought for sacrificing and seduced the women who worked at the entrance of the Tabernacle.

There were other problems confounding the people as well. Israel had not removed all their enemies from the land promised to them by God. Although they continued to battle with the Philistines, the Lord was not with them in their fight. They thought if they moved the Tabernacle closer from Shiloh to Ebenezer that it might help them beat the Philistines. In the transport of the ark, they were attacked. Eli's two sons were killed, and the ark was captured.

Every city where the ark was placed suffered with plagues, so the Philistines finally returned it to Israel. After the destruction of Shiloh, the Tabernacle was moved to the city of Nob. Because Eli knew of his sons' sins and allowed it, the Lord declared that no more of his family would serve as priests, even though that didn't happen immediately.

****

The Israelites weren't happy with a spiritual leader. They wanted a king. David was God's chosen king. The descendants of Aaron who served as high priests up to King David's reign were Eleazar, Phinehas, Abishua, Bukki, Uzzi, Zerahiah, Meraioth, Amariah, Ahitub, and Zadok.

The work of the priests changed with David. The kingdom of Israel and the kingdom of Judah were united under David when he became king. He moved the Tabernacle to Jerusalem, where descendants of Phinehas and Ithamar would serve as his high priests.

This marks the 14 generations from the time God made the covenant with Abraham to the time of David's reign as king. The promise to Abraham—for him to be exceedingly fruitful, for his seed to make nations, for kings to come from him, for his descendants to have the land of Canaan, and for Him to be their God—was intact.

Chapter Five

Zadok and Abiathar

Zadok stared out farther than his eyes could see, straining for a glimpse into the mind of David's latest challenger. There had been battle after battle. Even his own hands had blood on them. He'd fought with the 3,700 troops of priests, puncturing the hearts and bellies of his own people to ensure that David would be made king. He had lost count of the number of men he had sacrificed like the animals on the great altar to maintain David's seat on the throne. In all the killing, all he and his king wanted was peace, but peace still escaped them.

Zadok remembered the words his unassuming wife, Jaina, had said to him on the day they moved into the palace: "Don't let the power of another man intoxicate you," she warned. "Your purpose is to keep the word of God at the front of all the king does. You are not to be his counsel in worldly things." Zadok had tried, but he had failed in that charge many times.

Now, having lived in the palace and spoiled by the riches of it, Jaina, once full of faith, was addicted to the status and money afforded them by another man.

"Something must be done," she told him, adjusting her embroidered veil around her as she lounged. "If the king's son takes over, we'll be thrown out of the palace."

"Don't worry. God is on our side," Zadok said, patting her hand, which was weighed down with heavy jewels.

Zadok wanted to soothe Jaina's mind and keep her in the comforts she had come to love, but this war would be the hardest. He shook his head at the irony of it. After fighting so many enemies, is it just that a man would have to fight his own son? How can you raise a hand to kill your own flesh? He knew the greatest battle raged in the heart of his king. No matter what he'd given to his son, Absalom only wanted to take his place. Under his breath, Zadok gave thanks to Jehovah for the love of his only son, Ahimaaz.

"You sent for me?" Ahimaaz asked, interrupting Zadok's musings.

"Yes. Israel is divided yet again, my son," Zadok said, as they stood high on the palace terrace. "It seems peace is never with us for very long."

Ahimaaz's brow furrowed with confusion. "The tribes won't ever stop fighting one another. Sometimes I wonder why we keep preaching to people who'll never change their evil ways."

"It was Jehovah who designated us," Zadok explained to his son. "It was David who honored us and brought us into the palace. Ours is an awesome responsibility. We have to keep the people of Israel right with God, and we have to keep our king right with God."

"Prayers and sacrifices don't seem to make much difference, as far as I can see," Ahimaaz said, folding his arms. "The people don't respect God or the king."

"All this talk is worrisome," Jaina said, slipping her feet into her sandals. "I don't want to hear anymore. We'll all bear the burden from the actions of a few." She stood up and strutted out of the room with the adorned veil flowing behind her.

"You're too young to know what we've been through. It was only after many wars that David was able to bring the ark of the covenant to Jerusalem." Zadok thought back. "If only you could have seen the joyous celebration that we had that day. We wore our finest priestly garments, and we made sacrifices to Jehovah all along the way. The trumpets blew to high heaven, and the king danced with happiness in his feet."

"Yes, but how long did that last?" Ahimaaz asked, his voice full of sarcasm.

"At my age, I can tell you now that peace is a rare thing. When one enemy is conquered, it only seems to make way for another. When you finally get to a position of leadership, the battle is not won; you have to continue to fight to keep that position. Sometimes the ones you have to fight are family."

"What are you talking about?" Ahimaaz asked, puzzled.

Zadok turned to face his son. "The news brought back from Hebron isn't good," he replied sadly. "Absalom has courted and seduced the people of Israel behind his father's back. I've received word that he sounded the trumpet, and the unfaithful ones came running. They say he's gone so far as to declare himself king of Israel."

Ahimaaz's chest puffed up with indignation. "Absalom is a loser compared to the king. He isn't a warrior. How can the people turn against David?"

"In time, you will learn how silly that question is. Why wouldn't they turn against a mere man when they have turned against God so many times despite his punishments and his blessings?"

"This is outrageous!" Ahimaaz said, shaking his head in disgust. "Why aren't the people ever satisfied? How could they have turned their backs against the king so easily? It doesn't make sense. One day they love you; the next day they hate you."

"Youth and beauty are more intoxicating than strong wine, my son. Absalom is surely a majestic sight to behold: tall and commanding, a body like marble, and a glorious mane flowing from his head. David is old, only a shadow of his former self. The people of Israel have a long history of being fickle. They have short memories."

"That may excuse the foolish people; they don't have the same blood tied between them. That doesn't excuse the son's betrayal of his father."

"The same blood flowing through veins by itself does not offer protection. Love must flow along with it."

"Father, even without love there is honor. How can you explain the reason a son would turn against his father and want to take everything that belongs to him?"

"Family struggles are complicated. We've tried to keep it quiet, but it began after his sister, Tamar, was raped by her half-brother Amnon. After that, anger and the desire for vengeance filled Absalom's heart, so much so that he killed his father's firstborn son and fled to Geshur. He waited there for three years, wanting to come back to Jerusalem, waiting for his father to forgive him. Then he spent another two years waiting to get back in the king's good graces. Now that he's back in Jerusalem, it's plain to see that those years only brought him more bitterness."

"Why do you say that? The king has forgiven him; he has no cause to hate him."

"His hurt goes deeper than that, and he wants his father to feel the same pain. He wants the people to turn against the king as his father turned against him. That's why he went to Hebron under false pretenses. He went there to conspire against David, and it worked. The deceived people have crowned him king."

"Can't we just go there and talk sense to him? Maybe we can convince him that vengeance can only come from God."

"It would only be a waste of time," Zadok explained. "It's too late for that. It's the power he wants now. Revenge isn't enough. He knows that even though he's next in line to become king, David will pass over him and have the young son by Bathsheba succeed him to the throne."

"So, what do we do?" Ahimaaz asked, perplexed. "To which one of them should we show allegiance?"

"The answer to that question is very simple, my son. We'll serve the one who listens to God's word, and that is David. I will always be faithful to him. He is the only anointed king. The crisis before us is that he is in grave danger. Absalom is determined to kill him. If everything I've heard is true, he's recruiting a massive army to take over Jerusalem."

Ahimaaz balled his fists. "What are we going to do? We have to do something!"

"The king is going to flee tonight with all of his household, his servants, and those who will forever be devoted to him. He has 600 men from Gath to escort him."

"Why should David run away? We should stay here and fight Absalom!"

"No," Zadok said, shaking his head. "As in any combat, the man that gets closest to you is the most dangerous."

"But the king has the power of the whole army of Israel with him."

"A father who has suffered the loss of one son can't conceive of killing another. He'd rather give up the throne than see his own blood and the city destroyed in the process."

"Still, a son who betrays his father deserves his wrath," Ahimaaz said.

Zadok put his hand on his son's shoulder. "Only God can say what a man deserves. Our responsibility is to secure the ark of the covenant and meet him outside the city. I don't know what will happen, so we must be prepared. It's time for me to dress you in the clothes of the high priest. You shall succeed me after my death."

"Father, I want to fight for the king in the army," Ahimaaz insisted.

"That is not your place. As a descendant of Aaron, you have been born to serve God almighty. We must sanctify ourselves to carry the ark and join our king."

***

The wailing and the cries of David's loyal followers, who stood watching along the length of the street, supplied the background for the pomp of a king as David and his household made their escape from the city. Accompanied by the 600 men under Chief Ittaai, the procession out of Jerusalem was heartbreaking. David had fought hard to unify Israel, and now they were divided again.

Zadok stood at the edge of the wilderness on the side of the brook with his son, Ahimaaz, who stood beside Abiathar and his son, Jonathan, waiting with the Levites. They had the ark with them, ready to follow the king to a place of safety.

There, hidden in the bushes, Zadok's faith was jumbled up with his fear, making him nauseous and light-headed. He kneeled on the earth at the feet of his son and his nephew. Their positions as high priests were vital as well as delicate. It wasn't easy to serve the Lord and the king. Zadok remembered how King Saul had killed his uncle Ahimelech and his whole family of 85 priests. It was only God's grace that allowed Abiathar to escape. In this situation, Zadok had to wonder what would be their fate as his family was once again caught between two kings. The argument he had had with Jaina that morning replayed in his head.

"Zadok, come to your senses!" she'd shouted at him. "It's too dangerous! Why would you think of walking into the middle of a battlefield?"

Zadok continued to dress. "I can't abandon what God has called me to do," he answered, tired of telling her that he had obligations as a high priest that went above her needs and wants.

"Why can't you do what he called you to do in Geshon? That's our home, and we'll be safe there."

"You're asking me to run away at the time I'm needed the most."

Jaina folded her arms stubbornly. "I'm asking you to save your family. We'll all be killed because of the mischief of these men. You yourself know that this is a curse from God because the king took Bathsheba from her husband. I'm sick of suffering for the misdeeds of men. I want to have some peace in my life!"

Zadok shook his head in disbelief. His wife had no concept in her sheltered head of what real suffering was like, and he didn't have time to educate her.

"You'll be fine, and the Lord will protect David. I have no doubt about that," he said, tying the sash on his robe. "I'll be back when he comes to reclaim his throne."

Jaina's forceful façade crumbled, and she fell to her knees and began to cry. "I can't believe you're going to leave us here to be taken advantage of!"

That was the way Zadok left her, and now here he was in the brush hiding on his knees. He heard the horses' hooves clumping against the earth. He rose to his feet and stepped into the clearing when he saw David's chariot approach.

"We are going with you, master," Zadok said, rushing out to meet him. "We have the ark of the covenant. Its place is with you."

"I have no place to call my own right now, Zadok," David said, resting his hand on Zadok's shoulder. "Take it back to Jerusalem. It belongs in the Tabernacle."

"Pardon my objections, but it belongs with the king of Israel. We'll defend it and you."

David shook his head and said, "If the Lord sees fit, he will bring me back to see the ark and the Tabernacle again."

"I'll send Ahimaaz back with the ark, but my place is with you, my king," Zadok insisted.

"No, you must protect the covenant, or the anger of the Lord will come down on all of us. Stay in Jerusalem, you can help me better there. I will send word when I reach my destination."

Zadok bowed before him. "May the Lord bless you and keep you. The Lord make his face to shine upon you and be gracious to you. The Lord lift up his countenance upon you and grant you peace now and in the times to come."

"Amen," David said, riding off.

***

Absalom marched into Jerusalem and into the palace. He stood on top of the gables, roaring like a lion, his arms raised in victory. The crowd below cheered in approval. As usual, wretched sin rarely has to beg for an audience. The people were drunk, and wine mixed with adrenaline flooded their bodies, freeing their basest instincts as they watched Absalom lay with his father's wives on the palace roof. With no thought or hesitation, he committed the same acts of debauchery for which he held a grudge against his half-brother.

"We have to go to the Tabernacle and plead for God's mercy on our people," Zadok said to Ahimaaz, pushing his way through the unruly crowd. "We need to make sacrifices for the sins the people have committed. Go and get Abiathar and Jonathan."

The animals had been gathered, and the four men were walking to the Tabernacle when Hushai, one of David's spies, caught up with them.

Winded and out of breath, Hushai said, "Absalom has readied the entire army of Israel. They are going after the king where he's camped at the Jordan River."

"Bless you, Hushai, for your loyalty to David," Zadok said. Then he turned to Ahimaaz and Jonathan. "I need the two of you to get a message to the king. He must keep moving. He has to cross the river and go into the wilderness."

"Father, there is no one faster on foot than I am," Ahimaaz said. "I will get him the message."

"Godspeed, my son," Zadok said as the young men left running. Then he whispered a prayer. "Oh God of our salvation, protect our king."

"David is God's favorite son. He will protect him," Abiathar said to Zadok. "Gather the other priests, and prepare yourselves to come into the Tabernacle. We must praise the Lord, sacrifice burnt offerings on the altar, and thank Him for his blessings."

***

There was a fierce battle between the forces of father and son at the edge of the Ephraim forest. Absalom's army was routed by David's warriors. Twenty thousand troops died that day, and even more escaped into the forest. Absalom, sensing imminent defeat, fled in fear of his life. But riding through the woods on his swift mule, he was caught by the long locks of his hair into the spreading branches of a large terebinth tree. His mule kept running, leaving him there suspended and unable to disentangle himself. One of David's servants brought this information to Joab, the commander of David's army, and he gave the order that Absalom be put to death. When it was done, the trumpets sounded, ending the battle.

Ahimaaz begged Joab to let him be the one who would deliver the news of the victory to King David. Then he ran swiftly through the flat plains and arrived before anyone else.

He fell breathless on the ground in front of David. "All is well, my king," he exclaimed. "Blessed be the Lord your God, who destroyed those who rebelled against you."

"What about my son?" David asked.

"I don't know," Ahimaaz lied, refraining from delivering the bad news. "There was much noise and confusion."

Meanwhile, the second messenger arrived and answered David's question. "He's dead."

David tore his robe and began to weep. His army was victorious, and the takeover vanquished. He should have been jubilant that his throne was saved, but instead he was grieved over the death of his son. Witnessing the outpouring of sorrow, his sadness spread through the army, and they grieved with him. Together they mourned his son all the way back to Jerusalem. Any observer would have thought they were the army that had been defeated.

When word spread throughout the city of David's return, Zadok and Abiathar were among the ones that went to meet him at the city's gate.

"The revolt is over," Zadok exclaimed to David. "The people want their king back in his rightful place."

"Why haven't the elders invited me back into the city?" David asked.

"It's just a matter of timing," Abiathar told him, withholding the truth.

"What do you mean?" David exclaimed. "Are there any objections?"

"The men of Judah have some reservations," Zadok said, minimizing the situation.

"My own tribe," David said, shaking his head, confused. "It seems that those I expected to be closest to me are the most prone to hurt me. Zadok, you are my most faithful servant, one of the few I can trust. Take Abiathar with you. Talk to the men of Judah. I'm sure they don't want to be the last to welcome me back home."

"Yes, my king, I'll go and speak with them immediately. I'm sure they'll reinstate you," Zadok assured him.

"Be sure to let them know I bear no ill will against them for aiding Absalom. I'll assign Amasa to be the chief of my army in Joab's place."

"My king, are you sure that's a good idea?" Zadok asked. "Joab fought with you to defeat your enemies."

"Yes, he did, but he also ordered the killing of my son, knowing that's not what I wanted."

Zadok looked at all the broken spears, broken chariots, and broken men as he and Ahimaaz walked into the gate of the city to speak with the elders of Judah. The stench of blood and dead flesh made him think of the sacrifice of hopeless animals at the altar. That was in obedience to God, but what was the purpose in the detriment of men?

"War has become so predictable," Zadok said sadly. "No real resolution, uncountable loss, and immeasurable suffering. It's senseless. So much bloodshed because one man covets the power of another man."

"But men never seem to hesitate from its prospects," Abiathar said, looking around at all the destruction. "There's always another fearless warrior ready to take the risk, believing he can alter the inevitable, death with no reward."

The men of Judah were set at ease after speaking with Zadok. They invited David to come back to Jerusalem. Some even went to join him in the journey back home to the palace.

***

Zadok did his best to hold the children of Israel close to God. It wasn't easy, and he was growing tired as the years passed. He walked slowly to David's sleeping quarters, where the king was confined to bed, suffering from thin blood and body chills.

It seemed to Zadok that the king wouldn't have peace as long as he was drawing breath. The contest for the throne that had separated the people of Israel in the past had risen up in another one of his sons. He would have no choice but to tell the king that the tail of the lizard that had been cut off had grown back again.

Zadok walked past the servant who stood at the door of the royal quarters. Lying beside David was Abishag, the beautiful young maiden who stayed next to the king to keep him warm.

"Excuse us," Zadok said to Abishag, wanting to speak in private.

Abishag looked at David for his consent. When he nodded, she eased out of the bed and tiptoed out of the room.

"You rarely come to see me anymore, Zadok," David said, trying to pull himself up in the bed. "It must be trouble of some kind."

"I'm sorry to say that it is a problem and a very urgent one indeed."

"I'm an old man, and I'm sick. What more can this world ask of me? My days left are far fewer than those I've seen."

"God has been good to you, my king. Your peace is not far off, but there are matters at hand that must be taken care of. It's Absalom's younger brother Adonijah."

David sighed heavily. "What does the oracle say?"

"It says the throne is still in danger. Adonijah wants to take over once you are dead."

While they were talking, Bathsheba and the prophet Nathan frantically rushed in.

Bathsheba hurried to the king's bedside, visibly distraught. "Adonijah has crowned himself king! He told the people you are all but dead in your grave. David, you promised me that my son, Solomon, would be king!"

"How has this happened?" David asked, bewildered.

Nathan spoke up. "He sought help from your general, Joab, and Abiathar the priest. They agreed to crown him king, but Adonijah has no support from the elders or old warriors who are faithful to you."

"This throne has been my blessing and my curse!" David cried out. "My spoiled children have no love for me. They only want to take my place."

"What would you have me do, my king?" Zadok asked.

"Get my chief warrior, Benaiah, to be your bodyguard. There's no one else I can trust. I want all of you to take Solomon to the Gihon Spring. Let him ride on my mule. My personal servants are to accompany him. I want you to anoint him as king there."

"Consider it done," Zadok said, hurrying from the room as they followed him out.

***

In the three-mile walk from Jerusalem to the Gihon Spring, the people saw the boy on David's mule being escorted by the chief of the army, the high priest and Levites carrying trumpets, and the prophet Nathan, so they fell in step behind the king's servants. They wanted to see the crowning of the new king.

The procession passed through the guard towers and stopped there. Zadok motioned for Solomon to climb down from the mule.

"This place is where we get our life's' blood, the water that sustains us and the city of David," Zadok told the boy, eyeing him pensively. "This is a fitting place to crown the king who will sustain the leadership of Jerusalem." He put his hand on young Solomon's shoulder. "I anoint you with sacred oil of the Tabernacle." Then he poured the oil over the boy's head. He watched it flow down the sides of the 12-year-old's face. "Long live King Solomon!"

The trumpets blared in accordance, proclaiming Solomon's consecration. Then Bathsheba, Benaiah, Nathan, the servants, and all the people gathered with them shouted, "Long live King Solomon!"

There was a joyous procession all the way back to Jerusalem. The commotion caught the attention of more people, and they joined in the celebration, chanting, "Long live King Solomon!" By the time they reached the palace, the mass of people parading shook the ground beneath their feet.

Abiathar's son, Jonathan, saw the procession coming and rushed to Adonijah's feast. He was still celebrating his coronation and sacrificing oxen, goats, and sheep.

When the group saw Jonathan at the doorway with panic in his eyes, they asked, "What is all that noise about? Why are the trumpets blowing?"

"King David has made Solomon king," he answered. "He sits on the throne as we speak."

In that second, the party came to a complete halt, Adonijah's guests scampered out of the room like fearful mice caught in the cupboards.

"We're as good as dead!" Joab said.

Adonijah ran from the room, out of the palace, and straight to the Tabernacle, where he grabbed onto the horns of the altar and held onto them, pleading for mercy from the new king. Young Solomon granted his brother mercy, but he killed Joab for his betrayal. To Abiathar, he said, "Get thee to Anathoth, unto thine own fields; for thou art worthy of death: but I will not at this time put thee to death, because thou barest the ark of the Lord God before David my father and shared in his afflictions."

Solomon declared the priesthood singly to the family of Eleazar and his descendants, with Zadok as his high priest, thus fulfilling the word of the Lord to Eli in Shiloh.

***

Zadok was old, thin, and frail, but it was the heaviness of his heart that kept him practically immobile in bed. He was thankful that his wife hadn't lived to bear this burden with him. Lately, his thoughts flashed back to David, who he'd watched suffer so much disappointment and grief. Now he wore those painful shoes after the death of Ahimaaz, his only son, and had to hide his grief.

This day was different though. He rose early with a purpose he hadn't had in a long time. The water soothed him as he relaxed in the bath, his loose skin shifting along his bones as he washed. He dressed himself in his holy garments and slowly walked the familiar path he had walked so many times over the years. His grandson was waiting for him outside the Tabernacle, wearing the white linen priest clothes, as Zadok had requested.

"Azariah, have you kept yourself clean for seven days like I told you?" Zadok asked. Azariah nodded. "Have you bathed?" Azariah nodded again. "Good. Take off your shoes, and wash your hands and feet after me."

Zadok washed his hands and feet in the large bronze basin

at the door of the Tabernacle and waited for Azariah to do the same.

"It's time for you to put on the garments of the high priest."

"I can't take your place, Grandfather," Azariah said, pretending not to be anxious.

"My time is almost done," Zadok told him. "Solomon is going to build a new temple. You will be his high priest there. Today I will dress you as Moses dressed Aaron."

Azariah wasn't humbled by the consecration and the anointing. It made him feel like a child. He abided it, knowing that it was part of the surrender to the Lord. In truth, he had wanted to wear the fine clothes for a long time. As a priest, he had plenty of money, but money couldn't buy the attire of the high priest. He longed for the authority and respect that was given to the man who wore them.

Finally, he thought, feeling like royalty in the splendid garments. He gave a word to the people and blessed them; and after the sacrifices were finished, Zadok ate with his grandson and later celebrated with his family. Then he packed his belongings and moved out of the palace.

Chapter Six

Azariah

Azariah paced himself, measuring his strokes against the water, taking breaths intermittently, and sneaking glimpses at Solomon a half-body length behind him. Easily, he could have swam away from him and won the race, but he never did. He may not have had the wisdom of Solomon, but he knew enough to let the king win the contest, whether it was intentionally missing the bullseye by a few inches in archery practice or holding back his thrust when they were hurling javelins. Azariah may have been blessed with more physical power and speed, but Solomon was king.

Still, theirs was a genuine friendship. The king and the priest were drawn to each other not only because of their close proximity in the palace but because of their similar backgrounds. They were the son and grandson of men who were held in high esteem; and though finally free from their dominance and influence, they still lived in their shadows. Both had lived lives of great privilege and were spoiled as children, and now they were self-indulgent as men. They dined on the best food, drank the best wine, and slept with many beautiful women. The stark difference between them became apparent when Azariah had to take a wife once he was anointed high priest. Solomon had no such constraints.

Azariah had never wanted for anything growing up in the palace, but the riches amassed by Solomon were something he had never imagined. Ruling over all kingdoms from the Euphrates River to the land of the Philistines and to Gaza on the border of Egypt, Solomon severely taxed every one of them. It wasn't out of necessity; it was greed, pure and simple. Everything was in excess in the palace: luxuries, women, and food. Greed is contagious, and it spread like a disease among Solomon's close officers. Azariah was no exception. He, too, was afflicted by it.

Sitting in the second seat down from Solomon's right side at the long table covered with meat, fruit, and fresh bread, Azariah knew there was something important to be discussed because all the officers were present. Ahishar, the palace administrator; Nathan's sons, Zabud, the special adviser to the king, and Azariah, in charge of the district governors; Adoniram in charge of the labor force; and Elihoreph and Ahijah, who recorded all the activities in the courts, sat anxiously waiting to hear what Solomon had on his mind and how they would benefit.

"Gentlemen," Solomon began, "in these four years after my father's death, we have been blessed to have peace on all fronts. Through our alliance with Egypt, we are more secure; and as you all know, peace has been further bonded through my recent marriage." All the men around the table except Azariah cheered and raised their glasses to salute the king as he continued with his pronouncement. "It has also been a time of great prosperity," he said, with his glass still raised in the air. "The coffers are overflowing."

"Thanks to Jehovah it has been, my king," Azariah said, raising his glass with the rest of the men at the table, albeit with some hesitation. He was still worried about the possible consequences of Solomon marrying a woman outside of their faith. None of the other men seemed concerned. They all drank happily until Solomon put his glass down.

"The time has come to honor my father and build the Temple of the Lord that he wanted in Jerusalem," Solomon said in a more serious tone. "I have the instructions that he gave to me, the blueprints for the Temple that he received from the Lord to carry out. It's an awesome task that the Lord has chosen for me to fulfill, and I have pledged to do it with determination."

Ahishar thought about the funds it would take, funds he would have to surrender. "Are you sure we shouldn't wait another year or two?" he asked cautiously.

Solomon shook his head. "No, I've put it off long enough. Great stores of cedar, bronze, and iron were accumulated by my father before his death. Certainly, it will be a tremendous undertaking, physically and financially, but there are no dangers standing in our way."

"How are we going to designate the work?" Adoniram asked. "It will take many laborers."

"Of the nations conquered by my father, many of the people live among us—the Amorites, the Hittites, the Hivites, the Jebusites, and the Perizzites. They are under my command, and they can do the work. The children of Israel will supervise them."

A shiver ran up Azariah's spine when he heard that. It sounded distinctly familiar, almost identical to the stories his grandfather had told him about how their people were enslaved and made to build the temples and pyramids for the Egyptian pharaoh. Silently, he questioned whether it would be just for the people of Israel to become the slave master of others knowing the injustice of it.

"What will be their pay?" Adoniram asked, still fretting over the costs.

"They won't be paid," Solomon responded. "However, their basic needs will be met. They should be grateful that we have spared their lives and allowed them to share in our peace."

Azariah thought of his grandfather's warnings that the most critical thing for him to do was to put God first, lest he be struck down for insolence. That prompted him to speak up.

"We must be very careful in this assignment; it must be kept holy," he added soberly. "I'm not sure if we should have non-Israelites building the Temple."

"Your reservations are understood, Azariah, but unwarranted," Solomon said. "The Lord specified the instructions right down to the smallest details for the building of His Temple, but there were no restrictions on the laborers. The main concern for you is to make sure that all the materials are consecrated."

"We are all here at your service," Azariah replied, putting his objections to rest.

"Wonderful!" Solomon exclaimed. "Then the most glorious Temple on earth will be erected here in Jerusalem."

***

Much to Azariah's relief, Solomon followed the Lord's instructions to the letter. One hundred and fifty thousand men worked on the Temple, supervised by 3,600. The stone was finished at the quarry and then brought to the site. No hammering or chiseling was done inside the Temple. Azariah still had misgivings as he watched the slaves break their bodies cutting stone at the quarry, but his main concern was the amount of the treasury that was being used to build the Temple. At the rate they were going, there wouldn't be much left to build the grand palace that the king had planned for his new wife.

Azariah made a weekly trip to visit Zadok in Gibeah to fulfill the promise he made to him when he became high priest. It was beyond him why his grandfather would rather live away from Jerusalem. Outside his house, Azariah put down his package and dusted off his feet before he went in.

Zadok was lying on his bed, wearing a thick wool robe. Azariah handed the package to his servant, who ushered him in the room.

"What have you brought for me today?" Zadok asked, sitting up.

"Your favorites," Azariah said, kneeling beside him. "Cheese, grapes, and pistachio nuts."

"Very good, young man," Zadok said, rubbing his arm. "So, how is the progress on the Temple? If it's not finished soon, I may not live to see it."

"It's a heavy drain on the palace resources, and Solomon still plans to build a greater royal palace for the new queen."

"That woman Solomon married is going to be his downfall," Zadok remarked. "Obviously, he didn't have enough wisdom not to make that mistake."

Azariah came to his defense. "His reasons were twofold, Grandfather. He loves her, yes, but the marriage was to seal the political alliance we now have with Egypt."

"They aren't to be trusted," Zadok said, shaking his head in dismay. "You young people don't know your history or God's word for that matter. Jehovah's word forbids us to marry Egyptians. Do I need to remind you that they were our cruel captors for many generations?"

"That's all the more reason to make this treaty with them. We all want this blessed peace we have to continue."

Zadok's weak fist pounded his bed. "Jehovah's word forbids us to marry Egyptians or to make any other kind of agreements with them. You don't know what I've seen, and I no longer have the time or the strength to describe to you what devastation will come from raising the ire of God."

"You worry too much," Azariah, said, rubbing his grandfather's bony shoulders, while trying to calm his own fears. "We don't need to live in terror of our Lord. He has blessed us immensely."

"All that money and those material things have turned you from God," Zadok said, pulling away from him. "You care more for the collection of tithes than halting the corruption of men's souls."

Azariah snatched his hands back as if his grandfather's skin had burned his fingers. "That's not true. Solomon is faithful in his worship—that I can assure you—but every man has his vices. And even if we had 10,000 more priests, we couldn't control what the people choose to do."

"You are so wrong, my son. You and the king must lead by example," Zadok argued, his voice straining. "David was Jehovah's favorite son, and he too suffered for his transgressions. The wrongs done by Solomon are debts that will be paid—that I guarantee you." Then Zadok began to cough until he choked.

Azariah lifted a cup of water to his grandfather's lips. "Why don't you come back to the palace? You can be properly cared for there. Besides, I want you there. You are my most chief counsel."

"You have 80 priests under you. You don't need me. Besides, I know what goes on there. I can't stop it, but I won't be near it. I want to be clean when I meet my Lord."

"God forgives, Grandfather. That's why we make sacrifices to Him every day."

"Go home, my son. Go home to your family. I can't waste my breath on a man who can't hear the truth. I pray you teach your son better than I taught you."

****

Having taken seven years to build, the Temple for the ark of the covenant was beyond magnificent. It was surrounded by courtyards; and the dimensions were 90 feet long, 30 feet wide, and 45 feet high. It was divided into three sections: the forecourt, the outer chamber, and the inner Most Holy Place. The outside was built with stone and lined with outer chambers for storage of equipment and gifts. Inside, there were towering stairways with walls of cedar and cypress floors.

The center room where the ark was placed on a cedar wood altar was overlaid with gold, including the walls and the ceilings. Statues of two angels measuring 15 feet high stood in the inner sanctuary. Their wings spanned the width of the room, with the tips touching the wall.

The inner room was 30 feet by 30 feet and 30 feet high, with walls overlaid with pure gold. It had statues of angels with wings that reached from wall to wall, overlaid with gold. It was decorated with intricately carved figures of trees, flowers, and more angels, all overlaid with gold. All the dishes and utensils were solid gold. Three thousand tons of gold and 30,000 tons of silver were used in the Temple's structures, furniture, and utensils. Every inch of it was to the Lord's instructions and specifications.

Azariah had bathed and methodically dressed himself in his holy garments the way his grandfather Zadok had showed him so many years ago. If only he had lived to see this day, he might have been proud of him again. Five years ago, after the birth of his son, Joash, Azariah shared the happy news with his grandfather. That night, when Zadok went to bed, he slept peacefully and never woke up.

Tightening the sash around his waist as he looked at his blurred reflection in the polished metal mirror, Azariah realized how much slimmer his body was now. The building of the Temple had tested him. Neither he nor Solomon nor any of the priests had touched their lips to wine in all the years of the construction of the Temple. He hadn't laid with his wife in 30 days in preparation for the dedication. He spent most of his time at the Tabernacle in prayer; and all the material that went inside the structure had been consecrated. At long last, Azariah stood there in the city of David, ready to supervise the priests in carrying the ark from the Tabernacle to the Temple Solomon had built in Jerusalem.

"The people of Israel are waiting for us in Jerusalem," Solomon said to Azariah after arriving from the king's quarters.

"The Levites are ready," Azariah replied. They had all the contents of the Tabernacle in hand and the ark upon their shoulders.

Solomon moved to the front of the procession with the elders of Israel, the heads of the 12 tribes, and the chiefs of the clans following behind him. They were careful to make sacrificial offerings all along the way and burned incense with each step in order to please Jehovah. The trail was soaked with the blood of countless animals as the people danced and sang for the joyous occasion, feeling the Lord's presence and approval. Only the Levites strode solemnly in respect of God's words that lay inside the ark.

When the procession arrived at the Temple, the men walked through the enormous gathering of people and past the bronze altar Solomon had set up outside. There they took off their shoes. Only Azariah, the king, and the Levites who carried the ark and the utensils were allowed to enter the Temple. The ark was placed in the inner sanctuary under the wings of the angels.

While the priests were setting things in their places, the presence of the Lord became so thick among them, as if they were caught within a heavy cloud of smoke. The cloud encompassed the priests, blinding them to one another so they could only see God around them. It became so dense that they had to go out of the Temple, unable to breathe in God's goodness.

When they came out to where the people were assembled, the Levites called out thanks to Jehovah. Azariah and the lead priests washed their hands and feet to purify themselves for the dedication ceremony. The other priests, dressed in their fine white robes of linen, led the people in praise. One hundred and twenty of them glorified God on trumpets, harps, cymbals, and the lyre, while the choir lifted their voices, singing, "His Loving Kindness Is Forever."

Hundreds of sheep and oxen were sacrificed, and the people yelled praises to Jehovah. Solomon stood on the platform erected for this day, lifted his hand up to the sky, and prayed a fervent prayer on behalf of the people of Israel. When he finished praying, fire flashed down from the heavens and burned up the sacrifices, and the people dropped down to the ground on their faces in awe, thanking and worshiping the Lord.

Azariah proceeded with the dedication of the Temple with sacrifices after Solomon made a speech. The king offered 22,000 oxen and 120,000 sheep, more sacrifices than the bronze altar could accommodate. The celebration of praise and feasts of dedication went on for seven days, with crowds of people coming to the Temple from all over Israel to the border of Egypt. On the eighth day, they celebrated with the feast of the Tabernacle Festival. Sacrificing and celebrations lasted for 14 days. After that, Solomon sent the people home, happy and well-fed.

***

The Levites rotated in their service at the Temple, and there were more than 1,300 priests serving at any given time. Before dawn each day, the assignments of the daily tasks were decided and the altar was prepared. Some served as priests, others as assistants, gatekeepers, and musicians. At 9:00, the gates of the Temple were opened, with the blowing of the trumpets to announce the beginning of the morning service. The sacrificial lamb was slain and salted, the charred ends of the lamp wick were cut, fresh oil was added, and the incensed was burned. They presented the burnt offering and the drink offering and blessed the people, while trumpets blared. The singers sang the psalm of the day accompanied by the musicians.

After the morning service, the people could make private sacrifices and offerings. The evening service would repeat the ritual. At night, the priests kept watch throughout the innermost places of the Temple, including the inner court and the Temple itself. They also opened and closed all the inner gates.

The Sabbath began at sunset on Friday. On the Sabbath day, there was the weekly renewal of the showbread and an additional burnt offering of two lambs. Before the actual Sabbath commenced and the service of the outgoing priests ended, the service of the new course of priests and Levites had already begun. Both rotations spent the Sabbath in the Temple. The outgoing priest performed the morning sacrifice, and the incoming priests performed the evening sacrifice. After the evening service, the outgoing course handed over the keys of the sanctuary, the holy vessels, and everything else they had in charge to the new course.

***

Azariah sat at the table covered with meat from the peace offering, but he had no appetite. He was afraid. Afraid for the king, for the people, and for the life he had enjoyed from the day he was born. Solomon was spending too much money on the construction of the royal palace, and the conversation Azariah had had with the king earlier hadn't eased his worries.

"Are you not hungry?" his wife asked, sitting across from him, enjoying the meal.

"How can I eat?" he asked, pushing back from the table, "Everything we have is in jeopardy."

She wiped her hands and leaned forward, eager to learn more of what bothered him. "How can that be possible? Are enemies rising against the king? Is there talk of war?"

Azariah's brow wrinkled in confusion at all of her questions. "Why would you think that?"

"Everybody knows that Solomon is building a great army. There are thousands of horses and chariots coming into the city all the time. Young men who are needed to work are being forced to leave their homes and families to be at his service."

Azariah shook his head. "No, we aren't in danger of war. That would be much simpler. If it were his enemies threatening us, we would have no trouble claiming a victory. The danger we face comes from Jehovah. The people are obstinate. They refuse to follow the commandments given to Moses by God. They aren't making sacrifices like they should, and they aren't coming to the Temple to worship. With the amount of sins committed in this city every day, the altar should be overrun with cattle and sheep. It doesn't make any sense. Don't they understand the power of God? He can destroy all of us in an instant!"

"I've never heard you speak like this before. Has the Lord spoken or given you a sign?"

"None of us need a sign to know God is not pleased. Our history over the years is clear."

Azariah's wife leaned back into her chair and took a sip of wine. "Husband, you might as well know. The people are tired. They're doing all they can. I've talked with members of my family, and they say the taxes are too high. They barely have enough to feed themselves. Building the palace has taken a toll on them. They say they have been sacrificing for Solomon's pleasures for years. You ask too much. How can they possibly make sacrifices on the altar, too?"

Frustration rose up in Azariah's voice. "Can't you see? If I fail in my responsibility to the people, our family will suffer the consequences. I'm sure you don't want to give up the comforts we have."

"The people see how much the king claims for himself and continues to demand more. You have to use your influence on him."

"He listens to me less and less with time," Azariah said, lowering his tone. "He has so many others who whisper in his ear. If I push too hard, Pharaoh's daughter might have me replaced."

"If the king doesn't worship, what do you expect from the people. He's the biggest sinner in the city."

Azariah became angry again. "Show respect for the king! He's been good to us," he said in a huff.

His wife refused to back down. She had held her tongue for years. Now that they were talking about Solomon, much more needed to be said.

"It's no secret that he laid with the queen of Sheba when she visited and that the son she gave birth to belongs to him. There's plenty of talk going around that Solomon worships idols and pagan gods with his wives."

A wave of nausea came over Azariah. "That's not true. He knows better than to do that."

"You know better than I that he's not the king that your grandfather anointed. He's changed. Maybe all that wisdom is slipping away from all the wine he drinks."

"You seem to hear quite a lot of gossip," Azariah said, pushing his plate away in disgust. He could still smell the blood of the animal, despite the aroma of the cooked meat.

Azariah was torn. It was evident in the knots that tightened in his stomach. He was more aware of Solomon's sins than anyone else in Jerusalem. He had turned a blind eye to the king's hundreds of weddings with princesses from foreign countries and the presence of his constantly growing number of concubines. He couldn't deny Solomon's insatiable lust for women and how they drove him to sin. But how could Azariah stand in judgment of Solomon? His own lust for money and power were probably as voracious as Solomon's was for sex. So, Azariah kept silent. During the more than 20 years he had been high priest, he believed that he was no less guilty.

***

It was a quiet morning. Moisture from the night rain dampened Azariah's feet as he walked to the Temple. He could feel his age in the aches of his body, exacerbated by the extra pounds in his girth. His holy garments didn't flow along his flesh but held snugly to him. He nodded greetings to the attendants outside when he got to the house of worship. He removed his shoes and washed his hands and feet. He lit incense and bowed his head to pray.

"Have mercy!" he cried out, feeling a firm hand on his back. Half afraid to move, Azariah turned around to see Solomon standing behind him. "You almost stopped my heart," Azariah said with relief.

"I had another dream last night. It was more vivid and frightening than the last," Solomon said, sounding despondent.

Azariah put down the incense and turned to leave the inner room. The only words that were to be spoken in there were for

Jehovah. Solomon followed him through the forecourt out into the courtyard. There he motioned for the attendants to give them privacy.

"What did the Lord tell you?" Azariah asked, fearing what his words might be.

Solomon had not heeded his first warning. The Lord certainly would not be pleased. There was no doubt that a day of reckoning would come when God would punish Solomon as He had punished David, even more because of Solomon's heathen wives.

"He rebuked me for my disobedience," Solomon answered. "He's going to punish me for my weakness to beautiful women."

"Sire, the God of Jehovah warned us against marrying women from other nations where they worship idols. You turned away from God."

"Believe me when I tell you that no woman will separate me from the love of God."

"How can you say that, dear Solomon? You have 700 wives—wives from Moab, Ammon, Edon, Sidon, and the land of the Hittites. Then there are the 300 concubines. That's 1,000 women. If that weren't insult enough, you built shrines for their gods here in Jerusalem and worshiped idols with them. That was the most egregious of sins. Did you think that would please our Lord?"

"Haven't I built the grandest temple in all of creation to honor Jehovah? I haven't put any god above Him. Why should He take my kingdom from me and give it to one of my underlings? What more could I have done?"

"You could have done what you knew to be right," Azariah replied sternly.

"You know what it's like to grow old, my friend. I'm not the man I was. I can't please my wives in the way I used to. Worshiping with them makes them happy. It's harmless."

"Have you lost your senses? God is going to punish you and your family. All of Israel will suffer because of your actions. It's far from harmless."

"That wasn't my intention," Solomon said, trying to defend his actions. "I would never want to do anything to hurt the people of Israel."

"With all your wisdom, didn't you think there would be consequences? You had everything a man could want, but it wasn't enough. Your lust and weakness for women has brought the kingdom down. You should never have married Pharaoh's daughter. Not only did she turn you away from God, she made you in the mold of Ramses, who held our people captive as slaves."

"I'm sorry for that, Azariah. When it comes to love, I have no discernment. It becomes my master, and I do anything for it. It is my weakness."

Azariah continued to chastise him. "It was your faith that was weak. It's the struggles that make faith strong, and you haven't had any to speak of. Your vanity has cost the people terribly. You have made slaves out of those that chose to live among us. You oppressed your own people with burdensome taxes, and the country is practically broke from all the construction projects."

"What about the good that has come from my reign? The people have had decades of peace, and they are thankful to me for that."

"In truth, the people are disgusted with you. You have prospered, but they haven't. You taxed them beyond reason to build palaces and pagan temples. You've taken money out of their pockets to please women that aren't even of your own kind. You have given all your heathen wives everything at their expense."

The two of them stared at each other for a moment. Solomon realized that he had strayed from God's word, but he didn't want to admit his wrong. He was supposed to be wiser than any man. He was supposed to be the one with the answers to Israel's problems.

"I can clean up Jerusalem and put an end to all the pagan worship," Solomon said with renewed vigor. "Jehovah will be pleased again."

"It's too late, Solomon, the die has been cast," Azariah told him, long past the point of being disillusioned. "What I want to know is how will the punishment come? What did Jehovah say to you? Are we going to be attacked by a united army of our enemies?"

"I don't know, but there is some consolation. Because of the covenant Jehovah made to my father, it will happen after I die. He's going to strengthen my enemies, and they will take the kingdom away from my son, except for one tribe, the tribe of Judah. Because of my father and Jerusalem, His chosen city will always belong to Him."

Azariah closed his eyes and leaned his head back. "Then once again I say, 'Long live King Solomon.'"

***

Solomon died, and upon his death, his son Rehoboam became king in 931 BC. Lacking the knowledge and wisdom of his father and having a dearth of common sense, Rehoboam vowed to be more severe and demanding to the people of Israel in oppressive taxes and burdensome work than Solomon. The people rebelled against him, and ten of the tribes declared Jeroboam, one of Solomon's officials, the Lord's chosen ruler as their king. Only Judah and Benjamin remained loyal to Rehoboam. The kingdom of Israel was again divided. Jeroboam reigned in the north, and Rehoboam reigned in the south. God's word had been fulfilled.

Both kings were stubborn men with huge egos, forcing the Israelites to war against each other. To ensure his power and influence, Jeroboam discouraged pilgrimages back to Jerusalem to worship. He fired the Levite priests and ordained other priests who encouraged the people to turn from God and worship idols. He built two shrines, one in Bethel and one in Dan. He placed a golden calf in each of them for the people to worship. His sin of idolatry and irreverence to the Lord led to his death and the death of his family.

Rehoboam still reigned as the king of Judah and tried to be faithful to God; but after several years, he too abandoned the Lord. Because of Rehoboam's sin, after five years, God allowed King Shishak of Egypt to conquer Jerusalem and ransack Israel, taking all the gold. Rehoboam was humbled by God and replaced all the gold with bronze. But the rift between the king of Israel and the king of Judah divided the people for many generations.

***

Azariah's son Johanan followed him as high priest for King Abijah and King Asa. Johanan's son Azariah II served as high priest during the reign of King Asa, who rid the kingdom of Judah of all idols and made sacrifices to the Lord. Azariah II's son Amariah served as high priest during the reign of King Jehoshaphat (873-849 BC). Jehoshaphat was faithful to the Lord and appointed Amariah as the court of final appeal in cases involving the violation of sacred affairs. He sent the Levites throughout the land to teach the people God's law.

King Jehoshaphat's son Jehoram was as wicked as they come. His wife was one of the daughters of Ahab, and she led him into evil. Jehoram forced the people of Judah to break their covenant with God and worship idols. The Levites left the city of Jerusalem, and the descendants of Aaron did not serve as the kings' high priests for many years. Amariah's son was Ahitub II, Ahitub II's son was Zadok II, and Zadok II's son was Shallum.

The kingdoms of Israel and Judah remained split through the reigns of several kings, and wars continued between the Northern Kingdom and the Southern Kingdom. The tribe of Levi lived among the tribes of Judah and Benjamin. In 720 BC, the Assyrians invaded the Northern Kingdom, causing the Diaspora of the ten tribes living there. The kingdoms also remained basically corrupt until King Hezekiah (715 BC). Hezekiah summoned the Levite priests back to the Temple.

Chapter Seven
Shallum

Shallum paced back and forth outside his house under the mixture of gold, red, and blue hues of the early morning sky. His wife, Aaliyah, unable to sleep beside his tossing and turning, had come outside to grind grain into flour for bread. Even though she had servants to do it, she preferred to prepare the bread and the meals for her family. It was usually her quiet time to listen to her own thoughts, but Shallum had gotten up and had come out behind her, filling the pre-dawn air with his own musings.

"How do we know if we can trust this new king?" Shallum asked her and himself, doubting Hezekiah's intentions. "His father has done more devilment and corrupted more of our people than any other king. That same blood flows through his veins."

"Evil is not in the blood. It's in the heart," Aaliyah remarked, her shoulders rocking as she pressed the top stone firmly against the grain on the coarser larger stone.

Shallum turned on his heels and asked, "What kind of heart does a man have who rejoices at his father's death, waiting eagerly to take his place without tears?"

"If his father was Ahaz, who was so demented that he made his own son walk through fire, and he escaped that cruelty, his heart is resilient if nothing else. To survive, he had to be graced by God, so he must be a righteous man."

"When's the last time you saw a righteous king?" Shallum snickered. "Is it even possible?"

Before she could answer, Hilkiah, their son, who had been listening quietly in the doorway, spoke up. "If he wasn't sincere, why would he have sent for us to return to Jerusalem? We are still God's designated priests; and if he wants to worship God almighty, then we have to be there."

Shallum wasn't convinced. "I'm not ready to pack up my home and my family. I have to see what he has to say first."

"That's fair," Aaliyah said. "Just make sure you keep an open mind."

"I hope that he is sincere," Hilkiah added. "I don't like being out here in the country, living like a farmer and working like a mule. I want to live in the city."

Shallum ignored his son's comment, excusing Hilkiah for being young and naïve. "It doesn't matter where you live; your job is to do God's work. When the king starts another war, the safest place for you will be out here in the country."

"That's not completely true, Father. Our place is wherever the ark of the covenant is. Our job is to protect God's word."

Shallum continued pacing. He wanted to be left alone, and he had no problem living out in the country. He was at peace, and God knows that there is never much peace around a king who must fight to maintain his power. Unlike his son and his wife, he was a simple man. He loved tending the earth. It gave you something back for your hard work, not to mention the fact that he had become cynical over the years. He hadn't lost his faith in God, but he had lost his faith in man. The evil he had seen men do was most reprehensible.

Shallum was comfortable in his community and in his garden, but he doubted he would feel that way in the Temple. Away from the city, the smell of dirt and rain were pleasant to his senses, unlike the intolerable smell of blood and burnt meat for sacrifice. But Aaliyah was more like her son Hilkiah; the summon to the palace was a lovely melody in her ears.

"I thank God that we have a good king," she said happily. "If we're blessed, we'll never have to live out here halfway into the wilderness."

Shallum had listened to their complaints for years on end and was weary of them. "Look, my son, I'm sure you have something to do. I'm trying to reason with your mother right now." Hilkiah shrugged his shoulders, and Shallum watched as he trotted out of the courtyard. Then he turned back to Aaliyah. "We may not have been given prime land when we were sent here, but all our needs have been provided for."

"This is not what I call being provided for. My clothes are just above rags," Aaliyah giggled.

Shallum shot back. "If you want fine clothes, you can buy them, even if they serve no purpose."

"There would be a purpose in Jerusalem; I would be invited to the palace. When we married, I thought I was going to live the life of a high priest's wife."

"You are living the life of a high priest's wife because you are married to one," he scolded. "Maybe you should have waited for a king."

Aaliyah ignored his comment and his bad mood. Things were about to change for their family, and there was nothing Shallum could do to stop it.

***

King Hezekiah stood ready to deliver a message to the Levites at the entrance of the Temple. From the worn exterior, Shallum could see that it had not been kept up over the years. He had never been inside and wondered if it was as splendid as the stories he'd heard described it.

"Let's get closer, Father," Hilkiah said, pushing his way to the front. "I want to hear everything the king says." Shallum moved forward, even though he was skeptical about any words that would come out of the king's mouth.

Hezekiah raised his arms high to get the undivided attention of the priests, and then he began to speak.

"I'm pleased to see so many of you here at the Temple of Jerusalem today. As you all know, my father closed this house of God and turned away from our Lord. Now that I am king, I intend to reopen the doors of the Temple. I want you Levites to return and take your rightful place in the Temple as God's appointed priests. Sanctify yourselves, and sanctify the house of the Lord God of your fathers. I want all the idols in this country to be destroyed. The temples and shrines where the people practice idolatry must be demolished. The bronze serpent of Moses has been worshiped as an idol and must be destroyed. All pagan altars will be removed. We must clean and repair this Temple in Jerusalem. I declare that it will be restored as the principal place of worship, and the people will return here in pilgrimages.

"The people have dispersed like seeds blown in the wind," Shallum shouted toward Hezekiah. "It can't be reversed. Those days of unified worship won't be seen again."

"I have faith that it will," the king said, undeterred. "It will begin with the Passover being reinstituted."

***

It took the Levites eight days to clean out the Temple and remove all the idols and illicit pagan elements. It took another eight days to sanctify the Temple from inside and out. When the process was completed, the king extended an invitation to all the people of Israel, north and south. Although most of the tribes didn't accept the invitation and laughed at what the king was doing, the Passover was well attended.

The Temple courts were filled with joy, as the people danced, sang psalms and the songs of David, and praised the Lord for their deliverance from sin. The celebration continued for 14 days. Hezekiah ordered a tremendous sin offering of 1,000 bullocks and 7,000 sheep. There were so many sacrifices, including rams and goats, that the priests couldn't manage them all and had to be assisted by other Levites.

The priests returned to burning incense in the morning and in the evening. Hezekiah declared that the people would offer tithes again for the priests and the Levites and bring their own sacrifices for burnt offerings and thanks offerings. In only four months, the offerings from the people were so large that there wasn't a place to store all the produce and livestock. The king instructed the priests to build storehouses, and they too overflowed.

***

The invasion of Jerusalem by the Assyrians was a setback for Hezekiah and the Levites in the restoration of the Temple. The fortified cities of Judah were captured and held for ransom. The king emptied the Temple and royal treasuries of silver and even stripped all the gold from the Temple doorposts to pay, but the Assyrian king demanded more.

"I knew this would happen!" Shallum said, peering through a crack in the door where he and his family were staying in the area designated for priests. "Almost as soon as we returned to the city, we are invaded. We are sitting under the threat of the Assyrians. There is not a nation more powerful than they are right now. We are sure to face destruction."

Shallum was old enough to remember how the Assyrians took over Samaria, the capital of the northern kingdom of Israel. They killed anyone that stood in their path; and once they ravaged the city, they burned the remains. He should not have allowed himself to be taken in by promises and dreams. He should have stayed where he was.

"How can a man of God have such little faith?" Aaliyah asked, setting the table with lentil soup, bread, cheese, and figs. "Why don't you pray and ask the Lord to deliver his people?"

"What's the use? The invaders have already taken over the Northern Kingdom!" Shallum whined. "God didn't save our people there."

Aaliyah slammed her spoon down on the table. "You sound like our enemy! The Assyrians insult our God, and you don't profess His greatness. Hasn't He delivered Judah over and over again?"

Shallum stormed out of the house without eating and went straight to the Temple. He was angry, not with Aaliyah but with himself. She had shown him his faithlessness, and he was ashamed. He took off his shoes, washed his hands and feet, and went inside to pray. He was surprised to find the king already there, praying fervently. Then Shallum felt more shame

because of his distrust of Hezekiah. He cried because he was
the one who had not proven himself worthy of trust. He had
behaved too disgracefully to be there, so he left the Temple.

When the king sent his servants to the prophet Isaiah,
Shallum felt even more useless. He should have been the one
the king came to for intercession with the Lord. He should
have been the one to reassure the king and the people against
the threats and taunts from Assyria. He washed himself, went
into the Temple, and prayed and fasted there for three days. He
was there on his knees when Hezekiah came in with a letter.
He watched the king place the letter on the altar, kneel down
beside him, and begin to pray.

"Now, Lord our God, deliver us from his hand so that all the
kingdoms of the earth may know that you alone, Lord, are God."

Shallum heard through another priest that the prophet
Isaiah had sent word that the Lord had heard the king's prayer.
That night, the angel of the Lord came and killed 185,000 men
in the Assyrian camp; the rest fled at the sight of their soldiers
and withdrew. Shallum's faith was renewed, and he vowed
never to let it be shaken again.

***

Hezekiah saw the change in Shallum, declared him to be
his high priest, and relied on him for supplication. Having been
ill for some time, the king had called Shallum to the palace to
pray for him on several occasions. Even though the Lord saved
Judah, the high priest knew God wasn't pleased with Hezekiah.
He reminded the king that he had not followed all the laws
given to Moses; he had not taken a wife. But Hezekiah insisted
that his house was in order.

Hezekiah was far from the lustful king that Solomon, or even David, was. In truth, he didn't want to marry or have children. As Judah prospered, he had become more enthralled by his accumulation of riches than anything else. Shallum and the other priests prayed for Hezekiah to no avail, but the sickness seemed to get worse.

"Pray for me again, Shallum," Hezekiah said when he saw him enter the king's quarters. "I've been feeling bad for weeks now, and this painful boil is growing larger. I can barely move."

"I have prayed for you, my king, and I have offered a healing sacrifice for you," Shallum said sincerely. "I will continue to pray for you; but if it be God's will, you must prepare yourself."

Hezekiah's face contorted in distress. "Why would it be His will for me to die? I have done everything in my power to honor and worship Him. I praise His goodness every day."

"I cannot give you those answers, sire."

"Then bring the prophet Isaiah to me at once!" Hezekiah demanded, disappointed in Shallum.

Shallum sent word through another priest that the king was seriously ill and needed to see the prophet immediately. When Isaiah arrived at the palace, Shallum ushered him into the king's quarters.

"You've sent for me, my king," Isaiah said, moving close to the bed.

"Yes, I need a word from the Lord. What is this condition that ails me?"

Without hesitation or comfort for Hezekiah, Isaiah told him, "This is what the Lord says: Put your house in order, because you are going to die. You will not recover."

"How can you say that? How can this be?" Hezekiah cried out in anguish.

"That is the word from the Lord," Isaiah responded. "God is not pleased with you. You haven't been obedient in all he expects from you."

"What are you talking about? I brought the priests back, cleaned out the Temple, and brought the people back to Him."

"You've chosen not to take a wife."

"I don't want a wife!" Hezekiah retorted stubbornly.

"What are you saying?" Shallum asked, hoping to persuade him. "You can have any woman that you want, the most beautiful in all of Judah. You can have as many as you want."

The king shook his head in objection. "I can also live my life in the way I choose."

"Your majesty, you are not right with God," Shallum told him. "You must be fruitful and multiply."

"I have my reasons," the king said. "It was shown to me that any child of mine would disgrace me and mislead the people down an evil path again. I saw the evil my father did. I don't want the people to be subjected to that kind of leadership."

"It's not your place to try to control the fate of the people," Isaiah said firmly. "That is not in your power. Only God can do that. You must not interfere in His will because that is not your place. Occupy yourself with obedience to His commandments."

Hezekiah turned away from the priest and the prophet and faced the wall. "Please, Lord, I beg you. Please don't take my life in this way. Not now. I have tried to be a good king and a righteous man. I have righted the wrongs of my father. I have tried to glorify you throughout the land. I beseech thee, O Lord, have mercy on me, and let me live. Don't abandon me in my time of need!"

Isaiah left the room out of respect for the king while he pleaded with the Lord. He did not want to witness his weakness. On his way out of the palace, the Lord spoke to Isaiah, telling him that Hezekiah's prayer had been answered. "Go back and tell him that he will recover from this sickness."

Shallum was stunned when Isaiah came back into the room. His face had brightened. "What is it?" Shallum asked with anticipation.

Hezekiah stopped his wailing.

"My king, the Lord has decided to heal you," Isaiah told him. "He has granted you another 15 years of life."

"How do I know that the words you speak to me are true?" Hezekiah asked warily. "Can you give me a sign that I will be healed?"

"The shadow on the sundial will go back ten degrees," Isaiah answered.

The men waited there together. When the sun had gone down, the Lord returned the sun to the sky, and the dial moved back ten degrees. When Hezekiah saw it with his own eyes, he believed that he would be healed. Shallum's faith was further renewed to see God's miracle. Then Isaiah applied salve to the king's boil under a fig leaf, and it disappeared.

The king of Babylon, having heard of Hezekiah's illness, sent his son to Jerusalem with letters and gifts on his behalf. Hezekiah, still rejoicing in his healing, was excited to receive guests. Not only did he welcome them, he also proudly showed them all the treasures of his palace: gold, silver, jewels, oils, spices, and the arsenal. He did not give credit to God for His graciousness to him or to His people. Hearing about Hezekiah's actions, Isaiah prophesied to Hezekiah that all the things that he had shown to the Babylonians would one day be taken from that place, along with all the king's descendants.

****

After a few years, Shallum relaxed and dared to breathe more easily when Hezekiah took Isaiah's daughter as his wife. She gave birth to a son named Manasseh, the future heir to Judah's throne. There was peace in the land, and the wealth grew to heights not seen since Solomon was king. With the Temple as the epicenter for worship, more of the Israelites moved back to Jerusalem.

When Manasseh was 12 years old, Hezekiah died. Free from his father's influence, Manasseh wasted no time undoing all the restructuring that Hezekiah had implemented. He reopened all the local shrines and restored the worship of the heathen gods Baal and Asherah in the Temple. He consulted with mediums, wizards, and fortunetellers; and he practiced black magic. To take his evil another step toward the depths of hell, Manasseh took part in the cult of Moloch, which sacrificed young children. He even sacrificed his own children.

The people of Israel joined in his rebellion and refused to listen to the priests. Shallum delivered warnings from God, which they ignored. Then Manasseh was captured by the Assyrians. In chains, he cried out to the Lord and repented, "If you free me, I will lift up your name. I will worship you." The Lord had mercy on him and restored him to his throne. He ruled for 55 years.

When Manasseh died, his son Amon became king. Amon had watched the changes that his father made after his imprisonment—the removal of foreign idols and the worship of heathen gods—and he did not like them. Instead, Amon set about restoring pagan images and building altars for Baal and other heathen gods.

The wickedness in the city and in the people returned to Jerusalem. The priests and the Levites returned to their farms. Shallum was happy to be back in the country; but Aaliyah was not, and she fell ill and never recovered. In time, Hilkiah resigned himself to being back in the country and took his father's place as high priest for those who remained faithful to Jehovah.

Amon was so despicable that his own servants conspired against him and assassinated him in his living quarters after he had reigned for only two years. His conspirators were slain by the people, and his eight-year-old son, Josiah, took his place on the throne of Judah. Eight years after he became king, Josiah sent for Hilkiah. He wanted to learn about the God of King David.

Chapter Eight

Hilkiah

Hilkiah cleaned off the altar in the Anathoth sanctuary, marking another sin offering for the people that would not suffice for all the sins committed. What other choice did he have but to continue to come to this makeshift temple? This was his lot and the lot for his three sons: Azariah IV, Hanan, and Jeremiah. He put on his cloak, slid his feet into his sandals, and went to join his sons, wondering if anyone in the small group had bothered to listen to his message.

Hilkiah's body warmed under the sun, and the smell of the incense rose from his clothes along the walk home, with Azariah and Hanan leading the way. But the scent wasn't strong enough to hide the stench of the evil perpetrated by the people of Israel. Once again, they had allowed themselves to be corrupted by another depraved leader. At least now that Amon had been assassinated, there was a new king in Judah and hope for redemption, but the king was still a child.

The priest thought of Jeremiah, his youngest boy, who was sleeping so peacefully that he decided not to wake him up that morning. Jeremiah was different than his older brothers. He was always wandering off by himself on make-believe expeditions. He had the imagination of a storyteller and the energy of an athlete. Neither of these qualities suited him in the life of a priest. Hilkiah smiled when he saw Jeremiah running to meet them.

"Now you're up and about after the morning work has been done," Hilkiah said, wrapping his arm around Jeremiah's shoulder in affection.

"Forgive me, Father. I couldn't wake up. It was because of Jehovah speaking to me."

His brothers laughed loudly, and Hilkiah frowned. "Son, I'm too tired to hear about your dreams."

"It wasn't a dream. I thought it was at first, but then I realized it wasn't," Jeremiah said, unaffected by the way they always responded to his tales.

Hilkiah decided to humor him. After all, this child was the sun and the moon to him. "All right, Jeremiah, what did the Lord say to you?"

"He said, 'I knew you before you were formed in your mother's womb, before you were born I sanctified you and appointed you as my spokesman, a prophet to the nations. There will be those torn down and destroyed and others I will plant and nurture and they will be strong and great.'"

Hilkiah stopped in his tracks, but his heartbeat began to race. Jeremiah had come up with many stories, but this one sounded different in his ears.

"Azariah, you and Hanan go and cut wood for the burnt offerings," the priest said, wanting to talk with Jeremiah in private. He waited for them to get out of earshot, and then he said, "Now, what else happened in your dream, my son?"

"I told you, I wasn't dreaming. I told Jehovah that I couldn't speak as a prophet, that I am only a child; but He said that I shouldn't say that I am too young, that I must go to everyone He sends me to and say what He commands me to say. He said I shouldn't be afraid, for He is with me and He will rescue me."

Hilkiah didn't know how to respond. It overwhelmed him to think that the Lord was speaking to his son, that he planned to use him as a prophet.

"I am confounded with all of this, my son. I have no words," Hilkiah said, rubbing his temples.

Jeremiah kept talking. "He reached out His hand and put it over my mouth. And then He said, 'I have put my words in your mouth.'"

"Come into the house," Hilkiah said nervously, looking around to see if anyone had heard their conversation. "Have you told this to your mother?"

"No, Father, I got up and went running to find you as soon as I woke up."

Hilkiah ushered Jeremiah into the house, where his mother was humming a happy tune while she ground grain for bread.

"Stop and listen, wife. Your youngest son says that the Lord has spoken to him. He is to serve as the voice of Jehovah."

"You're not making sense, Hilkiah," she said without looking around. "You know Jeremiah is full of stories."

"It's true, Mother. Jehovah came to me. He said that He will carry out the punishment that He warned the Israelites about for worshiping idols and other gods. The terror will come from the north, and all the kingdoms will come to Jerusalem against all the cities of Judah."

That finally got Simona's attention. "That is crazy talk, Jeremiah. You must have a fever," she said, getting up from the floor to touch his forehead.

"The boy is fine," Hilkiah said, his pulse still racing. "I believe him. The warnings of destruction were given to us before this child was born. Our people have not been loyal to God."

"But what can a boy do to fix that?" Simona asked, alarmed and confused.

"Jehovah doesn't mind that I'm just a boy," Jeremiah said to them cheerfully. "He told me to get up, get dressed, and go out and tell the people what He commands me to say."

His words scared his mother. "The people don't want to hear awful news. They'll reject you."

"Our son has been called to speak for Jehovah," Hilkiah said with pride. "He has been given the gift of prophesy. If the people reject him, they'll be rejecting God, too."

"What are you saying? They're already doing that. If they don't hurt him, they'll run him away from us!" Simona said with her voice shaking.

"Don't worry, Mother," Jeremiah said to calm her fears. "I have the protection of the Lord. He told me I don't need to be afraid, and I'm not afraid. I'm going to speak outside of the sanctuary at the evening service."

***

"My youngest son, Jeremiah, is going to bless you all with a word today," Hilkiah said after the sacrifices were done. "The Lord has spoken to him, and He has a message for you."

Jeremiah stood at the steps of the courtyard and began to speak. "Oh Judah, listen to this message from God. The Lord of Hosts, the God of Israel says, 'Even yet, if you quit your evil ways I will let you stay in your own land. This is the only condition in which you may remain. You must stop your wicked thoughts and deeds, be fair to others, stop exploiting orphans, widows, and foreigners. Stop murdering. Stop worshiping idols. But don't be fooled by those who tell you that since the Temple of the Lord is here, God will never let Jerusalem be destroyed. I will make this temple like Shiloh. I will make this city an object of cursing for all the nations of the earth.' "

There was no response after Jeremiah gave his message—no praises or protests—the people didn't know how to react. They were stunned into silence. This wasn't anything they expected to hear or anything they wanted to hear. They wanted words on how they would prosper in the new season. They wanted to hear how their lands would be expanded, how their families would grow, and here was this child standing before them preaching gloom and doom. Hilkiah sensed their displeasure, but he dared not stand in God's way.

Jeremiah insisted on coming back the following day and the next. The number of people coming to hear his revelations had increased at first. Others had heard what was going on and were curious; they wanted to hear it for themselves. Then after a while, the crowd thinned back to what it was before, and then it got even smaller. Why would the people come to hear how they would be punished for their behavior? Then other Levites began to mock Jeremiah, but it didn't stop him.

"We can't have this," one of the priests said to Hilkiah "We are slowly losing support. How are we going to feed our families if the people don't bring sacrifices or pay tithes? You've got to tell Jeremiah not to be the bearer of bad news all the time and to say something to give the people hope."

Hilkiah shook his head, despondent. "I can't tell him what to say. He doesn't choose his words. God puts the words in his mouth."

Eventually, several of the priests got together and decided that something had to be done about Jeremiah. He would have to be sacrificed so that the sanctuary and the worship could be saved. Most doubted that he spoke for the Lord anyway. Why would Jehovah choose a boy still without hair on his face? Several of them devised evil plans to hurt Jeremiah, but a few faithful priests shielded him. Before things had a chance to reach a tragic point, Josiah called for the Levite priests to come to Jerusalem.

***

The priests gathered together for the three-mile walk to Jerusalem. Not all of them were pleased about the summons from the young king.

"How many times have we gone through this?" one priest asked Hilkiah. "First, the new king summons us back to the Temple. Then when he dies, his son closes it down before we can finish cleaning out the cobwebs!"

"It doesn't matter," Hilkiah answered. "If we are called back 99 times and sent back 100 times, we still must go. It is not about the king. All kings are temporary. It is about our obedience to God, who is forever and always."

"I wonder what brought this on?" another priest asked, "King Josiah has been on the throne for more than a decade. He probably wants the ark of the covenant back so he can benefit from the peoples' sacrifices. It will only take food out of our mouths."

Hanan interjected. "He was just a boy; he had to have time to grow up. I've heard that he wants to walk in the footsteps of King David."

"I'll believe that when I see it," another doubtful priest added sarcastically.

"Stop all the bickering," Hilkiah told them. "God has pulled on this young king's heart, and he wants to do that which is right."

The doubtful priest chuckled. "It's not him we're worried about. Amon's noblemen are still running things in Jerusalem. The young king is only a figurehead."

"If we don't have faith that God is with him and with us, why are we even here?" Hilkiah asked, leading them inside the palace gates.

Piercing eyes and silent mouths watched as the procession of priests walked into the receiving area. The young king nodded as they filed into the large room. Then he began to speak.

"I've asked you all to come here because there is much work to be done. And as the Levites, the priests of the people of Israel, you are especially suited for this task. I have cleaned out my house. I have removed all the noblemen of Manasseh and Amon. They have been replaced with God-fearing men. Now it is time for me to clean out my kingdom. I want you men, the holiest of men, to help me rid Judah and all of Israel of the shrines that worship false gods. I want to work with you to bring the Israelites out of sin."

Cheers and applause from the Levites filled the expansive room. They were relieved. Josiah was the king they were waiting for, and these were the words that they had yearned to hear.

Josiah addressed Hilkiah personally. "You, Hilkiah, will continue to serve as high priest at the sanctuary in Anathoth. And once we have purged this kingdom of the evil that contaminates my people, I want you to serve as my high priest at the Temple."

"It would be my honor," Hilkiah answered, more than pleased.

***

Hilkiah, his three sons, and hundreds of priests traveled with Josiah. Guarded by a small army, they went throughout the towns of Judah, tearing down pagan shrines and destroying idols. They burned the wooden images and smashed the molded ones. They went into the heathen temples and crashed the altars into pieces; the carved idols were thrown out. They even went outside of the kingdom to Ephraim and Simeon, where they tore down the shrines of Asherah and Baal, temples of human sacrifice, and temples of prostitution.

The priests who had presided over pagan worship were killed. They even dug up the bodies of pagan priests who had been buried in the cemeteries, and their bones were scorched on Jeroboam's altar. All the remnants of false worship, including the worship of the sun, moon, and stars, were burned. The priests carried the ashes with them to Bethel. It was there that they saw the golden calf in a shrine built by King Jeroboam. The Levites desecrated the temple in Bethel, and then they set it on fire, bringing it down to a hill of dust and ashes.

King Josiah was more than true to his word. All the pagan altars in Solomon's temple were removed. The ark of the covenant was returned to its rightful place, and the Levites were brought back to officiate over the worship.

***

Hilkiah and his sons sat together in the upper room of their home, reflecting on their mission with King Josiah.

"Now that we have removed all the pagan worship temples and shrines, we can focus on renewing the ministry in Jerusalem," Hilkiah said to his sons.

"I'll be glad when we can move our worship to the Temple," Azariah added. "That's where the ark is, and that's where we belong."

"Be patient, my son," Hilkiah said to him. "I don't know when that will take place; the Temple is still in poor condition."

"I can't stay here and wait for that," Jeremiah said to his father, pacing the floor. "I have to go out and take the word to the people."

"Jeremiah, you have already spread the word to the people during our travels when we were tearing down the heathen temples. Right now, it is not safe for you to venture out alone. Many of our people still like wallowing in their sin like pigs in mud. They do not want things to change."

"That doesn't matter," Jeremiah replied. "I still have to go."

"At least let our father send some priests with you for protection," Hanan added.

"I don't need their protection," Jeremiah said, self-assured. "More than a few have tried to attack me, but they have all failed. The fact is, I can only trust the Lord right now. As long as He is with me, I have nothing to fear. His power is greater than any person who can come against me."

"Where will you go?" Hilkiah asked worriedly, fearing for his son's safety.

"I'm going to the kingdom in the north, where the other ten tribes have been exiled. I want to let them know that they can come back home."

Hilkiah knew he could not stand in his son's way. He backed down. "If it be God's will for you to go, then I am at peace with it."

As Jeremiah took to the hills to spread God's word to the people throughout Israel, urging them to turn away from false prophets and gods, Hilkiah and his brothers were ministering to those in Judah.

***

Centralized worship of Jehovah had finally been brought back to Jerusalem. But even after ten years, the people were slow to return to the Temple. On the Sabbath, Hilkiah stood before the people and spoke.

He prayed a prayer of confession. "We have strayed from you word, Lord. We have sinned, and we have been disobedient. We come asking for your forgiveness and your mercy. Cleanse us from all unrighteousness so that we may present to you fresh faith. We want to hear your words, O Jehovah." He lifted up a scroll and recited the Ten Commandments and the laws that were given to Moses. Then he made the sin offering and burned the incense, as he had done so many times.

Even still, Hilkiah was worried. King Josiah's frustration with the progress was no secret. Besides that, he was not the only one who was dissatisfied. Several of his assistant priests were disgruntled and complained that they lived better in Anathoth than they did in Jerusalem. Hilkiah was weary of being the rope that tugged between the king and the priests. When he saw Josiah's court secretary, his official, and a scribe approaching the Temple after the morning duties, he wondered what new issue he would have to deal with.

"Shalom," Hilkiah said, greeting them at the outer door. "Are you here to make a sacrifice?"

"No, we are not," Shaphan the secretary answered formally. "As you know, the king strongly feels the responsibility to right the things that his fathered had wronged. He will not rest until he has brought the people back to worshiping Jehovah."

"I'm aware of that, Shaphan. My family is doing all they

can to make that happen," Hilkiah said. "Contrary to belief, we are not miracle-workers."

"More must be done," Shaphan said, eyeing the cracks in the worn-down structure. "The Temple is in disrepair. How can the king compel the people to return to a place that is as filthy and broken as this is? If the people are to be restored, then Temple must be restored first."

"I can't argue with that," Hilkiah responded. "The Temple needs repair. Unfortunately, we don't have the hands to accomplish much."

"The king recognizes that and has sent us here with instructions for you," Shaphan said. "You are to take the money that the gatekeepers have collected from the people and turn it over to his superintendents, a team of men he has appointed to refurbish and renovate the Temple. These men will purchase the supplies of timber and stone and hire the carpenters, builders, and masons. They will supervise and pay the workers. The king says that you should not worry about accounting for the funds as the men are honest."

Despite being skeptic of the enterprise, Hilkiah raised no objections. "The king has my full cooperation," he said willingly. "We all want to see the Temple brought back to its grandness to honor Jehovah."

***

Carpenters and masons were busy working all over the Temple. Their knocking and banging took the place of the music that usually filled the hallways and the courtyard.

"I don't see why we can't be the ones to supervise the repairs," Azariah complained to Hilkiah, resenting the interference in their domain. "We know what needs to be done. They aren't even supposed to enter into the inner chamber."

Hilkiah chuckled at his son's irritation. "You've been working here for ten years, and you never thought to try and clean up, my son. I am sure that it pleases God to see the Temple brought back for His glory. When they're finished, we'll consecrate the Temple again."

Frustrated, Azariah left to go fishing with Hanan and some friends.

While the superintendents were overseeing the clean-up of the outer room of the Temple, Hilkiah sifted through the debris left behind in the corner of a storage room. He turned over a cracked altar, and under it there was an unmarked wooden box. He hesitated before opening it. After all, who could know what manner of wickedness from the worship of Baal that it might contain? It had obviously gone unnoticed when all the idols and vessels were purged.

Slowly, Hilkiah lifted the top off the box, peeping through the side. He was surprised to see a scroll inside. He put the top of the box down and carefully picked up the scroll. For a moment, he didn't trust his own eyes, but he couldn't deny it. Was it possible that what was buried in the rubble, where the pagans' worship had taken place, was the law of the covenant, the lost Book of the Law? It was hard to believe that in his hands were God's laws, the very ones spoken by God and written by Moses.

Humbled, Hilkiah fell to his knees in prayer and supplication with the laws in his hands. Only a few minutes had passed before he realized how significant this was, and he rose to his feet. He gently placed the scroll back in the box, tucked it under his arm, and rushed to the palace.

Shaphan was working in his office outside the king's quarters.

"I must speak with the king immediately!" Hilkiah told him urgently.

"You're out of breath. What's the hurry?" Shaphan asked, wandering what his business was.

"This!" he said, placing the box on the table and opening it. "I found this scroll among the trash in the Temple. It's the lost Book of the Law given to Moses."

Shaphan didn't speak as he stared down at the delicate scroll. A few seconds later, he picked up the box and darted into the room where Josiah was being dressed by his attendant.

"What is it?" the king asked, wondering why Shaphan had rushed in without knocking on the door. "What's happened?"

Shaphan took a quick breath to gather himself before he spoke. "Hilkiah has found something in the Temple during the renovation."

"Well, what is it?" the king asked impatiently, "Don't keep me in suspense."

"I can hardly believe it, but it's the lost scroll of Moses, the Book of the Law!"

Josiah pushed his attendant away. "If that is what you say it is, then it is most certainly a sign from God! Read it to me."

Shaphan handed the scroll back to Hilkiah, who eased it open and began to read. The words had power and seemed to fill the room as Hilkiah kept reading. They were all in awe. The king tore the robes he had just been dressed in out of fear and consternation to the Lord. He knew the people would surely suffer for their iniquity.

"Almighty God, have mercy upon us!" the king cried out in anguish as Hilkiah kept reading. When he finished reading the scroll, Josiah was shocked and shaken. "I have been at odds with God's word, and the people have strayed," he said. "They haven't been walking in the path He instructed for us. His wrath is upon us because our fathers ignored the words written in that scroll. There will be a harsh judgment!"

"We have made great efforts to become right with the Lord, your majesty," Hilkiah said to bring him solace. "Surely that will make a difference."

"It can't be enough!" Josiah said, distraught. "I don't know how we can make amends. Go, Hilkiah, take Shaphan and my officials with you. Seek a vessel of the Lord, have them certify this book, and inquire of them of my fate and the fate of the people of Israel."

Then the king lay prostrate on the floor in his ripped clothes. Hilkiah hurried out of the room with the royal attendant and the king's officials behind him.

"Where is Jeremiah?" Shaphan asked once they were outside the palace. "He can tell us what the Lord says."

"He is away in Assyria, spreading God's word to the Israelites in exile. I don't know when he'll return to Judah," Hilkiah said, trying to think.

Shaphan was frantic. "What other prophet can we go to?"

Hilkiah snapped his finger. "Huldah the prophetess. She speaks on behalf of Jehovah."

"Do you mean Shallum's wife, the keeper of the king's wardrobe?" Shaphan said doubtfully.

"Yes, she's the one," Hilkiah said, nodding. "She has advised me on several occasions. She teaches the oral tradition of Judaism at the college. We can find her there."

The men rushed to the college and found Huldah there finishing a class. They waited until all the students had cleared the room before they spoke.

"Huldah, we come on behalf of the king about this scroll," Hilkiah said, taking it from the box to show her. "What can you tell us from the Lord?"

"This is absolutely the book of the covenant given by God and written by Moses' own hand," she said gazing down at the scroll. She looked up and stared out into space and began to speak as if she were in a trance. "Tell the man who sent you to Me, 'Thus says the Lord God of Israel: Behold I will bring evil and calamity on this place and all of its inhabitants; all the curses that were read to the king of Judah, because they have forsaken Me and burned incense to other gods, that they might provoke Me to anger with all the works of their hands. My wrath shall be poured upon this place, and shall not be quenched.'"

The men were stunned into silence at the message from God.

Huldah continued. "And as for the king of Judah, who sent you to enquire of the Lord, tell him, "Thus says the Lord of Israel concerning the words that were read to you: Because your heart was tender and you did humble yourself before God, when you heard His words against this place and its inhabitants, that they will become a desolation and a curse and did tear your clothes and weep before Me; I have truly heard you. Therefore, behold, I will gather you to your fathers, and you will go to your grave in peace, and your eyes will not see all the evil I will bring upon this place and its inhabitants."

***

Immediately, after Hilkiah and the royal messengers brought the word back to the king, he sent for the elders of Judah and Jerusalem and commanded them to summon the entire nation. Every one of the Israelites was to come to the "Sanctified House," the Holy Temple.

King Josiah stood on a platform before all the priests, the prophets, and the massive crowd of people and read aloud God's law of the covenant from the scroll that Hilkiah had discovered.

"Now that I have read to you the covenant that almighty God made with our people, from this day forward, there will be no other worship except that of Jehovah. All local sanctuaries will be destroyed. Jerusalem will be the central place of worship. All the laws written in this book are to be obeyed. I ask all of you to walk in the way of God and pledge yourselves to this covenant with all your heart and soul."

The nation of people solemnly agreed and pledged themselves to God. Josiah announced the Passover celebration in obedience to God. All the people took part in the observance. He supplied 30,000 lambs and young goats and 3,000 young bulls. Hilkiah and his attendants set aside a tenth of the animals, 2,600 sheep and goats and 300 oxen, to be given to the priests and the Levites as a Passover offering. So many animals were brought to the Temple for sacrifice that the Levites killed the lambs and then presented the blood to the priests to sprinkle on the altar.

Each tribe presented their pile of carcasses for burnt offerings to the Lord, first the lamb and then the oxen. They roasted the lambs and boiled the entrails of the holy offering in kettles and pots and rushed them out to the people to eat just as it was written in the Law by Moses.

The women were not included in the Temple choir of Levites, but they danced and sang, playing their tambourines during the worship. At the end of the day, the Levites prepared a meal for the priests and for themselves. This was the most inclusive and elaborate Passover since the time of Samuel. It was followed by the Feast of Unleavened Bread for seven days.

***

"I knew it wouldn't last long, only 13 years," Hilkiah lamented, rolling over in his sick bed, surrounded by his wife and three sons. "King Josiah was our only hope, and now he is dead. It was a mistake for him to ignore King Neco's message of peace and declare war on Egypt. Why he went out there without his royal robes and faced the enemy's arrow is a complete mystery to me. Jehoadaz was our only hope for survival; he was the only son of Josiah who is faithful to God. Now he sits in an Egyptian jail for refusing to bow to Pharaoh."

"Don't think about that, Father," Azariah said, wiping his father's brow. "Concentrate on getting well."

"Yes, hush all that fuss!" Simona added, patting his hand. "You'll tire yourself."

"Why should I want to get well?" Hilkiah said, pushing Azariah's hand away. "Jehoiakim, chosen by Neco, sits on the throne. He is the utmost of sinners. What kind of heathen lies with his own mother, his son's wife, and his stepmother? Then he adds insult to injury by killing the men whose wives he has violated and then seizes their property. He is an incestuous adulterer, a murderer, and a thief—not to mention that he has reversed his circumcision."

"You know better than I do that kings come and go, Father," Azariah said. "We have to make sure that God's word is constant in Judah and all of Israel."

"Ha! I wish you good fortune on that, my son. Jehoiakim is the king. He was placed on the throne to do Egypt's bidding. He taxes the people and gives the money to Pharaoh. How long do you think it will be before the people are back worshiping Baal again?"

"The people need us more than they ever did to keep the Temple holy," Hanan said. "We need your guidance, Father. The people respect you."

Hilkiah kicked his foot against his bed. "Don't be foolish! If they don't show reverence to Jehovah, who am I? I have given you the holy garments, Azariah. Put them on. You are the high priest. Let me alone. I don't want to witness the horrors that are sure to come. Haven't you listened to your brother Jeremiah's constant warnings? We will never have peace in this land again."

Jeremiah was angered and spoke up. "If the horrors are sure to come, why would God send me from town to town shouting warnings to people? There is hope! God is merciful, and He can soften toward the people."

"Jeremiah, there is no way to change prophesy. God has spoken. The only consolation in this life is family. Do as your brothers have done. Take a wife, and have some children to bring you joy in your youth and comfort in your old age."

Jeremiah looked down at the floor. "If what you say is true, then there will be no consolation for me except that which comes from the Lord. To spare me of the pain and worry, He has told me I cannot marry or have children. They would only be doomed with the rest."

"The Lord has blessed me, and I am very thankful," Hilkiah said, gripping Simona's hand. "I pray he will bless all of you. Now let me sleep."

The room grew quiet. Hilkiah went to sleep and never woke up again.

Chapter Nine

Azariah IV

Azariah treaded a fine line between his brother Jeremiah and the people of Judah—priests included. Jeremiah was prophesying the coming destruction of the Temple and the people, which was in contradiction to the prophesies of other prophets who had spoken of peace for the land. More than a few people wanted him silenced.

"You must be careful, my brother," Azariah said to Jeremiah. "Your life is in danger."

Jeremiah nodded. "There are many who want me dead," he said, kicking his sandal against a rock outside the entrance to the Temple courtyard.

Azariah sat down on the huge stone beside him. "Why don't you stay here in Jerusalem or Anathoth for a while? We can look after you and protect you."

"How can you do that, brother, when it's my own family who seem to be the angriest toward me?" he answered, referring to the other priests.

"The king is just as angry. He had the prophet Urijah murdered just for speaking against him. I don't doubt he would do the same to you."

"Jehoiakim has many more things to concern him than trying to quiet my preaching. He may not bow before the Lord in worship, but he will bow before his new master. The king of

Babylon's army has defeated the Egyptian and Assyrian forces in Carchemish. Nebuchadnezzar will take Pharaoh's place in the control of the king."

Azariah shrugged his shoulders. "What difference will that make? Jehoiakim's only allegiance is to the devil."

"Time will tell. He may not sit on the throne for long. I dare say another couldn't be worse."

The steady flow of people through the entrance of the Temple made Azariah nervous. He knew there were probably spies for the king among them. If Jeremiah were spotted in the area, it wouldn't be long before Jehoiakim's henchmen arrived.

"I still think it would be a lot safer for you if one of us traveled with you," Azariah said, his eyes searching for the possible informer among the crowd.

"No, your place is here in the Temple, and Hanan should be at your side. The Lord will protect me, that I am assured. He has instructed me to be the bearer of His message." Jeremiah got up and brushed off his robe. "I will speak with the people here today; and when I am finished, I will go back out into the cities."

Apprehensive, Azariah stood just behind Jeremiah on the platform in the courtyard of the Temple as he prepared to speak. This was his younger brother, but he seemed much older. Somehow, Jeremiah had outgrown him and Hanan. He had a larger calling from the Lord than they did. Azariah should have been jealous of the Lord's favor, but he lacked Jeremiah's courage. He preferred the comforts of home, the love of his wife and his little son. He admired Jeremiah for the work he was doing, but he would never want to stand in his shoes.

"People of Israel, you have committed egregious sins," Jeremiah began. "You steal, lie, and commit adultery and murder. You worship Baal, and then you run here to the Temple to throw a few offerings on the altar to be saved and then run off to do more devilment. There is no reason to burn sweet incense. I cannot accept the offering. These sins have robbed you. You stand before me with eyes that do not see and ears that do not listen. You have rejected the Lord, given yourselves to other gods in your land. For that, you will be slaves to foreigners in their land. The Lord says, 'The people have broken the contract made with their fathers. I will destroy this Temple. The evil I will send will be the fruit of your own sin.'"

The people groaned at the darkness of Jeremiah's message. Some of them walked away. They didn't want to hear of misery; they wanted to be encouraged.

A man shouted back at him. "Why do you curse us? We've come here to worship, haven't we? Isn't that what the Lord wants? We're not evil people!"

"You can't heal a wound by denying its existence," Jeremiah shouted back. "The priests and the prophets give you assurances of peace when war abounds. Don't assume that God won't destroy Jerusalem just because of the Temple that stands here behind me. The only way to escape disaster and destruction is to free your mind of wickedness; treat your fellow man fairly; and stop enslaving orphans, widows, and foreigners. And above all, stop worshiping idols. While God promises damnation, he still asks if you desire a path to a good road, the godly road you once walked along. There is still time to quit your evil ways, and the Lord will forgive and allow you to stay in this land."

The people grumbled and complained until Jeremiah had finished his message. It didn't matter that the people weren't receptive. He had to speak or the words would burn in him. He stepped to the side so the people could present their useless sacrifices.

***

"You have to do something!" Terah said, bursting into the house with the baby on her hips. My family won't even talk to me anymore. They treat me like a leper. They even refuse to take our son into their home."

Azariah held his arms out to hold his son. "Calm down," he said. "You'll have the child upset next. Sit down and take a breath."

Azariah was used to his wife being distraught after visits with her family. Though they consented to the marriage arrangement, they always had some criticism of her household. Being a loving daughter, Terah did everything she could to please and appease her parents. Her efforts didn't always bear fruit. For the first seven years of their marriage, she wasn't able to conceive. Her family had been cruel and dismissive, labeling her as barren until she finally gave birth to their son, Seraiah. They were happy with her now, but she still worried about falling out of their good graces.

"You must denounce Jeremiah, or the people will think you're against them," she raved. "He has everyone in a panic."

Holding the boy to his chest, Azariah scolded her in a low tone. "There's no way I can do that. Jeremiah is a prophet. He speaks for the Lord. You cannot expect me to denounce God's words. The people need to listen and heed all that he says."

"You know many of the people barely make sacrifices to the Temple as it is. Think of our son. If this keeps up, we'll have nothing to give to him."

"That isn't for you to concern yourself with," he said. "I'll take care of my family."

It seemed like more of his time was spent trying to assuage the fears and anxieties of the people who were unnerved by Jeremiah and his prophesies. Few of them voiced qualms about the king and what he had done, and none of them were moved to repent as Jeremiah had advised them all to do. Azariah didn't want to give up hope, but the words he had heard his brother speak on many occasions weighed heavily on his heart. How could Judah possibly survive now that King Jehoiakim was back on the throne?

Most of the kingdom and Azariah had prayed that the king was gone forever. From the very day that Jehoiakim came back, Azariah had become ill. He suffered headaches so painful that many days he could not get out of bed. Instead of the king complying with his victor in Babylon, he had become bolder and more defiant until he refused to be subservient to Nebuchadnezzar and returned his allegiance back to Egypt. So Nebuchadnezzar had come to Judah to squash Jehoiakim's rebelliousness.

Lying there, Azariah had flashes of the day that he watched in shock as Nebuchadnezzar rummaged through the treasures of the Temple and instructed his deputies to take the gold vessels that he fancied. It was all because of King Jehoiakim, who was sitting outside in a carriage bound in chains.

***

The city had gone from bad to worse, and now Azariah had gotten word that Pashur, a priest who was filling in for him at the Temple, had struck Jeremiah with his fist and had tortured him in the prison at the Upper Gate of Benjamin overnight. Early the next morning, Azariah pulled himself up from his sick bed, sent for Hanan, and waited in the upper room for Jeremiah to come back to Jerusalem.

Later in the day, Jeremiah arrived with his friend and disciple, Baruch. The strain showed in his face and his body. Azariah knew he probably didn't appear much better as they embraced.

"It's good to be someplace where I feel welcomed for a change," Jeremiah said, sitting down at the table Terah had prepared for them.

"We're happy to see you are safe and sound," Azariah said. "Hanan and I can't help but worry about you."

The two older brothers listened as Jeremiah described all that he had experienced. It was obvious that he was depressed and downhearted from his mission. The people mocked him and ignored his warnings. He was sad, not only for himself but for the terror he knew would rain down on them.

"I wish I had never been born," he said to his brothers. "I am despised wherever I go. People curse me as if I curse them. They don't know how many times I have begged the Lord to show them mercy."

"Trust me, there are many who hear you," Azariah assured him. "Tomorrow, on the day of fasting, you will speak with the people at the entrance of the Temple again."

"No, I won't," Jeremiah said sadly. "The Lord spoke to me and told me to take a scroll and write all the words that He had spoken to me concerning Israel and Judah and all the nations from the first day He spoke to me until this day. I dictated all of His messages to Baruch, and it is finished, but I will not read it. Only the Lord stands between them killing me. Hopefully, when they hear the word from a different voice, they will listen and understand that it is not my message, it's God's message."

"I pray that they do," Azariah said before he blessed the food.

***

Azariah was suffering another severe migraine the next morning, but he forced himself to rise from his bed to be a witness for Jeremiah while Baruch read his prophesies to the people. Looking out from a window of the Temple, he tried to gauge the reaction of the people while Baruch read from another window.

The people seemed confounded by the message, but they were not as rude as they had been to Jeremiah. One of the noblemen was struck by the message possibly because it was written on paper, giving more credence to it. The nobleman requested that Baruch accompany him back to the royal palace and read it the princes.

Baruch read the scroll to the princes, who were worried by the descriptions. The king heard about the reading and had Baruch come inside his parlor and read the scroll to him. Furious when he heard the words written in the scroll, the king snatched the scroll from Baruch, tore it in pieces, and threw the tattered paper into the hearth that burned in front of him. Then he threw Baruch in jail because of his impudence. When Baruch was released, Jeremiah dictated the words the Lord had given to him a second time.

***

"I'm afraid, Azariah," Terah said, hastily grabbing things to pack in her satchel. "The people have gone mad; they're turning on each other. Some are stealing everything they can. The rest are looking to take their anger out on someone. It's time to get out of the city. We'll be safer with my family."

"Have you lost your sense as well?" Azariah asked, pulling his things out of her bag. "You know I can't abandon my responsibilities at the Temple. That would surely be death for us. I fear God's wrath more than any man running wild out there in the streets."

"We have more reasons to go. My mother isn't well. She needs me. My father has guards who can protect us."

"Your mother has servants who can care for her. Haven't I protected you?"

"I want to be there for her. Besides, there's nothing you can do against an army if we're attacked again."

"Neither can your father's guards," Azariah snapped.

"Why do you always ask me to choose between you and my family?"

"I shouldn't have to ask you. You're my wife."

Terah wrapped up the belonging she had gathered and hurried to the door. "My main concern is for our son's safety," she said. "I promise you we'll return when things quiet down."

"I can't force you to stay here with me, wife, but I won't let Seraiah go with you."

"Don't be heartless to me!" she said, her eyes begging.

"You don't have to go," he told her. "Stay here. The Lord will cover us."

Terah shook her head and walked out the door. Seraiah, playing with his friends in the courtyard, noticed his mother rushing away."

"Mother, where are you going?" Seraiah called after her.

Terah tightened her veil over her face, moving quickly without looking back. Seraiah turned toward the door where his father stood. Azariah dropped his head and stepped back inside.

Seraiah ran to the door and opened it. "Where is my mother going?" he asked, puzzled. "Is she coming back?"

"She is going to stay with her parents for a while. Your grandmother is ill."

"Why didn't she let me go with her this time? I always go with her."

"She wanted you to go, but I need you here. You will be a man soon. There is much work to do to prepare you to take your place in the Temple."

***

Jeremiah kept up his warnings to the people and the king. Stubborn and still rebellious, Jehoiakim refused to yield to the word of God; and in his defiance, he also rebelled against Nebuchadnezzar, who he believed was weakened after a battle with Egypt. His judgment was wrong again. Nebuchadnezzar and his army laid siege to Judah and conquered the city; and sometime during the raid, the people of Judah killed their own king and threw his body over the wall of the city. Jeremiah's prophesy was fulfilled.

Jeconiah became king after his father's death. He reigned for 100 days, and then the armies of Babylon seized Jerusalem. He, his royal court, and his family were exiled in Babylon. Even more devastating was the drain of the wealthy and most skilled citizens of Judah, who were also exiled. Terah and her family were among those taken. Azariah was heartbroken but relieved that he had not allowed Seraiah to go with Terah.

Azariah watched helplessly as his father before him did as the Babylonian king desecrated and plundered the Temple and its treasures. The Israelites had insisted on having a king to lead them, and this is what it brought them. Obedience to God wasn't sufficient for them. They wanted a mortal man to lord over them, and now it had been to their detriment. As Jeremiah said, "My people have been lost sheep. Their shepherds have led them astray." It didn't take a wise man to see that they were at a crucial point. Their survival as a people was at stake. Azariah could feel his health failing. The only thing he could do was prepare Seraiah to take his place.

"It's time for you to take your position as high priest, my son," Azariah said solemnly. "I won't walk this wretched earth much longer."

"Don't say that, Father. Take some time off, and rest yourself. I'm praying for your recovery."

"Those are wasted prayers, I'm afraid. Even so, your appointment is much bigger than that. Before you wear the holy clothes of the high priest, there is much for you to understand. God bestowed this sacred honor upon your ancestor Aaron to carry throughout his generations. It is your responsibility to intercede for the people. Continual sacrifices must be made for their sins. The ark of the covenant is the most holy; it must be protected and treated as such."

"I know all that, Father. You have taught me well."

"You must be prepared for the greatest of evil. We are in a time the Israelites have never seen before. Jeremiah's prophesy will come to pass if the people don't renew their faith with the Lord and repent. We will be taken from this land into exile. The protection of the ark and God's word will rest heavily on your shoulders. Any missteps on your part can bring about instant death."

Seraiah nodded. It was in that moment that he understood his father's headaches.

***

"What is to become of this Temple and the people?" Azariah asked Jeremiah as they sat on the floor of the outer room. "The two years of occupation have taken their toll. Our mother is dead, our brother Hanan is dead. I have no wife. We are weak and torn beyond repair."

"Not true, my brother," Jeremiah said, patting Azariah on the shoulder. "This is God's punishment. It will be long and hard, but it will end.

"There's nothing and no one left to fight. Only the poor and starving are left here."

"Find your faith again, brother. I will tell you as I have said in a letter to those 10,000 who are captives in Babylon. We must build, plant, and multiply so that our numbers are not diminished. Be steadfast in your prayers to Jehovah, and beware of false prophets. After 70 years, he will return his people to this place."

Azariah brushed his feet against the dust around them. "I will surely be dead and buried by them, my brother. I can only pray that Seraiah will see that day when the Temple is restored again."

"There is hope that the city won't be totally destroyed," Jeremiah said. "My prayer is that Zedekiah will listen to my counsel and repent."

Except Zedekiah did not listen to Jeremiah's warnings. As defiant as his brother, he was disloyal to Babylon and joined

Egypt in hopes of bringing down Nebuchadnezzar. Jeremiah's only option was, again, to take his pleas for repentance out to the people, the Philistines, the Moabites, the Ammonites, and the Edomites; but none of them heeded his warnings.

***

Nine years into Zedekiah's reign, Azariah was dead, and his son, Seraiah, was now the high priest. Nebuchadnezzar responded to Zedekiah's insolence with vengeance. He marched on Jerusalem until his army had completely surrounded the city. In desperation, Zedekiah sent for Jeremiah and urged him to pray to God on his behalf. Jeremiah could only tell the king that it was too late.

"The prophesy has come to pass. The people remaining in the city will be attacked by Nebuchadnezzar's army, and all that do not submit to the Babylonians will be mercilessly slain."

The priests, tired of Jeremiah preaching gloom and doom to the people, asked the king for permission to arrest Jeremiah and put him to death. His prophesying was breaking the morale of the soldiers. Being spiteful, the king gave them his approval. They abducted Jeremiah and lowered him by rope into the dungeon of mud. He would have starved to death or drowned in the mire if a court official had not urged the king to allow him to rescue Jeremiah. Jeremiah was then brought before the king to give him the message from God.

"If you leave Jerusalem and surrender to the king of Babylon, the people in this city will be spared," Jeremiah told him, unfazed.

Even then, Zedekiah was stubborn.

"I cannot surrender. The people will see me as a coward. I

would be traitor to this throne. Your words have no use to me, and the only place I can offer you protection is in prison."

Jeremiah was sheltered in jail, receiving a loaf of bread each day until the famine and the fall of Jerusalem.

Chapter Ten
Seraiah

Upheaval spread over Jerusalem as the skies grew dark. Storms came, not deluges of rain, but of soldiers trampling the Israelites and burning down everything in their path. Seraiah spent his days and nights at the Temple, trying to soothe the people. Crowds gathered there all through the day, mostly those who realized that God's punishment was upon them. Nebuchadnezzar's army had surrounded the walls of the fortified city of Jerusalem. The very walls that had been constructed to protect the people had become a trap. Out in the country, they might have stood a better chance of escape.

There was no way out except to walk through the hundreds of thousands of soldiers waiting to attack. The terror was worse than any words Jeremiah had spoken or described to them. Not only did imminent death await them outside the wall, on the inside they were cut off from the fields without another source for food. As the months wore on with the Babylonian army camped outside the wall, the people's hunger turned into starvation. Desperate and out of their minds with no water or bread, some boiled and ate the flesh of their children.

Disease broke out and spread among the captive people, and they died horrible and painful deaths. The stench of rotting corpses filled the air. Men and women staggered through the streets delirious, wearing sackcloth in sorrow and mourning.

Some wore it in repentance for their sins. Their heads were covered in dust for the many who perished daily. Their numbers dwindled without any contact with their enemy. Jeremiah was helpless as he watched the sufferings of the people. Why couldn't they have heeded his warnings?

***

Another bad dream woke Seraiah. He had always had them as a child; but now anytime that he tried to sleep, his mind was filled with horrible scenes. It had gotten so bad that he dreaded sleep. He had begun to drink strong wine at night before bed so that he wouldn't remember the disturbing images. It was even worse whenever his uncle Jeremiah came to the Temple. His mind seemed to draw pictures of every horrid episode he foretold. Seraiah never discussed them with his wife, Carmela, although he suspected that she was aware of his restlessness.

Seraiah got up from the bed, dressed, and went to look for his youngest son, Hosea, who was six years old. He was different than his older brother, more easygoing, possibly because of the defect in his legs when he was born. One leg was two inches shorter than the other. He and Carmela had coddled him because of it, but they didn't need to. He ran and played as if he had two strong legs, and he had a loving disposition. Simply, his smile would make you smile, and his laughter made his father forget about his worries for a while. Seraiah found Hosea entertaining his mother with a rhyme he liked to recite.

"Good day, husband, did you sleep well?" Carmela asked when he walked into the room.

"Yes, I did," he said with the usual lie, lifting Hosea in the air. "How's my boy?"

"I am very well, Father," he answered, giggling.

They wrestled together for a few moments until the house servant came in and put the morning meal on the table.

"Go find your brother," Carmela told Hosea after Seraiah put him down.

Carmela watched her husband chew his food, noting the tension in his jaw, even after he stopped eating. She knew the pressure he was under. Everyone in the city was a nervous wreck. They wanted the man of God to intercede for them. They wanted a miracle.

Seraiah had only eaten a few bites when he heard the voices of his assistant priests outside.

"I have to go," he said, squeezing Carmela's hand. "Tell Jozadak to be sure he's at the Temple for the evening service."

Jozadak was only 12 years old, but Seraiah treated him as if he were a man. Time was short, and he had to be fully trained to accept his responsibilities. Smart and strong, Jozadak was loyal to his father. He was always ready to fight anyone who criticized him. Even though he was still a boy, he lived up to the meaning of his name, "Jehovah is righteous." Seraiah relied on Jozadak's strength to fend for the family when he wasn't there.

***

Seraiah knew the Temple would be ransacked and looted by Nebuchadnezzar's soldiers. His father had warned him about it many years before. Now he had a crucial decision to make. He'd prayed and prayed for guidance, but it seemed that the Lord had turned his ear away from him. Still, something had to be done. His family had been designated to protect God's word, not when it was favorable or convenient, but it was for all times. He couldn't just stand by and watch heathens desecrate the word given to his people.

Seraiah prayed again, "Please, Lord, forgive our filthy hands in what we must do today. We have pledged respect for Your word, but in this instance, we plead for understanding. Be gracious to us this evening; don't smite us for the unholy treatment of the ark." Then in the dark of night, without the poles and none of the fanfare and reverence that was used to carry the ark of the covenant, Seraiah had it removed from the Temple with the help of Zephaniah, the assistant priest, his older son, Jozadak, and two Temple guards. They carried it on an ox cart and hid it in the stable behind the high priest's quarters.

Seraiah paused outside the stable, and in a hushed voice he cautioned them: "Trust isn't plentiful under the threat of death and destruction, but I've placed what little I have in all of you." He faced the Temple guards. "You both have been faithful to the Temple, and I implore you to be faithful to God and His word."

"We are God's humble servants as well, master," one of the guards said. "I will stand guard here day and night if you need me."

"No, we don't want to draw any attention," Seraiah replied hastily. "We must pretend there is nothing in there of any value to anyone. Go home to your families. There's nothing else I can ask of you."

"We have no home to go to, master," the other guard said. "We do not even know if our families are safe or among the dead. There's nowhere to run and nowhere to hide. Let us stay here and be of service to you."

Seraiah exhaled heavily. "You may stay if you wish, but I have nothing to offer you."

"We expect nothing," the first guard answered.

"Well, there is plenty of that," Seraiah chuckled, attempting to lighten the mood. "In the meantime, return to the Temple. I'll be there later."

When they left, Seraiah spoke seriously to his son and Zephaniah.

"Jozadak, this ark is the covenant that Jehovah made with Moses. We, as members of the family of Levites, direct descendants of Aaron, have been entrusted to protect God's word. My father, his father, and his fathers before him have had to move this ark more than once to shield it from the desecration that has come to the Temple under rogue kings. As you saw, the gold has already been removed from it. I don't know what will become of the Temple during this invasion, but this ark must be safeguarded. No one is to be told."

"I will stand by you, Father, I will guard the ark with my life," Jozadak told him.

"My uncle Jeremiah's prophesies are being fulfilled. If the king of Babylon's actions from the last invasion are any determination of what will happen this time. There's a chance that we will be taken there as hostages."

"It is more than a chance at this point," Zephaniah added. "It is a certainty."

"That is what the prophesy foretold, Father," Jozadak said with wide-eyes. "Uncle Jeremiah warned that we would be slaves in a foreign land."

"If we are taken, son, the ark must be carried with us. Kings cannot be trusted to protect it."

Jozadak nodded in agreement.

***

Seraiah was heartsick. They had been under siege for months. Daily, the Temple was overrun with men, women, and children. They wanted to repent; they wanted to be blessed. They wanted to hear words from Jehovah. The one message that the people always looked for him to deliver, which was hope for tomorrow, was bereft of meaning. There were no animals to sacrifice and no bread or tithes to offer. Even Seraiah and his family barely had enough to eat.

Seraiah stood at the entrance at the Temple and spoke to the desperate and despondent throng that amassed there.

"God is testing our faith, children of Israel. I know things look bleak for us right now, but we will prevail. Jehovah did not come to our aid so many times before to look away while our enemies fight to destroy us. He loves us. All join me in prayer."

"We don't need prayers!" someone yelled out angrily. "We need food in out bellies. We are dying of sickness, and we are starving. Tell me, where is the love in that?"

A woman cried out earnestly. "You speak to God for us. Tell Him we are humbled before Him. Ask Him to deliver us."

"Don't you think I have?" Seraiah answered in frustration. "I ask for His forgiveness and relief around the clock."

"If He doesn't hear you, then what good are you?" the angry man yelled. "Maybe we need another high priest!"

It was no use responding. Talk wasn't going to change anything. If only they had listened to Jeremiah. Seraiah went into the inner room to pray again for mercy. Slowly, the people drifted away.

Most days, Seraiah stayed at the Temple from the morning service through the evening service, but the idle hours without sacrifices and incense to burn troubled him. No one needed him there. He went back home to see if he could help his family.

The courtyard was quiet when Seraiah got to his quarters. His wife, Carmela, who was always there to greet him, was nowhere to be found, and neither were his sons. Fear gripped his chest. His first thought was that they had been taken. The people were so desperate, and there was little they wouldn't do to survive.

Seraiah found Carmela on her knees in the silo, scooping up grain from the threshing floor. She looked up when she saw her husband's feet. Her face looked sad and gaunt, like that of an old woman, and her body had become thin. The sight of her made him feel weak and tired like an old man. The invasion had taken a toll on all of them. It was a struggle living in a war zone. Seraiah knelt beside Carmela and helped to gather the grain. It felt light in his hands and slipped through his fingers. He saw himself as the grain of wheat. All the comforts and superficial things he surrounded himself with were gone. He was naked in the world.

Seraiah watched Carmela grind the wheat into flour and then take it back to the courtyard. He followed her in silence. He kept watching as she mixed the oil and the water with the flour, pushing it and molding it into bread. The truth stared back at him. She was the one preparing a meal that would sustain them for a while longer. He wasn't much help to his family either, just plain useless. There was so much more that he wanted to do with his life, but now he could only wait and see what would become of him.

***

After 18 months of the invasion, just after dark, the moment they feared was upon them. The sound of the battering ram hitting the door of the city boomed loudly until the northern gate was broken off its hinges. Thousands of arrows rained in over the wall from archers to cover the infantry men who stormed into the city with their swords slashing at everything in their path. More gates of the city were torn down, and the horsemen in their chariots rode in, churning the dry ground into clouds of dust. They trampled over the people and beat them with sticks.

The Israelite soldiers fought back, but weakened by hunger and disease, they were defenseless. Flames lit up the darkness, and the smoke mixed with the dust, making the air too thick to breathe without choking. Countless spears covered in flames flew through the air. A chorus of screams swirled with the sound of swords clanging, as their attackers roared like beasts in a deadly symphony of flesh being cut and heads being hammered.

King Zedekiah and his army escaped through a gate in the king's garden, but they were captured on the plains of Jericho.

"We are alone," Zephaniah said to Seraiah inside the Temple. "The army is gone."

"What about the king?" Seraiah asked, forlorn.

"I've heard that he was taken to Riblah, where Nebuchadnezzar was stationed, and there he was tortured and killed."

"We both know there's even more misery on the other side of the wall," Seraiah said, falling prostrate before the altar. "All we can do is pray."

His prayer was a different one. This time, it wasn't for the Temple or forgiveness for the people. It was for the survival of his sons and the preservation of God's laws.

***

Jerusalem was brought to its knees in defeat. Nebuchadnezzar remained in Riblah and sent his chief general, Nebuzaradan, to knock it down completely. They started at Solomon's Temple; and they emptied it of the gold, silver, and bronze, the holy pots, bowls, and dishes used in the sacred services. They packed away the basins, censers, lamps, and goblets. They took down the bronze pillars, the 12 bronze bulls under it, and the movable stands. Once all the treasures of the Temple had been removed, the general gave the order for it to be burned.

Nebuzaradan pointed at Seraiah, who looked on in anguish. "You and him," he said, pointing at Zephaniah. "Come with me."

On the way out, Nebuzaradan ordered the guards of the Temple to follow him, too. Outside, they were put in heavy chains. When they were 50 yards away, the Temple was set on fire. The general kept moving with the priests corralled behind him like cattle. As they trudged along, every house, large and small, was set on fire. Then the palace was set ablaze. The flames burned for days as the people stared in disbelief. The walls were weakened and toppled down to their foundation. The entire city had been demolished.

Seven royal advisers, the chief officer in charge of the army, and 60 of his men still in the city were rounded up. They joined Seraiah, the priests, and the Temple guards in a makeshift prison. These military, civil, and religious leaders were brought to Riblah, where the king of Babylon had them all executed. All the treasures of the Temple and the palace, along with 10,000 captives of the wealthy, the elite soldiers, the skilled, and the expert craftsmen were taken into Babylon. The poorest and unskilled were left behind to tend to the land.

Chapter Eleven

Jozadak

The victorious became the conquered when Babylon fell to the Persian king Cyrus the Great. Jozadak hadn't considered what direction his life would take until that day. Before then, it would have been a waste of time, a fantasy of folly. His only certainty was that he would die in Babylon. He had made a life for himself there, knowing that his life back in Jerusalem ended on the day his father died. It was still the clearest memory of his life. It was his fourteenth birthday.

That morning, he'd watched his mother, on her knees, beg his father not to go to the Temple. Hosea sat in his chair, listening with tears in his eyes.

"You'll be killed! It's too dangerous!" Carmela cried, pulling on the hem of Seraiah's robe.

"My trust is in the Lord," Seraiah told her. "The city is being terrorized. If now is not the time to go to Him in supplication, when would that time ever be?"

Carmela held the cloth tightly in her hand. "You've prayed on this for years. There's nothing more you can do. The prophesy will not be changed. It's already come to pass."

"Carmela, you must be strong for Hosea," he said, jerking the robe from her hands. Then he motioned to Jozadak. "Son, come outside with me," he said, walking out the door.

Jozadak jumped to his feet, rushed out the door, and closed it behind him. "I'll go with you today, Father. I'm not afraid."

Horrible sounds of despair grew closer. Chaos and mayhem had engulfed the city. For a moment, Seraiah considered taking refuge back in the house with his worried wife, but he refused to be a coward in front of his sons.

"You're my eldest son," Seraiah said to Jozadak. "You are the one I trust for this awesome task. Your uncle Jeremiah foretold this day a long time ago. When I heard the gates of the city being broken, I took the most precious thing we have, God's word, and hammered it into the bottom of the wagon for safekeeping. It is concealed under a pile of cloth. We are sure to be driven out of the city or die in it. The ark must be carried with us. No one is to be told that it's there, not even your mother!"

"I won't say a word, Father," Jozadak promised.

"Good," Seraiah said, patting his son's shoulder. "I'll be back as soon as I can."

Jozadak stood back as his father ambled away. Once Seraiah made his way out of the priests' courtyard, Jozadak took a few steps to keep his father within his sights. He followed him all the way to the Temple, staying just far back as not to be discovered. He was hidden in the shrubs when the soldiers stormed toward the Temple. The horses and chariots stirred up so much dust that it clouded his view. That's where he was when he saw his father pushed out of the entrance.

Jozadak wanted to rush over and do something to help. He hesitated, knowing if he were taken, there would be no one to look after his mother, his brother, and the ark. He gawked in horror as they chained his father to Zephaniah, then another priest, and then the Temple guards. He stared in disbelief as they looted the house of worship and then set fire to it.

How could they be so evil? But it wasn't fury on their faces; it was a raging lust for debauchery and destruction. Jozadak knew they would persist unsatisfied until the whole city was up in flames. Panic-stricken, he raced back home. He had fallen more than once on the way, trying to run faster than his legs would carry him.

"We have to go," he said frantically to his mother and Hosea when he finally got back home. "They have taken father away in chains. They were headed toward the palace. We must catch up to them. I'll get the wagon."

"Help us, Jehovah!" she shrieked. The day that made her shiver with fear in the night had finally come.

Jozadak went back to the stable, where the wagon was already hitched to an ox. Inside the house, Carmela stuffed some clothing and bedding in a bag and a few of their belongings in a blanket that she wrapped up tightly and threw them over her shoulder. She grabbed Hosea by the hand and darted out the door.

Carmela was surprised to find the wagon packed with supplies, feed for the ox, and everything ready to go. She placed her bags on top of the wagon, Hosea on top of the ox, and led the way out of the courtyard. Their pace was slowed not only by the ox pulling the wagon but by the thick plumes of black smoke that hung low on the path out of the city. It should have been a cool March afternoon, but the heat from the fires made it feel like summer.

When they reached the palace, it was deserted and simmered like wood and rocks in an oven fire. They headed outside the broken walls that once safeguarded the city. They hadn't gotten far when they were stopped and questioned by General Nebuzaradan's men. Only the elite, educated, and the skilled were being taken into exile. Jozadak was relieved after Carmela was questioned and they were forced into the long procession out of Jerusalem. The numbers of people in the march enlarged by width and length, and the ground trembled under their weight as they traveled. Hosea wanted to walk beside his brother, but his legs grew tired after a while, and Carmela put him back on top of the wagon.

Jozadak watched the wagon shift and shake as the ox pulled it over the rough terrain. It boggled his mind that he was transporting something so essential and vital to the survival of the people, yet he felt as indistinct as a common fish in the sea of people that flowed along the side of the Euphrates River. The great number of them blocked out the horizon, and he could not see much in the distance ahead of him. He wished he could shove through the crowd to find his father and keep him within his sight, but he was contained in the small space, unable to move forward or backward. The march carried him along like a steady tide, with his sandals twisting in the sand and rocks beneath them.

***

The cavalcade of exiles had been moving for more than a week when they approached Riblah, the city that Nebuchadnezzar used as his headquarters. Situated near the center of the horde, the people were just about to set up camp when there was a burst of commotion. A man was rushing through the site, yelling, "They've been killed! They were slaughtered like lamb for sacrifice!"

"Who?" Jozadak heard someone call out.

"The high priest, the general, the governor, and all the officials that were chained up at the palace," the man answered.

Carmela screamed, and Hosea began to cry.

"It couldn't be true!" Jozadak said. "They didn't have a reason to kill him."

There was much weeping and moaning heard in the camp that night. Sorrow filled the air around them like the black smoke had filled Jerusalem. Tormented, Jozadak closed his eyes tight and prayed the way he had seen his father pray. He recited the words of God that his father had him memorize. It was that intense meditation that kept him focused on his promise to his father.

Jozadak lost count of the days that they trekked toward Babylon, but he knew it was nearly a 500-mile journey east to Babylon, along the Euphrates River, over sand and rock. He became more obsessed about his wagon. He wouldn't allow anyone else besides Hosea to ride on it. He slept on top of it at night, fearful that the ark might be discovered and anxious to safeguard it from thievery. A few commented that the wagon seemed full but noticed he never took anything from it. Some even found it peculiar, but then they excused it as the behavior of a boy who lost his father and was clinging to something that belonged to him.

For months, the Israelites walked, carrying their grief on their backs. The emotional toll was hard enough, being separated from loved ones and lost possessions, but the physical toll was a steady rival. The temperatures had risen higher across the desert as the weeks passed and food was scarce. The people prayed for rain, needing the water to refresh themselves and the animals. Sickness spread through the camp like weeds in a garden, choking the life out of the weak. Helplessness and sorrow walked with them every step of the way.

When Hosea fell ill, it nearly killed Carmela. The good-natured boy never complained. He died with a smile on his face. For Carmela, her own death would have been easier. If not for Jozadak, she would have gladly ended her life. He wasn't a man yet, so he still needed her.

The people rallied around them in sympathy and respect for Seraiah. Jozadak wanted to hurt the soldiers that guarded them. He didn't care if they killed him in the process. He'd seen what they could do. If they killed him, they would set his spirit free. The only thing that stopped him was his promise to his father. He needed to protect the ark and his mother for the rest of the journey and in the strange land they were moving toward.

***

Inside the walls of Babylon was a beautiful city. Jozadak wondered how such evil and violent men could not have spoiled it. But he doubted they could be comfortable in this place. It looked nothing like Jerusalem. The buildings were different, the language of the people there was different, and their worship was different.

Asa, another assistant priest who served under Seraiah and who had been separated from his family during the assault, helped Carmela and Jozadak set up their tent in the section of the city where the Israelites were to reside. Once Carmela was settled in, he sat outside with Jozadak to have a talk. He knew Jozadak, as Seraiah's son and a descendant of Aaron, was essential in his mission to restore the priesthood after the Exile.

"We must do what your great-uncle Jeremiah advised us to do," Asa told him. "We must build houses, plant gardens, and thrive."

"I haven't decided what I'm going to do," Jozadak replied rudely, resenting his interference.

"I want to help you, young man," Asa said to him, sensing his agitation. "Your birthright says you are the next high priest."

"What difference does that make here?" Jozadak said, still angry. "They only thing they seem to want is for us to lose our faith."

"You have an obligation to maintain the covenant."

"That was back in Jerusalem. There is no Temple here."

"Just because we're in a different place doesn't mean we're different people," Asa said. "We still have to follow God's laws. We are not past redemption."

Jozadak picked up a rock from the ground and threw it as hard as he could. "None of us will ever be the same again," he said. "We're right back where we started, as prisoners."

"You know as well as I do that on that path out of Egypt, we Levites were set aside to cover the children of Israel with God's word and be intercessors to cleanse the people of their sins."

Jozadak kicked the ground, taking out his fury on it. "It's because of the peoples' sins that we are here now. They're the reason my father is dead."

"That's why your position is more important than ever!" Asa said, gripping Jozadak's shoulders and looking him in the eye.

Jozadak shrugged and pushed Asa's hands away. "I don't have a position. Excuse me, I need to find work to cover my mother."

"Seraiah was like a brother to me. I will take your mother as my wife and care for her. I want to take you as my son and teach you. It would be an honor for me to care for your father's family."

"If my mother wants to marry you, that is her decision, but I don't need a father. I'm not a child; I can take care of myself."

"It's me who needs you," Asa said sincerely. "Help me preserve the word for our people."

Jozadak thought about the last talk he had had with his father and the promise he had made to him to guard the ark and the word of the people. He would do anything not to disappoint him.

"For my father's sake, I will help you."

***

The Israelites were given a certain degree of autonomy in Babylon. Self-governed villages were established where they were given the freedom to exercise their religion without force to accept the practices of their captors. They were given land where they could till the soil and provide for their families. The elders were allowed to handle the internal affairs of the people. They were also permitted to participate in the commerce of the city and accumulate wealth.

Babylonian society was much different from that of Jerusalem. It was more diverse, with opportunities for the people to become prosperous. Women were held as equals there. They could have businesses and retain the wealth they acquired. For many, the Exile was a change for the better. As the years passed, the longing to return home lessened. Material comforts with the peace of not having to defend themselves were embraced. Over time, the Israelites began to adopt the customs and manners of the Babylonian people. Even after all they had suffered as punishment, a few began to practice idolatry.

Asa, true to his word, married Carmela and built a home for them in one of the villages reserved for the Israelites, and he built a shed for Jozadak to store his beloved wagon. During the week, he and Jozadak worked together, writing down God's word that had been passed down orally for generations. They eventually started a school and taught other scribes.

Faithful ones wanted to worship God and looked to Jozadak as the son of their high priest to speak to them. Although they couldn't honor Jehovah with sacrifices in Babylon, they observed the Sabbath in a weekly communal service at home. They fasted, read the word, and offered prayers facing Jerusalem. As the people prospered, they built synagogues for their formal worship services. Large numbers came to hear Jozadak speak out of respect for his legacy and his uncanny recall of the words on the scroll.

Carmela spent her days going to the market to buy grain and then baking bread, even though she had a servant to do it. It was only when Jozadak's wedding was announced that she stopped. Both men were glad to see her happy again. Jozadak hadn't seen her smile for many years, maybe not since Jerusalem had been invaded. She spent days planning the celebration. Then one week before the marriage, her heart stopped. Some said it wasn't strong enough to hold her joy.

***

It was at Asa's urging that Jozadak took a wife. Her name was Etana, the daughter of a Levite merchant. Etana was an attractive young woman, but what Jozadak liked most was her independence. She earned her own money weaving cloth in a tailor's shop. Jozadak kept his emotions covered and wasn't affectionate or sentimental, but Etana didn't seem to mind. They were blessed with five children: two daughters, Diza and Gayle; and three sons, Elliot, Joshua, and Rabin. Etana liked the status she had as a priest's wife. With the tithes and offerings, they could afford to have someone attend to the menial duties in the home while she worked on growing her own business.

The years passed quickly in Babylon. Jozadak and Etana's two daughters were married and had children of their own. Disappointingly, their oldest son, Elliot, who Jozadak thought would secede him and one day be high priest, had married a woman who was not a Levite. That wasn't the only thing that disturbed Jozadak, though. It seemed to him that in some ways his own family was adopting the culture of Babylon and betraying God.

"You all are taking on the ways of our enemy," Jozadak said, scolding his oldest son. "We were not brought here to stay. You all are so hungry for money! Where is your hunger for God's word?"

"Father, are you angry because we are happy?" Elliot said. "Don't you want us to be happy?"

Jozadak wasn't sure what he wanted. He only knew that it wasn't in Babylon.

Then there was the issue of the ark of the covenant. There were many days when Jozadak sat alone working with Asa that he considered telling him about the ark concealed in the storehouse, but something kept him from revealing his secret.

At this time he had held it to himself for so long, he was almost ashamed to tell anyone.

Now it was 539 BC, and Babylon had been invaded and conquered by Cyrus the Great. As the new king, he issued a decree, freeing all the people of Israel to return to their home in Jerusalem. The king also said that with his help they were to rebuild the Temple.

All of these developments had Jozadak's head filled with doubts. Here he was, a man with the bulk of his life behind him. The journey back to Jerusalem was uncertain. Who would rule? Would the people turn against God and worship false idols as they had done so many times before? Would the people understand his hiding the contents of the wagon for nearly 50 years?

***

After days of meditation, Jozadak came to a conclusion. Before he confided in Asa, he had to share his decision with his wife. Lately, he found there was little time when he could speak to Etana alone. She was always in her store, working with the women she hired. Some of them spun from flax; some of them spun wool. He was proud that she had woven the linen for the fine clothes that he and the other priests wore during the worship service.

Etana was skilled in her craft. She could spin the finest thread from flax and weave it like an artist. Her linen was the most sought after in Babylon. Using almond leaves, she created many shades of luminous yellows. From the root of the madder plant, she got brilliant reds. From the bloom of the indo flower, she made a range of blues. And from the pomegranate tree bark, she created inky black. She would mix the colors into a rainbow of hues to dye the threads that she interwove with her fine cloth. Then she embroidered the cloth for extra detail.

Jozadak waited until the afternoon when the women had gone home before he went into the store. From the door, he watched Etana put flax onto the spindle and begin to spin, carefully drawing the fibers from the distaff that she held in her arm. She was humming the unknown tune that had become so familiar to him over the years. She pretended not to notice her husband, who had been pacing across the floor behind her for nearly an hour. She knew what he was deliberating over. It was the same decision that every family in their town was pondering: whether or when they would return to Jerusalem.

It had been over a week since King Cyrus had made his decree, and Jozadak had been waiting for her to broach the subject, but she still had not spoken about it. His patience had grown short with her; he had been waiting for this moment for nearly 50 years.

"Etana, what is wrong with you?" Jozadak finally asked in frustration. "You act as if you are oblivious to everything."

"This day doesn't seem to be much different from any other day," Etana said, continuing to spin. "I have a lot of work to do. The orders for fabric have piled up. I need to hire more help."

"I can't believe you!" he said, amazed at her nonchalant attitude. "Who cares about that? We are free to leave this place at last!"

"Do you think that you have a home back there waiting for you after all this time?" she asked.

Jozadak felt emboldened by Etana's words. Maybe she would be agreeable to what he felt would be the next step for them.

"I've given this much thought," he said. "I've decided that I'm not going back to Jerusalem. There is nothing left for me there."

Etana stopped her spinning. "I'm pleased to hear that, husband. We have made a good life here for ourselves."

"Why would we stay here?" Jozadak asked, dumbfounded. "We have no real freedom here. Have you forgotten we're captives?"

"The decree says we're free now," Etana answered. "We are free to go or stay. Our lives are here, our home is here, and we have raised our family here. Many families in our village are going to stay here in Babylon. They rely on you at the school and the synagogue. You should be proud of what you have accomplished here."

"It's doesn't matter whether we go back to Jerusalem or not. We can't stay here," Jozadak said, raising his voice. "You may have forgotten what they did to us, but it is fresh in my mind, as if it all happened yesterday."

"You yourself have said that was God's punishment for the disobedience of our people. Nebuchadnezzar was used by Him to fulfill the prophesy. Nothing will ever be the same, husband. My parents are dead; your parents are dead. The Temple has been burned, and no one even makes sacrifices anymore."

"That's why we have to move on. The wells have been poisoned here and in Jerusalem. I want to search for fresh water."

"What are you talking about?"

"I'm saying that I am not going back to Jerusalem and I am not going to live out the rest of my days in this place. The prophet Isaiah tells us the Lord said, 'Leave your country, your people and your father's household and go to the land I will show you.' "

Now Etana was upset. Why wasn't Jozadak asking what she wanted?

"Are you also saying that it doesn't matter to you what anyone else may feel about this?"

"That's exactly what I'm saying," he barked. "When I was brought here, I had no intentions of staying. We were to make good of our time here so our families would have enough for a new beginning."

Etana could see that there was no use trying to reason with him now.

"This is a conversation that we should have with all the family present," she said, returning to her spinning.

"You are right," Jozadak said indignantly. "We'll discuss it with the children on the Sabbath, after the evening meal."

***

There was a hush in the room during the evening meal. Jozadak's sons, their wives and children, and Joshua were there. His daughters were there with their husbands and children. It was at these occasions when he looked around the table that it was hard for him to fathom how much his life had expanded while he was being contained. Jozadak was sure that Etana had not held her tongue and there had been numerous discussions between them.

At the end of the meal, Jozadak stood up and said, "As you all know, King Cyrus has ended our exile. I was only 14 years old when I came here. I have spent 48 years here, knowing I didn't belong here. While all of you were born here, this is not your home; and never having set foot in Jerusalem, that is not your home, either. My hope is that we all move on and find a place that we can call home."

He paused and looked around the table at their faces. There was no hint of eagerness or excitement in the expressions that stared back at him. He nodded toward his son Elliot for him to speak.

"Father, I love and respect you, but I have been thinking about this situation, also. While you say this is not my home, it is the only home I have known. I have decided to stay in Babylon with my family. The husbands of my sisters have also decided to stay in this city. Our lives are here, we have built successful businesses, and our children are happy."

Jozadak said, "What you've accomplished here can be duplicated in another city, a city that welcomes you instead of imprisoning you. We have proven that we can prosper under bad circumstances, so we can flourish under neutral conditions."

"What you are suggesting is the same thing that Nebuchadnezzar had us do, leave everything we have and start again with nothing," Elliot said.

"Where is the sense of family, your sense of duty to Jehovah?" Jozadak asked, looking at each of his sons. "I'm getting old. The service to God and our people will soon be yours."

"I have already surrendered my right to secede you as high priest," Elliot said. "My wife is not a Levite, and my sons cannot serve as priests."

There was silence for a moment until Etana spoke. "If you feel strongly about your allegiance to the people of Israel, husband, then you must return to Jerusalem to rebuild the Temple."

Jozadak took a deep breath. "The Levites have tried over and over again to keep Israelites close to God, and they have failed over and over again. We can establish a new nation, loyal to God's word without the distractions of pagan worshipers."

"That's what you have done here, Father," Elliot said. "What about your loyalty to the people? Cannot you administer to those who want to stay in Babylon?"

"We cannot build a Temple to worship Jehovah on rented land," Jozadak said, stomping out of the room and out of the house.

Jozadak walked around in the darkness until the fervor of his temper eased. He reweighed all the options in his mind. There was nothing in his spirit that would concede to going back to Jerusalem. He hated the thought of separating from members of his family, but nothing in his spirit would accept staying in Babylon. His mind was made up. He wasn't going backward, and he wasn't going be stagnant. He was moving forward.

Etana was lying awake in bed when he returned. "I'm going to leave this place," Jozadak said, standing above her. "Those who want to come are welcome, those who choose to go back to Jerusalem have my blessing, and those who desire to stay in Babylon have my best wishes."

"You, husband, have my blessings and best wishes in your pilgrimage, but I am staying here with our children."

Blood rushed to Jozadak's head, and he felt faint. He dropped down on the bed beside her. He knew he couldn't change her mind. He hadn't been able to do that in all the years they were married. He laid beside her with the throbbing in his head keeping time with the beat of his heart.

***

Jozadak hadn't rested that night. He merely waited for daylight to come so he could go and seek Asa's counsel. Asa's body had become feeble, but his mind was still sharp. When Jozadak arrived, Asa was sitting outside in the courtyard, in front of the house he had built for Carmela so many years before.

Jozadak took a seat beside Asa to explain his dilemma. "There's nothing there to go back to. My life there is over. My destiny is not behind me."

Asa nodded as he listened, and then he spoke. "I am moved by the idea of returning to Jerusalem, and I am intrigued by the idea of finding a new land. The truth is that I'm too frail to travel past the center market, my son. My decision has been made for me. I would be remiss if I did not remind you of the prophesy of your uncle Jeremiah, much of which has come to pass. The word from God was that He would bring us back from this place after the Exile, that He would listen to our prayers, that our people would be gathered together once again."

"I'm not sure if the people have learned their lessons. I see wrong-headedness in my own family. The voice speaking to me tells me to travel further."

"Are you sure that is the Lord speaking to you?"

"All I can tell you is that it is the voice that has guided me all my life."

"And what of the prophecy?"

"Jeremiah's prophecy told us God said, 'Stand at the crossroads and look; ask for the ancient paths, ask where the good way is, and walk in it, and you will find rest for your souls'. But you said, 'We will not walk in it.' We're at a crossroad again, and I'm going to take a different direction, the path that I believe will lead to rest for my soul and the souls of our people."

"What if you are wrong? Where will the priestly leadership come from? Without you, do you trust the people will be guided properly? What about the designation for your family?"

"What can I do, Asa? If the Lord speaks to my spirit, I will return to Jerusalem later."

"You can have your sons go back in your place. Your time to serve as priest is at its end anyway. It is their time. Zerubbabel, the only descendant of the royal line of David, has been the prince of captivity. He is ready to take his place as king of Judah. He will be the leader among the first of us to return to Jerusalem. He has been called to rebuild the Temple. Your sons should be with him."

"Elliot has already said he's going to stay in Babylon."

"Then you must speak with Joshua and Rabin."

"Why is it my lot to lose those I love?"

"You're no different from anyone else in that matter. Truthfully, you have been highly favored."

Jozadak wanted to deny it, but he honestly could not. "Asa, you stepped into my father's shoes when we had no one, and I want to say I'm grateful."

"No thanks are needed, son. You and your mother blessed my life when I had no one."

"Well, there is something else, something I have kept secret for 50 years."

"I don't want to hear it," Asa said, shaking his head. "I'm too old to help carry your burden."

"You're right," Jozadak said, embracing him.

Jozadak walked back to his home, glancing at the shed between their houses. He would have to purchase another strong wagon for the journey. He was determined to restore the ark to its former splendor.

***

The thought of it was too much to bear; Jozadak couldn't lose all of his sons. He would need at least one of them to accompany him. If something were to happen on the journey, someone would have to protect the ark. After much contemplation, he decided that Rabin should come with him and Joshua would go back to Jerusalem. Rabin needed to learn more, and he had a young family. Joshua had been a good student, and he was physically strong and confident. He had the tools to go back and help Zerubbabel rebuild the Temple.

He waited outside the school door until Joshua was finished teaching his students.

"There's something important that I need to discuss with you," Jozadak said to him, taking a seat on the bench at the table.

"You don't have to convince me, Father, I'll go with you."

"No, Joshua, that's not what I wanted to say." He took a deep breath and told him. "The first group of our people is preparing to return to Jerusalem, and I want you to go with them."

"My place is with you," Joshua objected. "You'll need my help."

"No, son, you are needed to travel with Zerubbabel. As the prince, a descendant of David, he must take his rightful place on the throne. You, as a descendant of Zadok, will serve as his high priest. Jerusalem is in disarray. The tribes have been scattered. I need you to help in the rebuilding of the Temple. Jerusalem must always be the place of worship."

Joshua understood his father's reasoning, but it was hard to accept that they might never see each other again. "Why can't you come with us?" he pleaded.

"Now is not the time, son. Much gold will be needed to rebuild the Temple in greater glory. There are rich gold mines in Saba. Legends told to me as a child spoke of the queen of Saba, who brought two and a half tons of gold from there as a gift to Solomon. Once things are settled in Jerusalem and I have plenty of gold, I will return."

***

Jozadak read from the Scriptures and prayed for guidance before he delivered his message on the Sabbath. He wasn't sure of the reaction he would receive, whether the people would feel angry and betrayed as his family did or whether some might be inclined to follow him.

"People of Israel," he said, standing before the congregation, "this is a joyous moment for us! Our exile in this land has come to an end. We did not come to this place of our own free will, and many of us died on the way; but the Lord said that He would bring His people back home. The time has come for us to leave Babylon. We all have serious decisions to make about where we live out the remainder of our lives.

"For those of you who are anxious to return to Jerusalem, the first group of travelers, led by Zerubbabel and Joshua, will be leaving in five days. If you wish to be part of this group, you must quickly organize your affairs and pack whatever belongings you want to carry with you. If you need more time to prepare, there is no deadline, you can leave in later groups. For those of you who desire to stay in Babylon, you have that right. You are free to move about and conduct your lives as any other citizen in the city.

"As you all know, I came here as a child, and I have spent most of my life as a captive in this place. We have all done as the Lord directed. We planted seeds, and we grew. I have searched my heart and soul, and I have decided not to go back to Jerusalem. My destiny is not behind me. God has spoken to my spirit and has set a mission for me. My destination is not clear. I will trust in the Lord and let Him be my guide, just as our people did when they came out of Egypt. If there are those of you who would like to join me, you are welcome."

Then Jozadak prayed, "May the Lord bless you and keep you, now and in the world to come."

Jozadak was pleasantly surprised when after the service several families wanted to join him in his quest. Like him, most of them were Levites who had no land or family they knew of back in Jerusalem. They weren't interested in giving up their positions to rotate maybe once a year in the new Temple. For the first time in his life, Jozadak was looking forward to something.

***

There was excitement in the Israelite villages. Hope was in the air. Jozadak felt it, too, but it was bittersweet as he stood with his family and the others who gathered at the edge of the city to say farewell to Joshua. There were over 42,000 in the first group of Israelites journeying back to Jerusalem. Zerubbabel, with Joshua at his side, would be at the head of the march. King Cyrus had seen to it that the gold and silver vessels that Nebuchadnezzar had seized from the Temple were returned to them to be placed in the new Temple.

For a second, Jozadak thought about revealing that he had possession of the ark of the covenant and giving it to them to take back to the new Temple. Then he remembered the promise he had made to his father. He was sure there would be a struggle for power in Jerusalem, and the safety of the ark would not be guaranteed. Whenever things settled down, the ark would be brought back. His goal was to see it restored to its former glory. For that, he needed gold.

***

Goodbyes and cheers of praise rang out as the first group began their march back to Jerusalem. The people began to sing: "Lo, the winter is past, The rain is over and gone; The flowers appear on the earth; The time of the singing birds is come, And the voice of the turtle is heard in our land; The fig tree ripeneth her green figs, And the vines are in blossom, They give forth their fragrance. Arise, my love, my fair one, and come away."

Emotions ran high and tears of joy rolled down the faces of the women and many of the men. Jozadak and Etana watched the procession until Joshua was long out of sight.

"I want you to come with me," Jozadak said to Etana as they walked back to their village.

Etana stopped walking, grabbed his arm, and looked up into his eyes. "I'm happy here," she said earnestly. "Does that mean anything to you?"

Jozadak met her glance and said, "You heard my message. You know that I must go. You are my wife."

Etana dropped his arm, turned, and continued walking. "Then you have reason to divorce me. You are free to go."

"There is life outside this city," he said, walking close behind her. "You can be happy in another place."

"I'm old. Why should I travel across the desert to an unknown death? If you must scour the wilderness looking for peace, so be it. Leave me here in the peace I've found."

"You're a stubborn woman," he snapped.

"Yes, and you're a dreamer who refuses to wake."

Jozadak didn't have a response to that. What if it were true? Then he pushed those doubts out of his thoughts. If Etana didn't want to come, then, as she said, "So be it."

***

Careful planning had preceded the departure of Jozadak and his group. There were 219 Israelites; 98 Levites; and his assistant priest, Micah, who were willing to take this expedition with him. Among the group were families and individual travelers. Most of them were young and brave, looking for something new. They wanted to be free, to get away from the idea of rulers and powerful men dictating every aspect of their lives. They wanted to go to a place where they could thrive and establish their own rules.

Although they were a smaller band, it would be a great feat for them to cross the Arabian Desert. To limit some of the challenges, they waited for winter to end, after Passover, when it was months away from the monsoon season in the desert. During the delay, Jozadak tried to think of all the pitfalls they might meet, and he collected supplies to aid them on the trek. He hired a clan of nomads with 150 dromedary camels to guide them. He secured 15 oxen and 25 donkeys to carry the loads of provisions and personal belongings.

Well-wishers gave them gifts and money, things that would be of value they could trade at food depots, trade houses, and secured cities along the route. On the night before they were to leave, Etana and his daughters prepared a special feast in their honor at the house. The attendants busied themselves eating, unsure of the appropriate words for the occasion. The grandchildren were confused all evening, not knowing whether to laugh or cry.

The next morning, Jozadak's group met at the synagogue to pray and to say their final goodbyes. There was a lot less fanfare than when the large masses returned to Jerusalem. At the farewell, Jozadak wished that his family would not have come. He was sure it would break his heart to walk away from them. He was thankful that at least Rabin; his wife, Leah; and their two daughters would be going with him. Even so, guilt overwhelmed him when he saw Etana's tear-streaked face after saying goodbye to Rabin and her two young grandchildren.

As her youngest son and his family walked away, Etana knew that she might never see them again. She raised her hand and waved when Rabin looked back.

"You can still come with me," Jozadak said, wrapping his arms around her.

"My life is here," Etana said slowly. "You are free, and I am free from the sad boy who became a bitter man.

Gently, he pushed her away from his chest. "How can you say that?" he asked, bewildered.

"Because you never allowed yourself to feel love; and you

never trusted anyone enough to give them your love, not even your wife."

Jozadak bowed his head, unable to deny the biting words. "I'm sorry for that."

"Don't be sorry, Jozadak, be different in the life you've chosen."

Etana pulled away from Jozadak, and he lost sight of her in the throng of family and friends there to wish them a safe journey.

It was too late for second thoughts. Jozadak moved forward to take his place behind the guides waiting to march out of the city. The men outnumbered the women in the group, and there were only a handful of children. Most had considered the journey too harsh for anyone unable to fend for themselves between the severe weather and any menacing foes, be they human or animal.

Much different from the time that he left Jerusalem, where he felt so insignificant, Jozadak felt the responsibility that he imagined Moses felt as he led the Israelites from Egypt. These followers believed in him and trusted him. They cheered as the procession passed the Tower of Babel and then through the gate at the edge of the city. From atop one of the camels, Jozadak stared down at the wagon being pulled by an ox beside him, and he silently prayed that he would not fail.

***

Two days into the journey, Jozadak got a revelation. He was not a young man, and this trek would be nothing like the one he'd made from Jerusalem into Babylon. This journey, with its steep cliffs and deep canyons, would be longer and more treacherous than he had anticipated. His back ached from sitting for hours atop the camel, and when he walked, his feet ached. Dry winds with strong gusts blew against the caravan, slowing their pace, while toads and lizards scampered along at their heels. The elation felt by the group that buoyed him along the way quickly faded.

Many times, Jozadak thought of surrendering to the elements and turning back. It was Micah's daughter, Bayla, who renewed his fortitude. He'd prayed for strength, and she was heaven-sent. When they stopped their trudging and set up camp, she served him meals, kept water for him, and rubbed his feet. Her care and conversation eased the bleakness of the long, lonely hours.

Their first two weeks in the desert felt like two months. Jozadak shuddered in the cold of the night, unable to sleep. Already, he missed the comforts of the house and Etana's company. How did he walk away from 37 years of marriage so easily? How could Etana have let him go without complaint? Maybe he had made a mistake; maybe she was right. He hadn't appreciated the life he had had. The bitterness that boiled inside him after he heard his father had been murdered had soured, and from that point he hadn't allow himself to experience the sweetness of life. He had gotten lost in what could have been and what should have been and missed out on what was real.

Now Jozadak was tired, damn near distraught. What made it worse was he was out in the middle of nowhere with family, friends, and parishioners who saw his vision and believed in his dream. So far, he had only led them on a miserable obstacle course. "Help me," he cried out inside, lest the people around him hear the doubt in his words. He turned over prostrate on his mat and prayed.

A voice spoke to his spirit and said, "Stop your groveling and whining in self-pity. Rise up, for there are miles between you and your destiny."

***

The first 700 miles to Ur were difficult. To dodge the oppressive heat of midday, the caravan traveled mostly in the early hours of the morning and in the evenings before the temperatures fell to freezing. There was no rest after crossing a high range over rough terrain when another even higher peak waited ahead of them. At times, the sand felt like the sea as it flowed around their feet. At other times, dust storms swirled around their thinly veiled heads, filling their eyes, ears, nostrils, and mouths with sand.

There were complaints about the fleas, mosquitoes, and beetles that pestered everyone while they slept. There were the panic-stricken moments when a sand cobra or a scorpion crossed their paths. But it was the constant breeze that never stopped blowing that vexed them the most. It was never a refreshing or relaxing flow; it was always forceful and uncomfortable, alternating between a sweltering wind and a bone-chilling squall.

Lying on a mat under his tent-his feet cracked and bloody, and bugs flying around them-Jozadak was delirious from the heat. Through the opening, he stared up at the vultures that flew overhead, searching for bones upon the sand to pick. They were mighty birds, with a wingspan of nearly ten feet. He wished he could join them in the sky and fly high above the dry gust of sand and dust.

With each passing week as the season began to shift, the punishing temperatures rose even higher. They rationed the water to maintain a supply until they reached another city where there was food and a water depot. On one particularly miserable day, the heat was so thick and cumbersome, it felt as if they were walking into gale force winds. They had gone about 12 miles, and Jozadak didn't want to impede their progress, but he couldn't go much further with the pain of heat cramps.

Through gritted teeth, he called out to the guide in front of him. "We've gone far enough today. Look for a site to set up camp."

The guide signaled to the other men in his crew, and after a few more miles, they found a spot on the other side of a ridge. Jozadak was weak from exhaustion and dehydration from all the sweating in the heat.

"I've brought you some salt water," Bayla said, coming into his tent.

"Thank you," Jozadak told her, grateful for her kindness. "You didn't have to do that. Rabin will check on me after he gets his family settled."

"It's no trouble. I want to help take care you," she said, kneeling beside him.

It was her presence and thoughtful attention that reminded him that he had no wife to take care of him. It was plain he had taken Etana for granted. Jozadak took a sip of the water from the goat skin vessel and forced a smile. "You are no doubt a blessing to your mother and father, Bayla," he said. "How are they faring through this ordeal? I know it's not been easy on any of us."

Bayla nodded in agreement but answered confidently, "They are tired in spirit sometimes, but our faith that we are going to a special place is still very strong."

Jozadak was humbled by their trust in him. "I pray our faith and strength continually," he said, looking away from her.

The flap of the tent opened, and Rabin came inside. He frowned when he saw Bayla there. Whenever she was around, it pained him, a wanting ache. She was the color of a ripe fig hanging from a tree, sweet and waiting to be picked, but he couldn't partake.

"What are you doing here?" he snapped at her. "I'm sure your parents can use your help."

"Don't be rude, Rabin," Jozadak said, surprised at the shortness in his son's tone. "Bayla's brought me a little water while you were busy. We all have to help one another."

"She doesn't need to make a nuisance out of herself when there are plenty others who could use her help. I'm here to take care of you."

Bayla left the tent without saying a word. She'd sensed hostility from Rabin, even before they left Babylon. They didn't know each other well, so she shrugged it off as his being overprotective of his father. She figured that in time he'd get used to her being around.

***

A heavy storm came up suddenly the next day. The sand, unlike dirt, doesn't soak up the water from the rain. They had to keep walking with cloths over their eyes, searching for high ground. They dared not rest in a ditch where the water would flood. When it was over, the heat was slightly subdued, and they plodded along on the soft sand.

Jozadak had recovered some, but he still felt achy and nauseous. It bothered his conscience to ride on the camel while others walked. So even though he was prone to heat cramps, he insisted on walking most days. He moved steadily beside Rabin, who was having second thoughts about bringing his family through this ordeal.

"These callouses are like hoofs. These feet don't feel like my own," Rabin grumbled. "I can barely see my way through these storms with the threadbare hem of my coat. I struggle to breathe, only able to take in small gasps. My children are sick, and we are caught here with no refuge in sight."

"I have no words of comfort for you, son, except to say that this misery will be short-lived," Jozadak said, repeating the words he spoke to himself every morning.

"That's if we live through the misery," Rabin said, feeling hopeless. "Sand is blowing in the air like rain. I'm out here drowning on dry land, miles away from a drop of water, with my lungs filling up with grit and dust."

Jozadak wasn't surprised by his son's complaints. He'd heard the same gripes from several others in the group. But Rabin was his right hand, and Jozadak need him to stay encouraged. He grabbed his son by the arm and pulled him close to his side.

"There's something I must confide in you, Rabin. It's something I haven't trusted anyone enough to share for 50 years."

Rabin looked at him puzzled. "What is it?" he asked, bending down and leaning his ear toward his father.

Jozadak spoke just above a whisper. "When King Nebuchadnezzar invaded Jerusalem for the second time, my father became fearful that there would be no limits to their desecration of the Temple. In order to protect the ark of the covenant, he removed it from the Temple and hid it. Before he was taken by the king's generals, he instructed me to guard the ark with my life. I've kept my promise. I concealed the ark and brought it to Babylon. Many times, I have wanted to share this secret, but I couldn't chance it while we were captives. I tell you now because we are carrying the ark with us."

Rabin stared at him, wondering if he were out of his mind. "I can't believe you could keep something so important to yourself all this time! What about the other priests?"

"At first, I didn't know who I could trust. Then time passed so quickly, and with each year, it became harder to reveal."

"Are you going to let your followers know?" Rabin asked, still mystified.

"Telling them now might have the opposite effect. I might lose their trust. I'm telling you now because someone must know if I'm killed. You must live if I die. You must promise me as I promised my father that you will guard the ark and its contents with your life."

Rabin nodded obediently. "I will, Father, you have my word."

From that day, Rabin never complained again. He was humbled by the responsibility that his father had borne and that he now, too, would have to bear.

***

The nomads guiding the caravan discouraged robbers who hounded desert travelers for valuables, but they still had to pay taxes to pass through various territories. They had just passed the halfway point of the journey when they reached Ur, the place where Abraham, father of Isaac and all the Israelites, was born.

Ur was an amazing oasis in the desert, an essential capital city on the incense trade route. With its own seaport and man-made canal, it had a bustling population. The city had once been beautiful. That was obvious from the old towers, palaces, and shrines. Except now, the statues were crumbling, the gardens were ill-kempt, and the market square was nearly desolate. The city had no doubt been ruined by many wars over the generations. Nonetheless, it was the ziggurats, humongous pedestals that rose over 200 feet in the air, still standing, that boggled their minds.

From Ur, they traveled to Thaj and then on to Gerrah. That city was something to behold, magnificence the people had never seen before. No matter how much they disliked being held captive in Babylon, they could never deny its grandeur, but Gerrah was its superior. The homes, made of salt, were large and impressive, having walls and doors filled with precious stones of many colors and embedded with silver and gold. The people living there were Arabs who had been exiled from Babylon. Jozadak's caravan took a short respite from their trek, replenished their provisions, and kept moving.

Still traveling along the incense trade route, from Gerrah they went through El Riah, from there to Najran, and then to Thoma. From there, they were on the last stretch of the journey.

"What do you hope to do, Jozadak?" Micah asked when they were breaking camp. "Do you plan to start a nation of your own?"

"I don't know what I'm doing, my friend. I just know that after the hurt I felt in Judah, I couldn't go back. I never felt at home in Babylon. I was serving my sentence there like all of our people. I have to believe there is a place of peace and love for humanity. I believe we might find it in Saba. Some of our people, Levites, are already living there."

"I pray you are right," Micah said, gripping his shoulder. "We are here with you because we honor God and want to worship Him in the way He directed. Maybe then we'll have peace."

Jozadak nodded his head in agreement. "A wise woman once told me, 'Love and peace are where you make them.'"

Chapter Twelve
Rabin

Jozadak's caravan had come up against a host of challenges on the journey; but when the people saw the towers of limestone that surrounded the city, they breathed a sigh of relief. At last, they had reached the kingdom of Sheba, the place where the queen of Sheba reigned five centuries ago. *Saba* means "host of heaven and peace." It was Jozadak's hope that they would find a bit of both.

Saba was a prosperous place, specifically because of the frankincense that grew from the sap of a particular tree unique to the area. When burned, its rich perfumed aroma was offered to the gods. The scent was also heavy enough to cover the smell of death. It was placed on the body at funeral pyres. Myrrh was also plentiful in Saba and highly traded as a spice, with many medicinal properties in addition to being used to make fragrant oils that were necessary to prepare bodies for burial. Frankincense and myrrh were traded to India, China, Africa, and throughout the East, all the way to Egypt.

Tears of happiness burned Jozadak's eyes at the sight of the place they would call home.

"The people here look familiar to me," he told Rabin, unable to hold back his emotions. "It's as if I knew them when I was a boy back in Judah."

"We've just been in the desert for too long," Rabin said. "The heat has taken a toll on us all."

"No, son," Jozadak said, raising his fist in victory. "It's a sign from Jehovah. After all this time, we are in the right place!"

Their caravan kept moving until it reached the walled city of Marib, the capital of Saba. It was different than any other city they had passed through on the journey. The people there called it "the land of two paradises." They learned that it was sustained by the channels of water that flowed from a large dam. The land was lush and fruitful, and there was an abundance of livestock. The people were tall, their skin brown and olive, their hair wooly and straight. The buildings towered high in the sky. The smaller ones had three levels, and the palace had nearly 20 stories.

"This is the place where we will put down roots," Jozadak told his people after they entered the gates of Marib. "There is fertile ground here."

They shouted, "Glory to God!" relieved and grateful for their safe passage across the desert, all of them having survived.

The travelers were welcomed by a council of Levites who had left Jerusalem after Jeremiah prophesized the destruction of the Temple so long ago. Having lived there for several generations, they had established themselves well, participating in the trade that generated a great deal of wealth. They informed Jozadak that most people inside Marib lived happy and luxurious lives. They ate good food and enjoyed spending money on treasures and trinkets from India and China. With all the gold changing hands, Jozadak was assured that he would have no problem restoring the ark and building a Temple to house it in a manner that would please Jehovah.

***

There was little space inside the wall of the city for setting up camp, and the costs for the whole group to stay at an inn would add up quickly. Rabin suggested that he, his father, and Micah make an offer to purchase a large inn to house the group. They discovered that money and goods trade fast on the incense coast, and they were able to make a bargain with an innkeeper on a slightly rundown building just inside the wall.

The inn was seven stories high, with a staircase in the center that supported the structure of the building. The ground level was used to store timber, grain, and fruits. A separate portion of it was reserved for animals and excrement from the relief rooms. On the second floor, meals were served. The third floor was for important meetings and worship services. Above that level was reserved for living space.

The ordeal of crossing the desert and having to rely on one another for survival bonded the group. Their connection to one another was the only familiar thing remaining in their lives. On the Sabbath, they came together for worship on the third level of the inn.

Jozadak read from the Torah, prayed, and then gave them a message of encouragement.

"In David's psalm, he said, 'Praise be to the Lord for he showed his wonderful love to me when I was in a besieged city. In my alarm I said, I am cut off from your sight. Yet you heard my cry for mercy when I called to you for help.' Children of Israel, we have been through many trials and had many troubles, but God has been faithful to us. As we were freed from Egypt, we have been freed from Babylon. The Lord has led us to this place, and I pray His blessings upon us as we seek to honor Him. There may come a day when we return to Jerusalem, but this day we have a new land of milk and honey here in Saba."

The group shouted praises to Jehovah and sang songs of joy.

"We can all stay here together for however long it takes for you to get settled," Jozadak told them in the eating area. "There are no workers here, so we'll have to maintain for ourselves."

From the time they left Babylon, Jozadak's followers revered him, not only as their priest but also as their leader. In this same space, he settled their disagreements and schooled the children in the word of Jehovah. With the support of fellow Levites who were well established in Marib, most of the families in the group were able to find work and homes of their own in a year's time.

***

Once Micah moved into his permanent dwelling, he agreed to sell his interest in the inn to Rabin. It was an opportunity for Rabin to establish himself out of his father's shadow. Rabin then offered the empty rooms to traders seeking lodging. It turned out to be a successful venture for him. After a while, he could have gotten a home for his family, except to hire someone to manage the inn would cut into his profits. So for the time being, he kept his residence on one of the higher floors of the inn on the same floor as his father's.

For the most part, Rabin was content and had no regrets about leaving Babylon or not going to Jerusalem. Saba was overrunning with wealth, and he was determined to get his share of it. Managing the inn was only the beginning. By the time the new synagogue was completed, there would be more tithes and offerings coming. The one thing that continued to vex him was Bayla's presence. She was always fawning over his father, bringing him meals, and washing his clothing. He wondered what she hoped to gain from all the attention she showered upon him.

A portion of his irritation was because he was jealous. It was not simply because Bayla was beautiful; it was the obvious devotion that she felt for his father. Why would she choose to favor an old man when he would have gladly accepted her favor? Many nights, he dreamed that she was his wife and woke up unsatisfied with Leah lying by his side. He decided that the best solution was to encourage one of the young Levite men who traveled with them to take her as his wife. Uriel would be the perfect match for her. He lived on the edge of the city raising livestock, a good distance from the inn and his father.

***

On Rabin's suggestion, Uriel went to speak with Micah to propose marriage with Bayla.

Micah was delighted. He and his wife, Danya, had noticed that their daughter spent too much of her time helping Jozadak and that she needed a husband of her own to focus her attention on. Micah was surprised when his daughter objected to the match.

"Uriel is a good man and a hardworking man," Micah told her, hoping to change her mind. "He has done well here in Marib and can provide well for you."

Bayla bowed her head, looked down at the floor, and replied, "I don't doubt that, Father. It's only that I love someone else."

Danya stayed silent, her fears were confirmed. Micah dropped his head in dismay. He, too, had suspected that his daughter felt more than kindness toward Jozadak. He had prayed that the interest of this young man, Uriel, might give her another option to consider.

"I won't force you to marry Uriel if that's not what you want," Micah said gently. Bayla was his only child, and her happiness meant everything to him.

"I'm sorry, Father," Bayla said earnestly. "I can't marry a man I don't love."

Micah walked out of the room, leaving Bayla and her mother alone to talk.

"Daughter, you must think this through," Danya counseled. "I know you are very fond of our leader, Jozadak. He has been so important in all our lives, but you mustn't confuse feelings of gratitude with love."

"I'm not confused, Mother. It wasn't my wish to love him. It happened naturally, like a wildflower that comes from the earth without any urging."

"He's much older than you, child. If you marry him, you most likely will become a widow."

"Only Jehovah can say that," Bayla said, confidently. "I only know that he is the man I want. If it is only for a short time, I will be happy with that."

Danya was bewildered by the depth of her daughter's devotion to Jozadak. What brought this on. Maybe Jozadak had been dishonorable in his behavior. She couldn't help but wonder if Bayla had been seduced by him.

"Has the priest spoken to you of his love?" Danya asked, afraid of the answer.

"No, Mother, he hasn't."

Danya was even more confused. "Then why would you pass over Uriel who has professed feelings for you without knowing if Jozadak even wants you as his wife."

"I don't ask anyone to understand my heart. I only ask that you accept what it feels."

Danya sighed in resignation. "It is your life, my daughter, and your choice. I love you and want you to be happy in whatever you choose.

***

Bayla slept intermittently during that night, anxious for the sun to rise. At last, no more secrets, she was free to be open and honest. Her parents had not given her their full approval, but they hadn't rejected her feelings. At the first sight of day, she dressed, gathered the water for the family, and rushed to the inn to find Jozadak.

Jozadak was teaching a small class of students behind the inn. Bayla sat down under a mustard tree and waited for him to finish his lesson. When the young boys had scattered away, she hurried over to meet him.

"Uriel has spoken to my father about marrying me!" she said, sounding excited.

"That's wonderful news, my dear. I'm happy for you and him," he said, rolling up the scroll.

Bayla shook her head. "No, you don't understand. I told them I could not marry him."

"Why is that?" Jozadak asked, puzzled. He knew Uriel was a good man.

Bayla couldn't believe that Jozadak didn't know why.

"Because I don't love him. I love you. I want to be your wife."

Jozadak's shoulders dropped from the heaviness of her words. "I'm sorry if I have done or said anything to mislead you, dear Bayla. You mustn't reject Uriel's proposal for any devotion you have for me. He is a fine man."

"Yes, he is, but I don't love him. I love you. Don't you feel some love for me?"

"The kind of love you speak of is gone from me," he said sadly. "I doubt that I will feel that love again."

"That's not true. If your heart still beats in your chest, you can feel that kind of love again."

"Dear child, my heart is like stone, rock hard, there is no tenderness in me and no room for love like that. I've had my chance, and I wasn't very good at loving anyone but the Lord above."

Bayla pulled the sleeve of his robe. "I'm not a child. I'm a woman who loves you. Take another chance, and love me."

"I'm an old man. There isn't much I can offer you," he said, shaking his head. "Most of my money has been spent; I have nothing but hope in my pockets."

"I know what you have, and that is all I want," she insisted.

He kept objecting, trying to dissuade her. "I could only be another father to you."

"I have a father; I don't want another," she replied, more forcefully. "I need a husband who will love and protect me."

Jozadak was fond of Bayla. If he were a younger man, he would not have hesitated to take her as his wife. He was lonely and probably needed her more than she needed him. He and Etana had divorced to free each other, but he had never thought about marrying again.

"I must pray to Jehovah," he said, walking away from her.

Jozadak went straight up the stairs into the room where they held worship service, dropped the scroll, and fell to his knees.

"I need to hear Your voice, O Lord," he cried out. "What would You have me do? I am not worthy of the love of this young woman. How can I deny such sincerity? How can I deny I want that second chance she has offered me? I've been selfish for so long. This makes me feel even more selfish. I didn't ask for this precious gift, but something inside me wants to hold it tightly against my chest. I have not amounted to much. No one would call me a great man. I am simply a lowly servant to You. I lie here asking for You to show me a sign that I have Your blessing, and I realize that it is already before me. It is only You who would open up that lovely heart to love me; and so I praise You, honor You, and thank You."

***

The walk to Micah's home seemed much farther than usual. Each step brought Jozadak closer to the answer that would determine how he would spend the rest of his life. He had no idea how Micah would react to his request. What he did know was if he stood in Micah's shoes, he would certainly not grant his blessings on such a match. He hesitated at the door of their home. How could he face his friend, his assistant priest, his business partner, and ask him for his daughter's hand. He knocked twice, softly, and waited.

"Come in, my friend!" Micah said, welcoming him. "Sit down with me."

Danya was standing next to the table. Her expression revealed nothing. She served them wine and left the room.

"We have discussed countless subjects since we have known one another," Jozadak said, staring down at a gash in the wood of the table. "This is something that I never imagine we would have to talk about."

"I must agree with you on that," Micah said. "I thought your idea of coming here to Saba was the peak of the unexpected."

"I want you to know that I did nothing to encourage Bayla. In fact, I tried to discourage her when she came to me. She is beautiful, kind, and loyal, all very easy for a man to love." Then Jozadak looked his friend in the eyes. "I would consider it to be an honor to have your daughter as my wife. I would care for her as the most precious blessing the Lord hath bestowed on me. Still, as my closest friend, and out of respect for that, if you object to the marriage, I will yield."

Micah sighed and then took a deep breath. "In honesty, I would have preferred a younger man for my only daughter, a man with more years in front of him than behind him, but you are a good man, Jozadak. I know that from the years that we have worked side by side. She says she loves you and wants to be your wife. I only want her to be happy, and she says that will make her happy. I trust you to care for her and protect her as I have. You have our blessing."

Those words gave Jozadak new life. He was filled with a joy he had never felt before. His life and his future had never meant more to him than they did at that moment. Was it possible that the happiness he thought was stolen from him had actually been given away? Perhaps he had wasted much of his life brooding. He wouldn't waste another day.

***

Anger raged inside Rabin when Jozadak took Bayla as his wife. When Rabin complained to his father, he tried to label it as the righteous indignation of his disregard and betrayal of his mother, Etana. If he made any effort to hide his displeasure, no one could tell from all the protests he spread among the congregation.

Rabin spewed venom in his messages on the Sabbath. "The prophet Malachi said, 'For the man who does not love his wife but divorces her, covers his garment with violence, says the Lord of hosts. So guard yourselves in your spirit, and do not be faithless.' If a man breaks with the wife of his youth, he does not follow God's word. There are those among us who have wronged those who loved them. Jehovah requires us to repent of our sins less we reap His punishment. We people have suffered enough for the sins of our neighbors, brothers, and fathers. We all must be accountable."

Jozadak was not perturbed; he walked as if his feet no longer touched the ground. Rabin watched his father behave in a way he had never seen before. His resentment grew, and he absorbed all the bitterness that Jozadak released.

"Did you ever love my mother? Did you even love your children?" Rabin asked in a sharp tone after their morning prayer.

"I was a different man then, son. I was too angry to feel real happiness. For that, I am sorry. Any fault in the way things ended with your mother belong to me. Nevertheless, God has given me another chance."

"May we all will be so blessed," Rabin replied sourly.

"I don't know why you're behaving this way," Jozadak

said. "Your mother and I were both free to marry. That was the decision we made."

Rabin grunted. "What other choice did she have?"

"I begged your mother to come with me, you know that."

"Maybe this was all some ruse just to get away from her so you could have a younger wife," Rabin sneered.

"Watch your tongue! Respect that I am your father!"

"That's easy to forget since you only seem to think of yourself."

"That's not true. Having you with me on the journey was the reason I kept going. We share a responsibility greater than ourselves. Let's not be divided by this. You have so much to celebrate with your wife and the new life she carries. We have both been blessed."

Rabin bit his lip. He had a lot more he wanted to say, but it was evident that his father didn't care how he felt. Rabin stood there staring in disgust. Jozadak reached out to him, holding him in a firm embrace while his arms hung limp at his sides.

Over the next few months, Rabin tried to behave better, except it wasn't easy for him to stop complaining when he had to see Bayla every day, especially with Leah big with child. His other preoccupation was the baby soon to be born. The first thing in the morning and the last thing he did at night was to pray to Jehovah for a son. When his third child was born, another daughter, he stopped praying.

***

The birth of his third daughter, Ava, was a huge disappointment for Rabin. He sulked for months, bemoaning the absence of a son to secede him as priest and inherit the wealth he worked so hard to accumulate. Leah tried her best to brighten his mood.

"We can have another child, Rabin," she said, nursing the new baby. "We must stay in prayer. Hannah's prayers for a son were answered. Don't lose faith."

"Do you know how I've prayed? The Lord doesn't hear me."

"He hears, I promise our next child will be a male."

Rabin stormed out; her words were as useless as his prayers. He spent less time at home and refused to hold Ava. Leah tried to pacify him, but she too was disheartened as he became more distant toward her.

When Jozadak announced that Bayla was pregnant, Rabin chewed the inside of his mouth. When she gave birth to a son, the bitterness in his heart rose into his throat, burned the sore in his mouth, and he wore a constant scowl on his face.

Jozadak named his son Tobiah, meaning "the Lord is good." The boy was a fresh breath of air that renewed and revitalized Jozadak. He reveled in the baby's presence, for he was untainted by the past and knew nothing of family resentment. Jozadak thanked God for the eyes that looked at him with love and not scorn.

All the while, Rabin's jealousy was like an infection, growing to a fever pitch and making him sick. He dreamed of plots of how he could hurt the child who stole the affection from his father, affection that he had never received. He waited for the moment that he would find relief from this affliction that presented itself in this innocent baby.

That day came one bright morning when Rabin saw Bayla working the soil in her garden beside their home without the baby tied to her breast. He knew that his father had gone early to the school to teach. The servants were at the river doing the washing. He eased down one floor into his father's living quarters and crept into the room where Tobiah was sleeping.

Rabin stared at the baby, feeling some regrets. This boy should have been his son, could have been his son if his father hadn't have kept everything for himself. Rabin placed his hand onto the blanket covering little Tobiah. With the fabric in his hand, all he needed to do was pull it over the child's face and press down until his breath was smothered out of him. There would be no fault, no incriminations. The baby would have simply suffocated in his blanket. Rabin gripped the blanket tighter and slowly inched it toward the baby's neck.

Then a shriek startled him. "What are you doing in here?" Bayla shouted, running over and snatching Tobiah from his bed. "I don't want you near my baby!"

Rabin face was flushed with the heat of guilt. "Is there a law against me to lay eyes on my little brother?"

Bayla covered Tobiah with his blanket, shielding him tightly in her arms. "You don't have to pretend that you care for him or me. Your eyes show you despise us both."

Rabin snapped at her. "Why did you have to come and spoil everything? Our family was fine without you!"

"I haven't taken your father's love from you," she said, unfazed by his contempt. "It's your bitterness that separates you."

"No, it's you! You fool him into thinking he's a young man again. You have turned his head away from his own blood!"

Bayla never flinched. "He is my husband, and this child is his blood. You can't change that. Besides, the way it looks to me is that you have turned away from your own blood. Do you even lay eyes on your daughters or your wife anymore?"

Rabin was indignant. Who did Bayla think she was? "You have no right to question me!" he declared, staring down at her.

Looking him dead in the eyes, she responded, "And you have no business in this room with my son!"

Rabin glared at her, enraged. He had lost his chance, and she probably would take care that he didn't get another. He turned and stormed out.

***

Gradually, Rabin withdrew from his responsibilities at the makeshift meeting room. He spent less time reading the Torah, spent less time teaching, and avoided his rotation in leading the worship services on the Sabbath. Initially, he did it to spite his father, but he found passion in making money. Wealth became his measure of himself as a man. He concentrated the bulk of his energy on enlarging his fortunes.

When the synagogue was near completion a few years later, it didn't matter much to him. He was more pleased that he would be free to use his inn fully for his purposes, as it was becoming one of the premier trading hubs in the city.

However, for Jozadak, it was a time of great celebration. Finally, there was a building where he could place the ark of the covenant. He had kept his promise to Seraiah, his father. It would take some time before the gold needed to restore it was accumulated, but he was making progress. He was also aware that the second Temple was being built in Jerusalem and that that was the rightful place for the ark. But for the time being, he wasn't sure when or if he would return the ark. He had heard from traders who passed through Saba that the Israelites were more loyal to Jehovah, but he knew that whoever reigned as king could quickly influence them. That was the precise reason he had not revealed to anyone that he had possession of the ark.

Nonetheless, there was a setback for his plan in Saba. Rabin was turning his back on his responsibility as a priest to the people. When they left Babylon, Jozadak had taken for granted that Rabin would secede him as priest. He had hoped that they would oversee the construction of a grand Temple and that Rabin would become high priest. That expectation seemed more unlikely with each day.

The disappointment caused by the rift between him and Rabin was lessened by Tobiah. He was the joy in his father's heart. Jozadak delighted in every moment they were together. He saw himself in his young son, the boy he was before Seraiah was murdered. Tobiah loved to hear the old stories his father told him about the Israelites and life back in Jerusalem. As the years passed, he became Jozadak's right hand at the synagogue.

Rabin on the other hand grew more distant. Through trade and his businesses, he had more dealings with the monarchs of Marib. He got a glimpse into the intimate relationship between money and politics. Once his ambition achieved the measure of wealth that he wanted, he acquired a taste for power, not the power or standing from serving as high priest in the small city of Levites, he wanted to be a Mukarrib or a federator, a ruler with the consultations of a council. He would leave his business for weeks at a time to enjoy the company of the king of Saba, the principal mukarrib of the combined cities.

Coveting that which belonged to another man robbed Rabin of his satisfaction, and he was always searching for something

to fill it. He dressed in the fine silks that traders brought
from China, and he loved to wear the turbans from India that
signified his nobility. He paid high prices to lay with countless
women, always looking for one who was more beautiful than
Bayla to counter the envy he carried for his father's wife.

Chapter Thirteen
Tobiah

Bayla convinced Jozadak to move away from the inn, telling him how much she wanted a house with space for her to plant a larger garden. She never mentioned the incident with Rabin or him being a threat to her and their son. Jozadak found them a home in a peaceful spot where frankincense and myrrh trees grew wild all around it.

When Tobiah finished his daily lessons, he worked with Bayla in the garden, sowing seeds for their crops of vegetables and grains. She planted while he guided the plow pulled by two oxen. At first, she encouraged him to work in the garden so she could keep a close on eye on him, not trusting Rabin or his motives. Then it became clear as Tobiah became a young man that he had an affinity for working the land. As smart as he was strong, he figured out how to connect their land to the irrigation canals to increase their water supply, increasing their yields double-fold.

Tobiah had a generous nature and shared their harvests from the land with the people of the expanding group when he prayed for them. More and more were attracted to his genuine kindness and love of God's word. Within a few years, the congregation overflowed at the synagogue every Sabbath, and some began to come to him for prayer during the week. He joined his father in counsel and in compiling and transcribing the word for the people. Jozadak could see that Tobiah was even more of a blessing to the Israelites than he was to him and Bayla. It was also as plain as the sky above that Rabin's allegiance to God's word was fading like the sun at dusk.

Jozadak accepted the fact that Rabin probably should not succeed him as high priest. The time had come for him to share his story about the ark of the covenant with Tobiah. Although his son was still a youth, Jozadak trusted him more to protect the covenant than he did Rabin. He blamed his older son's hunger for money and material things on the life they had had in Babylon. It was the distraction of that city, with its prostitutes and the dismantling of their worship rituals, that destroyed their culture. He hated to admit it to himself, and he would never confess it to another living soul, but it turned out that Marib wasn't much different than Babylon.

***

It had been a long time coming, but it seemed sudden. Jozadak couldn't get out of bed. His bones were locked in the position of a baby lying in its mother's womb. The truth was he had never fully recovered from the trek across the desert. It began with his toes curling beneath themselves and the knuckles of his fingers becoming gnarled. Over the years, his body had gradually shrunk in stature as his back bent and his knees buckled.

Bayla had tried countless concoctions of roots and herbs that she poured down his throat and rubbed on his body. Nothing seemed to give him relief from the pain that tied him in a knot. Priests from surrounding villages came and prayed over him to remove the evil demons that plagued him. Rabin even sent for a Sabaen physician who tried bloodletting to drain the source of his illness. The treatments only made him weaker. His breathing became more and more shallow, until one day it stopped. Bayla insisted on preparing his body by herself, and they buried him in a cave on the foothill of their land.

Tobiah, barely a man at 19 years old, was prepared to fill the role his father had spent years grooming him to hold, except Rabin stood in his way. Although he rarely attended services on the Sabbath anymore, Rabin declared that as the eldest son he should succeed his father as priest in the synagogue. Despite his enormous wealth, he claimed his double portion of inheritance from his father's estate.

Losing most of his inheritance to his brother didn't matter to Tobiah. He was more upset about Rabin wanting to return to the synagogue. He spent hours digging in the dirt and breaking rocks at the edge of their land trying to vent his frustration. Bayla, still wearing her mourning clothes of sackcloth, walked down to console him. Out of breath and covered in dirt and sweat, he thrust the spade into the ground.

"Tobiah, what is troubling you so?" she asked. "As a priest, you are not to waste time mourning. This is the moment you must stand in your father's shoes. He prepared you for this."

"I know that, Mother. I'm ready to step in his place. The problem is Rabin. Why is he pretending he wants to serve the people? All he wants is to put more money in his pockets. He cares nothing about God's word. I can't let him do this," he said, bringing his hammer down heavy on a rock.

"Don't let your brother sway you from the promise you gave your father, son. The people are depending on you."

"How can I keep that promise if Rabin stands in my way?" Tobiah asked, disheartened.

"Your father led us across the desert for months through dangerous miles to come to this place. He could have gone back to Jerusalem, but he did not want to struggle with heathens or those who worship pagan gods, those who sullied the Temple over and over again. He didn't want any political interference in worshiping the way God commanded us. Your father was searching for a place of peace to build a house for God, one where the Lord would be pleased to inhabit. He wanted the faithful Levites and other children of Israel to join him. Now that your father is gone, this will no longer be a peaceful place. Fighting Rabin for the synagogue will only draw you into his evil web."

Tobiah thought about what she said for a minute. Then he said, "Father wouldn't want me to abandon my obligation. He trusted me."

"You can keep your promise to your father better by walking away. That is what he did when he walked away from Jerusalem and Babylon. Outside of these walls, there is fresh air and a fresh start. There is no need to be jealous or squabble over territory. You can build your own synagogue, a synagogue that is holy, maybe even a magnificent temple."

The quest appealed to Tobiah. It was a challenge, a chance to show he was a grown man. One condition gave him pause. He was determined to take the ark of the covenant with him, and he wasn't sure if Rabin would have objections or even reveal to the people that they had concealed it all these years.

***

Unannounced, Tobiah showed up at Rabin's trading depot where he was busy drinking wine and admiring his new purchase of jewels.

"Hello, brother," he said, startling him.

"What brings you here?" Rabin asked smugly, wondering where he found the nerve to show his face near the inn. "I don't have time for social visits. I'm a busy man."

Tobiah was undeterred by his rude attitude. He was used to it by now. "I have a proposition for you," he said confidently, "a business deal of sorts."

Rabin folded his hands together. "You have my attention," he said with a sly smile. "There's nothing I appreciate more than a lucrative bargain."

"It's no secret that you would like to be rid of me and my mother," Tobiah said frankly.

Rabin chuckled. "I must admit I'm not good at hiding my feelings."

"You can be free of us and gain possession of our father's house in exchange for one thing."

Intrigued, Rabin sat up in his chair. "And what might that be?"

"The ark of the covenant," Tobiah told him.

Rabin laughed loudly, "Are you serious? You would give up our father's house for a rotten wooden chest filled with stones and torn scrolls?"

"If you have no objections, yes."

"You are as foolish and sentimental as he was," Rabin said, laughing again. "Take it and be gone—the sooner the better."

Tobiah turned on his heels and walked away, containing the impulse to jump for joy. Rabin was the foolish one. He should have known nothing was more valuable than the promises of

God. Tobiah and Bayla packed up their belongings and the considerable amount of money they had earned from farming their land and selling their harvest in the city. With the ark secured safely in a large cart, they traveled south and bought a plot of land among other Israelite farmers in a town halfway between Marib and Sanaa.

***

Bayla and Tobiah tilled the soil and planted wheat, dates, and a host of vegetables. Shut out from the synagogue and the school in Saba, his work on the land helped to occupy Tobiah's mind and body. Still, there were days when he wondered if he'd done the right thing, walking away from all his father had built in Saba.

"Time is passing, and nothing is happening," he said, staring out into their field of few sprouts.

"You may not be able to see it, son, but there is a lot of growth going on under the surface. Be patient, and you will see the harvests from your labor."

"What about the temple? It's not the same as raising a crop. How can I start from nothing?"

"You must remember when Joshua led the people into the Promised Land, they didn't have a lot to start with. Your father believed you could take his place. You have to believe that, too. God is with you, and you will be the leader in this place. His promise is to you: 'I have given you every place where the sole of your foot will tread, just as I promised to Moses.'"

Tobiah studied alone late every night, with a lamp lit with olive oil. He held Sabbath worship service on the edge of his field. What began with a few neighbors grew to 100 people, then 200, and then 300. He met a young woman named Gail, and they were married. They had a son, Baram, and a daughter, Carmella.

Years later, they received word that Rabin was suffering from a terrible skin disease, a punishment from laying with loose women who he and his fellow merchants traded. Leah had taken over as the mistress of business, as Rabin's mind was failing; but the synagogue Jozadak built was in disrepair, and few attended.

Tobiah considered returning to keep his father's work intact, but all the seeds that he had planted were flourishing. Through that initial piece of land, the fruits provided for him, his mother, and his wife and children. That piece of earth became the foundation on which they built their city. Tobiah's tribe enlarged. And through the sacrifices and tithes of the people, he returned it to the earth, expanding their territory, and they were blessed. It was indeed a land that flowed with milk and honey.

Although the king of Saba ruled the country, Jehovah was the center of their lives. In time, Tobiah and the people built a temple, and the ark of the covenant was placed inside of it. Tobiah continued to compile the Scriptures and taught his son and the other priests everything that Jozadak had taught him, the word of God and their history. Israelites made pilgrimages from nearby cities for the celebration of Passover and fasted and prayed on the Day of Atonement. The people, somewhat isolated from the influences of the inner gates of Marib and its foreigners, remained faithful to God and His word and kept His laws.

***

Tobiah's son, Baram, took his place as chief priest. Baram's son, Eliam, followed him as chief priest. His son, Shlomo, followed him, and his son, Jacobo, after him. Then Jacobo's son, Enoch, who was followed by his son, Axel, then his son, Rabson.

Rabson was chief priest when the Qataban, Hadramout, and Main declared their independence from Marib to establish their own kingdoms. Beginning in 200 BC, civil wars disturbed the peace, as the states rivaled for control of the incense trade. Rabson's only son was born in 170 BC. His name was Nathan. He became chief priest in 149 BC, when Rabson died after being bitten by a cobra.

Chapter Fourteen
Nathan

For centuries, prosperity reigned in Marib and the surrounding cities. Nathan, as chief priest, was a recipient of that prosperity. When he was born, there was nothing left to buy or to build. His lot was to enjoy the ample fruits of his father's labor. He was pragmatic in his post, being moderate in his teaching and messages to the people. The only thing he yearned for was delicious food, and he indulged himself without restraint.

Still, nothing corrupts and corrodes civilized man more than money, greed, or the lack thereof. The kingdom of Saba still had a monopoly on the production and trade of incense. The huge caravans that carried the commodity across the desert returned with large quantities of gold. Arabic-speaking tribes of nomads settled there, and as their numbers increased, they established rival kingdoms. The Himyarites from southwest Arabia and disloyal tribes were steadily encroaching on the southeast region of Saba toward Marib.

"Conditions in Saba are deteriorating," Nathan explained to the council, a group of Levite priests who met monthly to discuss issues related to their city. "There are serious decisions to be made," he said solemnly. "This land that we have loved and nurtured for hundreds of years lies in the path of the Himyarites, Arabs, and other rival kingdoms who have set their sights on Saba. The time has come for us to decide our fate."

"We don't have any choice but to fight," Omar declared forcefully. He was one of the more defiant members of the council. Young and headstrong, he had never seen the horrors of war.

"For you it may be easy to walk away from this city," he said, addressing Nathan. "You don't have to worry about feeding your family. As the chief priest, you receive the first portion of our hard work. It's not that simple for me. My blood is in this land."

"We are a peaceful people," Nathan said, interrupting him. "We have no army. To have any chance of survival, we must align ourselves with one side. And in the end, we will owe our allegiance to one king or another."

"I still say that we fight," Omar shouted with his fist in the air.

Nathan folded his chubby hands and rested them on top of his ample belly. He didn't have any firsthand knowledge about warring either, and he had no interest in finding out. He wore his laziness as the only badge of honor he wanted to acquire. Even as a young man, he had no desire to mount a horse or wield a heavy sword trying to kill some fierce adversary.

"We are surrounded on all sides," Nathan said, remaining calm. "There is a chance we will be left with nothing. I advise all of you to sell your fields while they are valuable and there are buyers. If you wait too late, bandits will take it without recompense."

"You talk like a fearful man," Omar said, taunting him. "Have you no faith that God will be with us in battle?"

Nathan ignored the insult and said, "Need I remind you that we are not the mass of Israelites who left Egypt for Canaan?

We are separated from our people. This is not the land that was chosen for us."

Then Nathan's nephew, Ozni, an over-achieving young priest who usually asked three questions after every statement Nathan made, chimed in. "I think we should refer to the words of the Lord given to Jeremiah. 'Then I Myself will gather the remnant of My flock out of the countries where I have driven them and bring them back to their pasture and they will be fruitful and multiply. I will raise up shepherds over them and they will tend them and they will not be afraid any longer, nor be terrified, nor will any be missing.' I ask you, fellow Levites, why must we be a nomadic people when there is land that was designated for us? Maybe this is the time for us to return to Jerusalem."

Nathan's eyes rolled back in his head at the stupidity of the suggestion. "That's if you don't mind being ruled over by heathen kings. We can stay in Saba for that," Nathan said, directing his response to his nephew. "The Israelites who returned to Jerusalem after the Exile were first ruled by the Persian Empire until Alexander the Great conquered them. When he died, the Greeks were defeated, and they were back under Egyptian rule. Today the Greeks are back in power over Jerusalem. There is no Israelite king. We all know that whenever we have been occupied by foreign powers, the people stray from God's word."

"We Levites are the shepherds called to tend to them," Ozni argued.

"Stubborn sheep lead the shepherd astray and the rest of the flock unprotected," Nathan told him firmly. "Now let's return to the business at hand."

"I still say we defend what is ours," Omar said, a little more subdued.

"The hills are not on fire. We have time to wait," Palti, one of the older priests, added.

Nathan took a deep breath. Not one man around this table had grasped a word of what he told them at the beginning of the hour. They were wasting time, and the growl in his belly was urging him to conclude the meeting.

"Listen, fellow priests," he said, "this freedom and independence that we have treasured, that has kept us close to God, will be in danger much sooner than we believe. I have fasted and prayed, and God's message to me is to move from this city. He will give us a new land in a different place."

Palti spoke again. "Stay in prayer, Nathan, and ask the Lord for a sign, so the message will be clear to the rest of us."

"Rest assured, I will," Nathan replied sarcastically, standing up to leave.

Nathan climbed on top of his donkey to ride the short distance to his home. His feet were swollen and tender under his expanding girth, so he seldom walked anymore. He looked forward to a hefty meal of goat meat flavored with tasty herbs and marjoram that would erase the unpleasantness of the council meeting. His wife, Sharon, knew he would be upset as usual after these meetings and would set the table accordingly. She had learned over the years that whatever joy he did not find in the Lord, she could supply it in a generous plate of food and a goblet of sweet wine.

Nathan could smell the bread and stew wafting through the air as his donkey stumbled along the stones leading up to his house. His stopped at the basin filled with water and washed his hands and face before he went inside. His family was already sitting at the table. Sharon got up and helped him remove his cloak. He said a brief blessing over the food and sat down to eat. No one spoke. Nathan insisted that conversation over supper caused indigestion.

"You are still a wondrous blessing to me," Nathan said to Sharon, wiping his mouth after he had emptied his plate.

"Thankfully, the Lord blessed us with two daughters to help me," she said, smiling at Rina and Talia. They were ten-year-old twins, their firstborn. In her arms, she held their infant son, Deron.

Nathan glanced at his children and smiled. "Yes, we have been blessed here in Saba, my dear wife, but we may have to leave soon. Trouble is in the air."

Sharon looked down at her baby son. "Hopefully, we will have a few more years here to let the children get a little older."

"We can only hope and pray," Nathan said, nodding.

* * *

The sign or omen that Nathan and the other priests prayed for was eventually shown, but not in the way they expected. For years, the displaced Israelites had contemplated whether they would submit to an invader or battle against them. They had discussed how they would defeat an enemy who came against them. They debated whether they would fight with swords, lay traps, or retreat. In all those deliberations, they had given no thought on a strategy to contend with nature.

When the war broke out between the people of Raydan and the kingdom of Saba in 145 BC, the battles across Marib trampled the water tunnels on the mountains and weakened the

Great Dam, causing a major breach. The fighting continued, without respite to repair the dam. Then the flooding started. The crops were washed away, along with most of the greenery and the trees, turning the paradise into a marshland. Vegetables and grain couldn't grow in the sands that flowed into the fields.

An emergency meeting was called for members of the council to discuss the crisis.

"Well, Palti," Nathan said mockingly once they were seated at the table. "Is this sign clear enough for you?" There was silence in the room. Even Omar had nothing to say. "Now those of you who have land, have nothing. It's worthless. Nothing can grow here."

"What if the flood was a punishment from God?" Ozni asked thoughtfully.

"What are you talking about now, Ozni?" Nathan asked angrily, losing his patience.

Ozni put up his hands in submission and said, "We as Levites were not to own land. We didn't follow God's ordinances."

Nathan shook his head at his nephew's ignorance. "That meant we did not receive an initial portion of the land divided among the tribes," he explained. "Once the land was allotted, we were given land by the tribes to live on. Besides, that was during a time when there were 12 tribes for us to administer to and a tabernacle for us to officiate over. Look around you. We have to feed and provide for our own families now."

"Surely, the dam can be repaired as they were once built," Omar offered. "As a people, we can't keep walking away from our homes. We'll have no legacy for our children."

"When will it be rebuilt? The war isn't over," Nathan hollered across the table. "Then how many years will it take to repair the dam? How long are you willing to wait to see who will be your next king?"

"Is leaving the only option? And where would we migrate?" Ozni asked, looking around the room for more suggestions.

Nathan answered, "The ground here is unstable. We must go where we can put down roots and be secure. If there are no objections, I suggest that we travel southwest, cross the Red Sea, and go into Axum. Israelites also migrated there when Jerusalem was invaded and the Temple destroyed. It is a fruitful land where our farmers can plant new fields of wheat. There are trees of frankincense and myrrh, gold, and spices that our merchants can continue to trade. Most importantly, we can worship Jehovah freely."

There were no more comments. The men stared at one another across the table. Nathan waited for Omar to gripe, but he didn't. He paused for more questions from Ozni, but he had none.

"It seems you have left us nothing to argue, Nathan," Palti admitted.

"Thanks be to God, I have achieved the impossible," Nathan said with a chuckle. "We'll speak to the people on the Sabbath."

***

Nathan read from the Torah, "Hear these words from the song Moses recited to the Israelites before he died, 'He spreads his wings over them, Even as an eagle overspreads her young. She carries them upon her wings—As does the Lord his people! When the Lord alone was leading them, And they lived without foreign gods, God gave them fertile hilltops, Rolling fertile fields, Honey from the rock, and olive oil from stony grounds! He gave them milk and meat—Choice Bashan rams, and goats—And the finest of the wheat; They drank the sparkling wine.'" Then he closed the scroll.

"Children of Israel," he exclaimed, "pack your things! There is yet another journey ahead of us. It will not be as long as some of the others we have taken, but we must be prepared. You will need provisions for more than a week's time."

They weren't happy about it, but the people didn't have any other options. War and water had swamped Marib, rolling over and destroying everything they had spent centuries building. Nathan put Ozni in charge of transporting the ark, which was to be carried with the first group of migrants. They would be 1,500 in number. Nathan, as their spiritual leader, had no choice but to lead them. Some rode donkeys, some rode horses, others on camels, but most were on foot. They traveled west for two days until they reached the gulf. There, they boarded fishing vessels to carry them across the Red Sea. There were ten ships with 150 passengers on each ship.

That short voyage was the most frightful 50 miles that Nathan had never experienced. The ships fought against the northerly winds of the summer and the current. He prayed in those five days more than he had in the last five years. Their boats reached land at the port of Adulis. It was blistering hot and dry. Nathan felt like a lump of dough baking in an oven.

The ship carrying Nathan and his family was the first to dock. The gangplank creaked under the strain as he stomped off. Sharon, with Deron tied to her chest and holding the hands of the twins, nervously followed.

"This ground is as thirsty as I am," Nathan said, squinting his eyes in the brightness of the sun. "I don't see anything around here where we can eat or drink."

"It doesn't look like they get much rain here," Sharon said, kicking the mixture of sand and dirt with her sandals.

"You're about 40 miles from the city," the seaman told them.

"We'll need a caravan to carry us into Axum," Nathan said, between heaving breaths. "I don't have the strength or the energy to traipse all over the desert."

The seaman directed them to the trading depot where they could hire a guide to escort them to the city. Once they were united with the rest of the group of travelers, they proceeded on the 12-day trek to Axum. It was an arduous hike along steep slopes. Nathan did most of the complaining about the heat, although he rode atop a camel for the entire journey. Sharon should have been the one making a fuss; she had the children, and had to contend with the job of keeping Nathan's belly full. She was thankful for the help from the other women who worked together to prepare meals for the whole group.

Nathan's breathing became easier the further away they marched from the Red Sea. Closer to the city, the temperatures were much more agreeable and the ground less parched. Magnificent stone pillars stood tall at the entrance of the city. Once they were inside, their guide showed them to a place where they could buy food and set up camp.

***

The next day, Nathan washed and dressed in his finest cloak. He hired another guide to take him to the four-towered castle where the palace was located to meet with Nagey Bsente, the king of Axum. Nathan had never seen such riches. He understood perfectly why some of the Levites who had migrated there earlier had declared themselves royalty, but ambition had not been his strong suit. Two attendants led him into the King's Hall, where Bsente sat on his throne.

One of the attendants announced him. "This is Nathan, chief priest from Saba."

The king waved his hand for him to come closer. "Welcome to Axum, Nathan," the king said, his voice deep with authority. "What is your business here?"

"Your majesty, my people and I were displaced by the flood waters over the Marib dam. We bring you gifts of purple cloth embroidered with gold. We are an industrious people; we are traders, farmers, and skilled artisans. We hope to find refuge in your wonderful city."

Nathan passed the cloth to one of the attendants, who then handed it to the king. Bsente held it up, admiring the workmanship.

"Axum has grown into a strong empire from the efforts of its productive citizens," the king said, rubbing the cloth with his hands. "Your people would have to be committed to sustaining this growth."

Nathan bowed. "We welcome the opportunity, your majesty."

"Then you are welcomed to Axum. Of course, there will be duties paid to support our military. It is necessary for us to have a strong army. Greatness has its enemies."

"I understand," Nathan said, nodding in agreement.

"Why don't we continue this meeting in my chambers," the king said, smiling, "Here in Axum, we consider ourselves to be gracious hosts."

Nathan trailed the king and his attendants out of the room and down a long hallway to a small banquet room. A large grin spread across Nathan's face when he saw the lengthy table covered with delicious food and honey wine. Nathan offered a blessing before they were seated. He concentrated on the eating while the king did most of the talking. Bsente indicated that a number of the young Israelite men coming into the kingdom would have to serve in the military, the army or the navy.

When Nathan couldn't consume another bite, he took a big gulp of the sweet wine and switched the subject. "A serious concern for our people is the freedom to worship without any influence or restrictions. I hope that won't be an issue in Saba."

"There are other Israelite tribes here who worship as you do," Bsente said. "We are all respectful of others' rituals. Now, I'm sure your people are anxious to put down roots. Are you prepared to make an offer on land?"

"Yes, we are, your majesty," Nathan said proudly. "We have not come empty-handed."

"Splendid," the king said. "One of my officers will assist you in the bargain and show you to a prime area where your people can settle." With the business settled, Bsente motioned for his attendant to escort Nathan out. "You must come back to the palace and become acquainted with the other noblemen of the kingdom," he said before Nathan reached the door.

"Thank you, your majesty," Nathan replied, hiding his glee as he was led out of the king's chambers.

* * *

The council of Levites designated an area in the center of their territory that would be reserved for the Temple. Around it, those with considerable wealth built tower houses with walls of colored stone, like the others in Axum. They were at least five stories high, with windows framed with marble, teak, and ebony to see enemies from a distance. Nathan had thin layers of alabaster rock cut and placed in his windows, like those he saw at the palace.

The members of the tribe who were farmers lived in stone and mud homes with thatched roofs, close to the hillsides where they farmed. They learned how to build dams and canals to direct the flow of water onto the terraces of the hillsides where they planted their fields. Fortunately for them, Axum had two rainy seasons that enriched the soil and gave them two crops a year. The rains also supplied them with good grazing land for the cattle.

Nathan became a regular visitor at the palace; and as the chief priest of the Israelites in Axum, he was soon accepted into the group of noblemen. More than the status, he enjoyed the feasts. He grew larger and larger as Sharon plied him with more food to keep him at home.

Word of their success spread back in Saba, and more of Nathan's tribe migrated to Axum. Their area developed into a small town. They all prospered. The land was fertile, yielding plentiful harvests of wheat and barley. Some raised cattle and sheep, others mined salt that traded ounce for ounce with gold. A few of them hunted elephants for tusks and rhinoceroses for their horns to trade the ivory. With their increased wealth, they acquired tastes for the luxuries traded from China and India—

silks, satins, perfumes, spices, and glass dishes. When Nathan and Sharon celebrated the marriages of Rina and Talia, the festivities were fit for royalty.

A portion of the tithes and offerings was designated for the new temple. Axum builders and architects were hired, and Omar and Palti were chosen to oversee the construction. It was not a tall towering structure. It was wide and only two stories high, but it had elaborate carvings out of rock around the exterior walls that told their story from Egypt to Babylon to Marib, and now to Axum. New priestly garbs of violet and white were worn at the dedication of the temple and the ark of the covenant was placed inside. Although no animals were sacrificed, the tribes rejoiced and thanked God for their blessings.

***

Building the temple was an impressive accomplishment for the Israelite tribes in Axum. Nevertheless, as time passed, the congregation seemed to dwindle. On the Sabbath, there were fewer worshipers than they had when they came to Axum. Attendance at the synagogue shrunk as well. Some preferred their sons to work in the fields or learn a trade instead of wasting time reading the Scriptures. Worse, some started offering sacrifices and worshiping the pagan gods Beher, the god of the sea; Maher, the god of war; and Hawbas, the god of the moon.

Nathan should have been alarmed and should have chastised his flock for going astray, but he didn't have the stamina. As he got fatter, he became even lazier. He even left Deron's education for preparation to succeed him as chief priest to his nephew, Ozni, so the questions that always filled Ozni's head were passed over into Deron's.

"What is wrong with the people? Why aren't they faithful to God's word?" Deron asked Ozni while they cleaned the temple after a poorly attended evening service. He had become stringent in his thinking under Ozni's tutelage.

Ozni finished adding oil to a lamp, and then he answered. "Our people have become rich and can afford to indulge in sin. When they were poor, they were more faithful in prayer because their needs were greater."

"We have to do something, or God will punish us again," Deron told him urgently. "We have to remind our people of Jehovah's retribution when we are disobedient. The first commandment says, 'Thou shall have no other gods before me.'"

"Sacrifices must be made for our sins," Ozni said, looking toward the ceiling. "We have been free to worship in our own way for centuries, but we haven't returned to worship in the way God instructed us."

Deron paused for a moment in thought. Then he said, "It's time that we restore the ark of the covenant and offer sin sacrifices."

"Your father is the chief priest, Deron; he has to lead the people back to God's word," Ozni responded without much optimism.

Deron frowned in disgust. Now a willful teenager, he despised his father for his slothfulness and gluttony. He kicked his foot in the air, frustrated, and said, "As chief priest, he should hunger for God's word instead of stuffing his mouth with platters of food."

"Don't doubt your father, Deron. I'm sure he wants what's the best for the people."

"Come to the house with me, and we can discuss it with him over supper," Deron said eagerly. He knew his father hated nothing more than to have his meal interrupted with conversation. It would be the best time to get him to agree without any fuss.

***

Nathan rolled his eyes when he saw Ozni walk in behind Deron. He didn't know what brought his nephew there at mealtime, but he didn't want to hear about it. Sharon was finally about to put dinner on the table. The aroma had been seducing him for hours, and he was not in the mood to be delayed from indulging himself.

"I pray you two are not about to spoil the delectable meal my wife has painstakingly prepared for us," he said, making no effort to hide his irritation.

"No, Father, that is not our intention," Deron said quickly. "We will be brief. Ozni and I believe that measures must be taken to bring our people closer to God. It is our suggestion that we resume animal sacrifices for sin offerings."

Nathan slouched in his chair. "That is a messy business. We've progressed passed the ritualistic ceremonies of 1,000 years ago. The people bring offerings and tithes and portions of their harvests and cattle."

"God's word hasn't changed, Father," Deron said, moving closer to his chair. "The people are not obeying the Torah of Moses. They are marrying outside of the tribe and worshiping pagan gods again. Those are the very things that brought down Jehovah's wrath and sent us into exile. We have to get right with God."

Just then, Sharon walked in with the platter of goose piled high with bread and fruits.

"Ozni, you have my blessing to do whatever you decide," Nathan said, anxious to end the conversation and eat in peace.

Content with his answer, Deron and Ozni sat down at the table to eat.

***

On the next Sabbath, after Nathan finished the morning worship service, Deron spoke to the people. "Children of Israel, in thanks for all the blessings that have been bestowed upon our people in Axum, we are going to fulfill the promise of Jozadak when he left Babylon, and we're going to restore the ark to its former glory and build an altar for sacrifices." The response was split. Some of the people hailed shouts of support, and others silently listened. "This is an awesome task that will require all of you to contribute in one way or another," he told them. "We will follow the directions given to Moses in the Scripture."

To Nathan's surprise, the people responded enthusiastically. The men chopped wood from acacia trees on their land. The women brought offerings of blue, purple, and scarlet linen. Some offered animal skins and spices.

Palti's son, who was a carpenter, replaced the rotted and weakened wood on the bottom of the damaged ark where it had sat on damp earth after the flood in Marib. They built two altars, one for the inside of the synagogue where incense would be burned, and a large one for the outside of the temple for sacrifices. To Nathan's dismay, a substantial amount of tithes was used to buy gold for the holy vessels. He suspended the project before they bought enough gold to cover the outer surface of the ark. Out of reverence, the ark was kept closed. Ozni told Deron that none of them were worthy to look upon God's word.

Special garments were sewn according to the word given to Moses for Nathan and Deron. The only thing missing was the ephod, the chest piece that held God's oracle, the Urim and Thummim. They had been lost when Seraiah was taken and killed. White linen garments were sewn for Ozni and the other assistant priests. Holy oil was prepared to anoint and sanctify all the contents of the temple. Male oxen and sheep without any defects were gathered and housed near the synagogue.

On the Day of Atonement, a huge crowd was present for the return of the old traditions to the worship service. The priests washed their hands and removed their shoes. Nathan did not want any part of the messy killing, passing the responsibility to Deron, since it was his initiative in the first place. Outside the temple, seven bulls, seven rams, and seven lambs were sacrificed for the people's sins. A butcher cut the meat, and the innards were burned on the altar.

The people came inside the first floor of the temple, the men on one side and the women on the other. Deron read from the Torah and delivered his first message to the people.

"This is the beginning of God's redemption for our people. We have strayed from God and his word so many times, but Jehovah is a forgiving God. He allows us to cast our sins down and burn them away in the flames. We must always remind ourselves from where we have come. We cannot live our lives separate from God. We must be steadfast and be obedient. As faithful as God is to us, we must also be faithful. If we do that, he will continue to bless us and protect us."

Deron lifted his arms and said the words of David. "Praise be to you, O Lord, God of our father Israel." He began to chant the phrase, and the people joined in with him.

From that day, he burned incense daily at the temple and was available to the people for prayer and individual sacrifices. He was faithful to God and his priestly duties. He sought no business ventures or tilled the land around their home. Nathan was pleased with his son. Tithes had increased greatly, and he was free to spend more time socializing with the other noblemen.

***

It was Ozni who helped Deron select a wife. He chose Hannah, the young daughter of a farmer. He felt Deron didn't need the distraction of a woman who was accustomed to all the benefits that money could buy. He hoped Hannah would be more concerned with pleasing God than with gaining status. Hannah loved Deron and was a good wife to him. He loved her, too, but after years passed without her bearing any children, Nathan wanted her to be divorced. Deron fasted and prayed for months, all summer and into the winter, and Hannah became pregnant.

After the following harvest season, Deron's first child was born, a son he named Abbott. Nathan hosted a huge feast in celebration. There was every kind of fowl you could think of—chicken, geese, and ducks—and even goat and beef were served. Nathan ate heartily from the thigh of a ram. Exhausted from the festivities, he went to bed early. That night, his belly bloated from all the meat, pressed heavily on his heart, and crushed it.

A tall monument was erected over the place where Nathan was buried. Sharon blamed herself for her husband's death. She had fed him to death because of her desire to keep him home to herself. Her own heart had been crushed in the process. She punished herself by refusing to eat. She grew thinner and weaker, despite all the twins' and Deron's efforts to get her to eat. Within three weeks, she was gone.

Hannah would never bear another child. All their love was showered on Abbott. Deron kept him close as Ozni had done with him, teaching him all the laws that had been handed down to Moses. Abbott was intelligent, a deep thinker, and he loved working with his father to solve the disputes between the people in their town. He became a judge before he followed his father as chief priest.

Chapter Fifteen
Abbott

Abbott couldn't think of a single thing to ask God to bless him with. He had been blessed beyond his imagination. He had a beautiful and faithful wife, Joelle, who had given him three sons, Yusef, Zachary, Myron, and two daughters, Aliza and Gabby. Having received a substantial inheritance from his grandfather Nathan, he was quite wealthy. He had also inherited his grandfather's position in the town as a leader and was now head judge. Before his thirtieth birthday, his father yielded his position in the synagogue and consecrated him as high priest.

The expansion of the temple, which had been under construction for decades, was now complete. He had watched it all the years he was growing up as it was meticulously carved out of humongous stones. At last, it had now revealed its magnificence from the rock and stood in full view ready to be consecrated. The pledge to God by his father, his father before him, and his father before him to build a house of worship worthy of God's word had been fulfilled.

Even though his father forbade it, Abbott had dared to look inside the ark once, and he regretted it. The inscription was barely visible and made no sense to him. For as long as he could remember, he had thought of the moment he would read the words given to Moses and touch them with his hands, but the supernatural stones turned out to be just stones. The mystique disappeared, and the fervor he felt to acquire more gold to renew the ark diminished.

With all the responsibilities that Abbott had in the town, he wasn't as strict as his father had been with him in the teachings of the Torah to his children. He allowed his sons freedom in choosing the direction for their lives. Only one of them would be needed to follow him as high priest, with worship services limited to the Sabbath. Furthermore, they had cousins who were eager to serve as assistant priests. Deron disagreed with his reasoning; he felt all of his grandsons should be prepared to accept the honor for which they had been designated.

Abbott's sons were as distinct as the three corners of a triangle. Yusef was restless and easily bored. Having his head buried in scrolls and Scriptures was torture. Even as a youth, he preferred to spend his time in town, watching all the business conducted at the markets. When he came of age, he worked as a merchant, a successful one. Making money was a sport, and he was a fierce competitor. He traded frankincense, salt, and gold and was branching out into the dirty business of ivory. Nothing was off limits if it paid him a profit. He would vehemently deny it, but gold had become his god.

Zachary was the middle son and was smaller in stature than his brothers. A dreamer with a hero complex, he enjoyed the extra attention he got from his grandfather. It made him feel special and important. The stories Deron told him became thrilling adventures to him, and he longed for the excitement of fighting wars and crossing deserts. Jerusalem captured his imagination, and with the new Temple erected, he thought of it as a place where he could achieve his own measure of greatness. After all, he was a descendant of Aaron.

Myron, the youngest, was the most studious, although he was a free spirit. He was fascinated with learning about a host of things outside of the Torah. Open-minded and curious, he loved to participate in intellectual conversations among wise men from Persia who studied the stars and the religions of other cultures. When he wasn't studying or teaching at the synagogue, he visited other temples, where he compared his beliefs and shared thoughts with the magi who followed Zoroastrianism, a religion based on the struggle between good and evil.

Abbott's oldest daughter, Aliza, a dutiful daughter, was the light in his life. When she danced, she moved like a flower blowing in the wind. It was a sad day for him when the arrangement for her marriage was made; her presence in the house gave him a sense of serenity. Gabby was another story; she made him nervous most of the time. She was his firstborn, and she was the one who announced to him and Joelle the pregnancies and births of her brothers and sisters. People in their town believed she had the gift of sight. They would come and ask her about family and business concerns. Gabby always told them that she could not see the future, her insight came from Jehovah, who spoke to her in her dreams.

Abbott hadn't found a suitable match for Gabby. Despite her physical beauty, a lot of the men were afraid of her because of her gift as a seer. With all the servants doing most of the chores in the house, she spent her time molding clay for pots and dishes. She had become quite an artist, and her pieces were well sought after. Gabby was the one who usually caused the most controversy in their community but never enough to disturb the peace that covered their house. That peace was lifted on the day Myron gave a sermon to the people on his first rotation of the Sabbath worship service.

Myron stood beside the altar, wearing his priestly robes, hands raised.

"Children of Israel," he said with authority beyond his age, "Jeremiah, who prophesized the exile of our people, who was ridiculed, ignored, and despised when he foretold the destruction of our people, also provided us with another prophesy. The Lord declared to him, 'The days are coming when I will make a new covenant with the people of Israel and the people of Judah. It will not be like the covenant I made with their ancestors, when I took them by the hand to lead them out of Egypt, because they broke my covenant, though I was a husband to them. This is the covenant I will make with the people of Israel after that time. I will put my law in their minds and write it on their hearts. I will be their God.'"

Abbott, who was sitting a few feet away, was caught off guard with Myron's message. He straightened his back and sat at attention, wondering why his son was diverting from the subject that they had discussed.

Myron lowered his hands and spoke intently. "During our exile in Babylon, Daniel, wearing sackcloth and ashes, fasted and prayed in supplication for forgiveness and mercy for our people. It was during this prayer that God sent His angel Gabriel with an answer. He touched Daniel and revealed to him that in 70 sevens of years, or 490 years, when the 'times of the Gentiles' has been fulfilled, the Messiah's kingdom will be established. This great charismatic leader, this military head, will defeat all of Israel's enemies and bring all Jews back to Israel. Today, Israelites, I say to you that the signs of the

Messiah, a descendant of David, the one who will be our savior and liberator, are here before us. In his prophecy, Daniel said this 'anointed one,' would come to confirm the covenant and put an end to sacrifice and suffering."

Abbott shifted uncomfortably in his seat as he listened to the sermon Myron was delivering to the people. His son knew that he wouldn't approve of him confusing the congregation with all the dreams, speculations, and nonsense from the peculiar people he wasted time with.

"This anointed one," Myron continued, "Will not come as a god or a demi-god, nor will He be supernatural. He will come as a human being. He will be a great judge and create a government that will be the center of all world governments. The Temple will be rebuilt, and centralized worship will be established there."

Abbott stood on his feet. He had to stop this irresponsible interpretation of God's word. They didn't have any problems in Axum. Why get the people stirred up for no reason?

"It's time to pray," Abbott said, squeezing Myron's right elbow as he motioned for the men in the choir to sing.

Myron considered ignoring the interruption and continuing, but out of respect for his father and the temple, he ended his message and gave a blessing to the congregation. Then Aliza played her drum and did a dance.

When the floor of the temple cleared, Abbott grabbed Myron's arm and yanked him outside, tearing his sleeve. "What is wrong with you?" he shouted, close enough for the warmth of his breath to be felt on Myron's face. "Have you gone out of your mind? What fallacy were you preaching to the people? God directed us in the way to worship and to offer sacrifices to him. Those sacrifices are what keep bread on the table!"

Myron was calm. "I only reminded them of Daniel's word, Father. You know he was not a fake prophet. He was a rigorous student of the Holy Scriptures and the prophecies of Jeremiah. He foretold the rise of the Medo-Persian Empire and the Greek and Roman empires. He predicted all the prosperity, conflicts, and wars of Syria and Egypt."

Abbott was dumbfounded. "Why would you try to get the people confused over something we don't know to be true?" he asked, still holding his arm tightly. "What are you trying to accomplish?"

"It's because we haven't heeded the word of God that we have suffered as a people. I want to remind them of God's word."

"I yielded to you to speak truth to the people, to teach them and pray for them, and you stood there and questioned our beliefs!"

"No, you're wrong. That's not what I did," Myron said, backing up and pulling his arm free. "What did I say that was wrong?"

"You talked about a messiah who would be a regular man, a savior for the people!" Abbott yelled, exasperated that Myron was oblivious to his mistake.

Myron didn't understand his anger and asked, "What's wrong with that?"

"We are forbidden by God to worship any man. God is the only true King."

"He will be the King of kings," Myron said, attempting to explain. "We won't have to make sacrifices and offerings for our sins, for He will wash them all away."

Furious, Abbott pushed Myron forcefully. "Go on away from me! I'm not going to listen to you twist the Scriptures to suit you and those charlatans you've let fill your head with foolishness!"

Myron looked at Abbott in amazement and dashed away, leaving his father at the entrance of the temple. Abbott joined the rest of the family, who were waiting under a cactus tree.

"Is everything all right, Father?" Zachary asked, observing their disagreement, but out of earshot.

"Don't talk to me right now," Abbott said, trudging ahead of them. "I can't stand to hear anymore foolishness right now."

***

It was eerily quiet at the table when the servants brought in platters of food. When they left the room, Gabby and Joelle poured the wine and sat down. Still upset about the morning message, Abbott looked around at each member of his family, his eyes lingering on Myron at the opposite end of the table. Myron avoided his gaze, his head bowed, waiting for Abbott to speak. In a stern tone, Abbott gave the blessing for the meal.

Before anyone could take a bite, Abbott began his speech. "I take full responsibility for indulging my children. I have not demanded much of them. All that I have asked is that everyone in this home love and respect the Lord and His word."

Joelle put her hand on top of his to calm him and poured more wine into his goblet. "Our children are good children, husband," she said, smiling at him sweetly. "They all love and respect Jehovah. Myron meant no harm today. Let us eat now. We can talk about this later."

Abbott nodded and conceded for the moment. Relieved, Joelle motioned for them to begin eating. The silence returned to the room, save for the sounds of chewing and cups tapping the wood of the table.

It was hard for Abbott to hold his temper, even after the satisfying meal. He sat back in his chair, unsure if he wanted to continue the conversation about what Myron had said to the congregation. As Joelle had said, no harm had been done. He could fix it next week when he delivered the message.

Then Gabby spoke up, "Father, the prophecy is coming to pass."

Abbott pounded his fists on the table. "What prophecy?" he asked, annoyed again. "There are so many of them, they're like birds in the sky!"

"The most important one, the one that tells of the Messiah, the anointed one," Gabby answered steadily. "The time is approaching. It has been 14 generations since the Exile, 70 seventies. It was given to Daniel as Myron said."

Abbott stomped his foot. "How can you say that, Gabby? How much do you know about it?" he asked, wishing she would stay out of it. "We have an obligation to deliver the word of God, not lead our people astray with speculation."

Except Abbott knew it was not pure speculation. Even though he had refrained from speaking about it, talk was circulating all over. He and several other priests had already been summoned to the palace to meet with the king to discuss the implications of a messiah.

"I want to go back to Jerusalem," Zachary said. "If the Messiah is to be a great military leader, I will fight in His army."

"Shut up, stupid boy!" Abbott said, frowning at Zachary. "Why would you want to go *back* to Jerusalem. You've never been there. It's not the place you've read and heard about. We have no country there. The Romans seized it more than 50 years ago and rule it with illegitimate kings."

"Illegitimate kings are everywhere," Myron said, turning to Yusef. "Even here, Levites are declaring themselves royalty."

"Does God's word speak against earning a living, brother?" Yusef said snidely.

"Maybe it's time to return to the place where we have a legacy," Zachary said, fixated on going to Jerusalem. "Herod is a Jew. Maybe we can trust him."

Abbott looked at Zachary as if he were out of his mind. "How can you trust a man who executed his own wife and children? Besides, he is not Hebrew; he was only raised as one. His people are converts. You know the dangers we have suffered from the influence of outsiders."

Zachary refused to let it go. "Father, he has rebuilt the Temple and expanded it. He must be a religious man."

"That was for his own ego," Abbott argued. "He has nearly broken the people with the heavy taxes he lays on their backs to build his monuments. He serves at the wishes of Rome. Israelites cannot worship freely in the country God designated for them. Jews have to pay him if they want to be independent of the state religion."

Zachary kept on defending Herod. "I heard he took care of the people during the famine, that he fed them from his own stores."

Abbott kept up his derision. "Stores put up with their own monies. How can you unselfishly give to a man that which you took from him?"

"None of what's going on there will alter the prophecy," Gabby said, breaking into their squabble. "The Scriptures say that a messiah is coming; and whether we go to Jerusalem or not, our lives here will be changed."

"That's enough of all that talk for one evening," Joelle said, waving her hands. "Why don't we talk about finding wives for you boys so I won't have to listen to all your complaints?"

That broke the tension, and they all laughed.

"Don't forget a husband for Gabby," Abbott added. "This house is so full of pots and dishes that if we don't get her married, I won't have a place to lay my head."

"Tell us, Gabby," Yusef said, teasing her, "which one of us will find a match first."

"It will be you, dear brother," she answered as she got up from the table. "Then only one other of us will be so fortunate."

Gabby's words sobered them. The brief moment of merriment was over. Gabby quickly left the room and stepped outside to get some fresh air by herself before she was pressed for more details. It wasn't easy to accept that she would never have a family of her own.

***

The sun had barely found its place in the sky when Abbott left the house the next morning. He was in such a rush, he probably could have gotten there faster on foot than the donkey pulling his cart. Several other priests, noblemen, and junior kings were all meeting at the palace to discuss strategy with King Basen.

The men were already sitting at a table covered with fruits, cheese, and wine when Abbott was ushered into the receiving room.

"Join us, Abbott," the king said, pointing to an empty chair on his right, next to Lemuel.

Lemuel was a priest at a small synagogue on the edge of the city of Israelites. His congregation was mostly farmers, and he did a poor job of masking his envy of Abbott's position and the tithes that he received.

Once Abbott had taken his seat, King Basen started the meeting.

"There are many developments that we have to cover today," he said formally. "The first of which is the situation in Meroe. Kandace has acted boldly, and her army has performed well in the past; but the Roman military occupying Egypt have attacked the Kush people in Nubia. If they are defeated, the Romans will not stop until they have moved on us. They pay handsomely for our resources, and I am sure they have it in their minds that it would be financially feasible to eliminate the kingdom of Axum. If the Kushites are not strong enough to defend their trading network from the Romans, then we have no choice but to take it over. We cannot allow the Romans to come that close to our territory. It is a matter of us protecting our sovereignty."

"We may need to send a large troop of our military there as a safeguard," one nobleman said. "It might encourage Augustus to think twice."

"I agree," the king said, lifting his golden goblet. "We will let him know we are ready and able." He drank from his cup and took a breath. "Now, for the next subject on the table. There are rumblings about a new king of the Jews." He turned toward Abbott. "It seems the subject was touched on at your Sabbath service yesterday."

"Yes," Abbott said, fidgeting in his seat. "My son Myron was a little overzealous."

"I commend your son," Basen said. "We can't ignore the uproar that is starting in Jerusalem or pretend that it won't affect us in some way. Axum has prospered with the people who have migrated here from Saba. This is your home. I wouldn't like to hear that your people are not content here."

"We have no reason to consider leaving Axum, sire," Abbott said, forcing a smile. "Our people are very satisfied, but there is a preoccupation with prophecies that are centuries old."

King Basen nodded. "My concern is Herod and his quest for power, especially with the amount of support he garners from Rome. Are the Israelites willing to go to war for him?"

"It's the influence he brings from Rome that has divided our people," Abbott answered. "Herod isn't secure in Jerusalem; he is in an awkward position. The country is divided between the Pharisees and the Sadducees, and they both hate him. He refused input from the Pharisees on the Temple construction, and he replaced the Sadducees' high priests with outsiders. He is badly in need of local allies. We may be able to curry favor with him."

The king's brows furrowed. "Who are these Pharisees and Sadducees?"

Lemuel, eager to participate in the discussion, interjected, "Your majesty, they are political factions that disagree on religious philosophies. There are deep conflicts among the Pharisees and the Sadducees."

"So the people are hungry for leadership," one of the noblemen added. "Which one of them will serve to our advantage?"

"I don't want either part of them," Abbott complained. "The Pharisees think of themselves as the elites. They think they are better than the rest of the Hebrews. They hide behind the laws they profess to follow so stringently, but the faith they practice is not pure. They rely on the unwritten word that has been twisted by many tongues. They pick and choose their philosophy like a woman buying vegetables in the square. They take what is pleasing and leave that which doesn't satisfy them. They are virtuous to a fault, or at least they pretend to be."

"This is true," Lemuel said, glancing over at Abbott. "Cleanliness of the heart cannot be attained by the washing of hands or refusing to defile yourself among your fellow brethren. It comes from within. A clean heart has love, not disdain for another."

"Do you mean that your people here have no connection to either of these factions?" the king asked. "Have they no relation to your tribe?"

Abbott took a deep breath before he spoke. "The Sadducees are family to us. They too are descendants of Zadok, the high priest. Like us, they are the designated spiritual leaders."

To Abbott's surprise, Lemuel snapped angrily, "The Sadducees are worse. They are pagans in disguise. They are only more rich men who revel in the culture of the Greeks and want to dictate to those of lesser means. There is nothing a rich man loves more than controlling the poor like children. That is when the power of money becomes evident. They, too, consider themselves to be pure, only accepting the written word given from Moses. The rest is simply contrived traditions of men who followed him."

The king chuckled at the discourse between Abbott and

Lemuel. "Obviously, the conflict between the people isn't isolated in Jerusalem," he said.

"The times have changed, and it's a challenge to apply the word to our lives in this day," Abbott said, thinking about the conflict in his own household.

"Different factions interpret the word to suit their purposes," Lemuel said intensely. "Neither one has a claim—"

Abbott interrupted him. "A servant to God must not have his own purpose. He must move on the will of God. We can't look back at what was and what should have been, trying to stuff our feet into sandals that don't fit. We must stay where we can worship without the interference of politics and money."

"Money always interferes," Lemuel said in a salty tone, "or in some cases comes first. Many of the priests are greedy. They want to make their own money. They want the power that comes with it. It was your father, high priest Deron, who told me that politics and religion do not mix. You cannot elevate yourself and God at the same time."

"I think we've said enough on that subject for one afternoon, gentleman," Abbott said, picking up his wine goblet. "There is no urgency for now. Let's not borrow the worries of tomorrow and spoil this delightful day."

He pasted a smile on his face, but on the inside, he was seething. All of this upset over a prophecy that had yet to come to pass. The meeting ended with him restating the loyalty of the Israelites to the king and to their home, Axum.

"It seems you have some concerns of which I was not aware," Abbott said to Lemuel once they had walked a mile from the palace. "You embarrassed us in front of the king."

Lemuel stopped walking, looked him in the eye, and said,

"Priests cannot speak as one when there are vast differences between them. Your family has immense wealth. Outside of the city where the farmers live, we priests are not so fortunate. We don't receive the tithes that you do."

Abbott shrugged his shoulders and asked, "Am I to blame for that?"

"I find no fault in you, Abbott. You are rightly high priest. But I find no way forward in you either. Jeremiah's words told of the change that is to come."

"God's blessings be with you," Abbott said, climbing into his cart to ride.

Trouble was in the air, and there was nothing Abbott could do to squelch it.

***

"You know how your father is, Myron," Joelle said to her son sitting on the rug across from her. "He doesn't like to rock the boat. Give him some time, and he will listen.

"His mind is closed to anything outside of the Torah," Myron grumbled, watching her embroider the fine red cloth. "Not everything we need to know is written in a book."

"You've been spending too much time with those astrologers with their heads stuck up in the sky," Abbott said, overhearing what they were saying as he walked in the door.

"They are followers of Zoroaster, Father," Myron replied. "They have a love of wisdom and a quest to search for the truth."

"I don't care what they love. They're pagans."

Myron shook his head with dismay. "I wouldn't call them pagans. They are wise men who read the Scriptures. They have been studying Balaam's prophecy of the star that will come out of Jacob and Daniel's prophecy of the date for the coming of the Messiah. They feel that the time is near and have been watching for the star."

"Many have, and many more will claim to be the 'anointed one,'" Abbott said, mocking him, "this king of the Jews."

"They've seen the star in the east. There is an entourage of magi from Persia, China, and India, kings, nobles, and priests from Yemen, traveling to follow where the star leads. They have arrived here in Axum. King Basen has announced that he will be going along and bringing his military escorts as well. I am going to buy myself a strong horse tomorrow. I plan to join them on the journey."

"And what of your responsibilities here?" Abbott asked, bowled over.

Myron stood on his feet. "Zachary can handle things without me."

"How soon will this happen?" Joelle asked Myron.

"In a few days, Mother."

"All the family must be gathered together," she said, throwing her cloth to the floor and rushing from the room.

***

Joelle had the servants prepare a huge feast before Myron was to leave. The whole family was present, including Aliza and her husband. They were all excited about the news and the prospect of Myron going back to Jerusalem and seeing the new Temple.

It was only Abbott who sat there fuming. "I don't see why you have to be running around the desert with a bunch of heathens," he fussed. "If the prophecy comes to pass, don't you

think we'll know about it here in Axum? The whole thing is a
huge waste of time and money."

"You're right, Father," Myron said, too excited to be
bothered by anything Abbott said. "The truth won't be hidden,
but I want to witness it for myself. The money doesn't matter
to me."

"We can't survive in this world without money," Abbott
griped.

Myron snickered. "I don't know why you're worried. The
people give you tithes that you don't even have to work for."

"God's word given to Moses said the people should give
of their earnings to the priests, and we must do God's work to
receive it," Abbott said, feeling defensive.

"I wish I could go with you, Myron," Zachary said
wistfully. "Isn't it possible that our responsibility is to go back
to the Temple and return the ark to its rightful place? We are
the true high priests."

That doesn't matter anymore," Abbott shouted. "Too much
of our blood has been shed at the doors of the Temple. It's all a
charade now. The high priest in Jerusalem is usually the highest
bidder for the job. Our place is here in Axum. The people
here are loyal followers to God's word, and our ministry is
growing."

Chapter Sixteen
Myron

The entourage of magi, priests, noblemen, and royalty on horseback traveled from Axum to Egypt and then to Jerusalem. The long route was taken to avoid conflicts between the Romans and Persians. Three months passed from the time they left Axum to when they crossed Herod's walls into Jerusalem. Their entrance into the city caused somewhat of an uproar among the people. They were curious as to what business this diverse group of men—obviously from several different countries, given the colors of their skin and the variety of their clothing—would be conducting in Jerusalem.

The conspicuous group of men strode their horses through the crowded marketplace in the center of the city. Carpenters, metalworkers, potters, weavers, tailors, farmers, and bakers were gathered to sell their wares. There they stopped, and King Basen, who was at the front, concealing his identity, approached one of the vendors selling his harvest.

"Where is the newborn King of the Jews?" Basen asked him. "We have seen His star in the east and have come to worship Him."

"I don't know who you are talking about," the man said, bowing his head. "I haven't heard anything of this. I'm only here to sell you the best olives in the city."

"Where is a place where we can eat and rest for the evening?" one of the magi asked him.

"There is an inn at the end of the market," the man told them, pointing them in the direction.

When the entourage was halfway down the road, the vendors next to the man rushed over to see what the travelers wanted. It wasn't long before word of the curious men and their quest spread quickly through the market and then reached the palace.

King Herod was outraged that these men would be referring to someone else other than him as the king of the Jews. He needed to determine where this threat to his throne was coming from. He sent for his priests and scribes. When they arrived, he questioned them thoroughly and was informed about the prophecy of the "anointed one" and where He was to be born. Hastily, Herod sent for the group of magi, kings, and priests, to speak with him at the palace.

The impressive group was escorted through the camp of Roman soldiers by Herod's officers to the western side of the Upper City, where the palace was surrounded by a fortress. The structure was a wondrous sight to behold. It was elevated on a platform rising close to 1,000 feet. There were two wings, with a luxurious garden between them. Bronze fountains, canals, and ponds accented the grounds.

The group was led to the king's stables where they could have their horses watered, fed, and stored. There were guards in every area of the palace. Basen was the only one indifferent to the opulence of the inside of the palace as they walked to Herod's reception area. Inside, the king sat waiting, flanked by his personal bodyguards.

"Welcome to Jerusalem," Herod said from his throne, as the league of men stood before him. "Once I learned of such a prestigious group visiting the city, I wanted to greet you and find out if there is any way that we here in Jerusalem can be of service to you."

"We have seen the star," Myron said, stepping forward. "We have come to worship the Messiah, but we don't know where to find Him."

Herod forced a fake grin and said, "First, I insist that you all be my guest at the palace."

"Thank you, your majesty," Myron said graciously. "We won't be trouble to you for long. Do you know where we can find this child?"

"I have been told by my religious leaders that He will be born in Bethlehem," Herod replied. "Tomorrow, when you have refreshed yourselves, go and search for Him there. When you find Him, come and back and tell me the location so that I too can go and worship Him."

"You have been most helpful, your majesty," Myron said to Herod.

The men were led to a huge banquet room. There were no women at the feast table that lasted for hours. They were served chicken, duck, pigeons, and goat, with plenty of wine. Afterward, they were entertained with dancing girls and acrobats. The entourage rested themselves, but they decided to leave the palace after sunset.

Once they were outside the gates of the city, they saw the star. As they rode toward it, the star moved. They followed it all the way to Bethlehem, where it stopped over a small house. They climbed off their horses and went inside.

There they found the small child with his mother, Mary. She told them that His name was Jesus. All of them, the kings, priests, magi, and the noblemen bowed before Him and presented Him with the gifts of gold, frankincense, and myrrh. Myron was in awe that such a small child could already be considered the Messiah. He thought of all the prophecies related to this child, the events that might come to pass and said a prayer.

When all the men in the entourage had a moment to gaze upon the child, they went to an inn to rest for the night.

Myron was frightened by a dream and the message that was delivered to him. He woke up in a cold sweat. He thought about Gabby and the burden of dreaming of things that might come to pass.

"I had a vision or a strange dream last night," King Basen said. "It may have been an angel speaking to me. I'm not sure. I was told that we should not to go back to the palace, that Herod seeks to find the location of the child and kill Him."

"I had the same dream," Myron said.

"I did also," one of the magi added.

Myron felt better when he realized that most of the men traveling in the entourage had had the same experience.

"We have come here together, but it may be more prudent for us to disband and travel in different directions," Basen said to his traveling associates. "Herod is going to be looking for us to tell him where the child lives." Then he addressed Myron, "You're welcome to return back to Axum with me under the protection of my officers."

"Thank you for the kind gesture, your majesty," Myron said, bowing. "But I want to spend a few weeks in Jerusalem before I return."

"You must be careful not to be recognized by Herod's soldiers," Basen warned.

"I will," Myron said, riding away from them on his horse.

***

Myron had heard so much about Jerusalem all his life that he wanted to explore the city, meet the people, and learn as much as he could before he went back to Axum. To be safe, he searched to find a different place for lodging and a stable to store his horse. From the stares he got, he realized that the next thing he needed to do was find clothes that would help him blend in with the people in the city. Before going to the market, he asked the innkeeper if he could exchange his vibrant pants and cloak for a tunic and robe that would not draw attention. His shoes were still a little conspicuous, but he could buy a more appropriate pair of sandals at the market.

There were Roman soldiers patrolling the area when Myron got to the market, so he moved about with downcast eyes to avoid their scrutiny. Perusing the open-air market, he scanned all the foods and wares for sale by the farmers and the craftsmen. He ventured into a few of the tent shops and found sandals like the ones worn by the locals before he sat down to listen to a tale from one of the storytellers. It was a fable about a lion and a mouse.

Feeling hungry, Myron bought bread and stew to eat. Sitting on the ground under a tree, he overheard a conversation between a group of local men. That's when he learned that King Herod was furious that the band of wise men searching for the baby Messiah had not returned to the palace as he had instructed them. He had since made a pronouncement that all male children in Bethlehem under the age of two years were to be killed. Myron thought it was strange that the men spoke so casually about Herod's murderous callousness. Apparently, they had become accustomed to the whims of an evil and wicked king.

After his meal, Myron left the market in his new sandals and started his hike to Jerusalem. It was an uphill trek for the first half of the distance along a rocky terrain. Closer to Jerusalem, when he had gone around the Mount of Olives, the walk was downhill. From the heights, he could see the Temple Mount amidst the beams of light cast from the sun reflected back from the gold-adorned structure. Almost there, he passed through the thick stone wall into the Lower City, where the poor of Jerusalem lived in houses crowded together on tiny dusty streets.

Alive with the cacophony of voices and animals yelping and clomping along through the road, the city was full of activity. Myron could smell food cooking and bread baking as he muddled his way through the maze of small houses. His leather sack of water was empty, and after the two-hour walk, he was parched. He ventured into a courtyard where he saw a group of women at the well. They whispered and smiled as he came toward them.

"You look thirsty," one of the older women said.

Myron nodded. "Yes, I am. I've just walked here from Bethlehem to visit the Temple."

The young woman next to her offered him a dipper of water and said, "My father was one of the 1,000 Levites who worked as masons and constructors to help build the Temple."

"I'm also a Levite," Myron said. "I have traveled here from a long distance."

"You must come and have supper with us," the older woman said. "My husband loves to meet fellow Levites with quests from faraway places. The Temple isn't going anywhere this evening. It will be there in the morning."

"Thank you. I would like that very much," Myron said, thankful for the invitation.

"Come with us," the older woman said. "I'm Beth, and this is my daughter, Darrah."

"I'm Myron," he replied, nodding to the younger woman.

Myron followed the women as they carried the large pitchers of water on their heads to a tiny house where a man was sitting on the ground outside, chiseling a face on a large rock.

"This busy man is my husband, Pascal," Beth said, patting the man on the shoulder. Then she turned to her husband. "We met this young man at the well. His name is Myron. He's a fellow Levite who has traveled a long way to see the Temple."

Pascal looked hard at Myron, appraising the young man.

"It's a pleasure to meet you, sir," Myron said, kneeling beside him.

"Supper will be on the table shortly," Beth said, pushing the door for Darrah and walking in behind her.

"Where are you from, Myron?" Pascal asked, squinting his eyes up at him.

"I come from Axum. My family migrated there after the Exile."

Pascal was intrigued. "You came all that way by yourself?"

"I met some others along the way," Myron answered, unsure of who he could trust.

"Are you here to stay?" Pascal asked cautiously.

"No, sir, I heard so much about Jerusalem from my grandfather when I was a boy that I always wanted to come and see it for myself. Now that the Temple has been expanded, I thought the time was right."

"Well, it is something to see. I worked with the Levite builders for 14 years. We were the only ones allowed to enter the inner halls," Pascal said, shaking his head as he thought back. "We worked long and hard days to see that there was no interruption in the sacrifices and the worship services."

"That must have been a great honor for you."

"I guess I'd have to say yes and no. They've fashioned the whole place like Rome, and the Romans have no morals. The city is full of prostitutes and drunkards. From what I've seen, the Temple was built to bring him more money. I don't go there. We have hundreds of synagogues in Jerusalem where a pious man can worship."

"The city is not at all like I had imagined it," Myron told him, glancing over at the run-down houses next to them. "Your neighbors are very close."

"Most Levites don't have land. The poor don't have much to offer," Pascal said, standing up. "Thank Jehovah, we can still put a decent meal on the table. Come on in, young man."

The table was filled with a lentil stew, and Myron could smell the onion and herbs that wafted above the bowl. In the middle of the table, there were cheese, olives, and fresh figs. A jar of curdled milk sat at the end of the table. Pascal sat down next to his wife on the mat and said a short prayer. Myron sat down next to Darrah.

Myron noted that the room was still, with no servants hovering over them to pour water or wine, but it was one of the most enjoyable meals he had ever had. He wasn't sure why, but he felt more comfortable eating with these strangers than he did at the table with his own family. Most likely, it was the company of Darrah beside him, who smiled pleasantly when she caught him staring. When they had finished eating, Pascal went back outside and chiseled some more on his rock. Myron joined him while the women cleared the table.

"Tell me about your home," Pascal said, staring at his rock.

"Axum is a beautiful place," Myron said wistfully as he visualized it in his mind's eye. "It's lush, with colorful flowers and strong trees among lofty hills. There are people from all parts of the world there because of its profitable location for trade. In the city, there are palaces, temples, and great houses that are as vivid as flowers. The buildings are tall, five stories and even nine stories high, to see far into the distance. We have busy shops and markets like you do here in Jerusalem, but there are few poor people in the city of Axum. You do not have to try hard to become wealthy. My brother Yusef is proof of that.

"The weather is agreeable, and the soil is rich and fertile, with good pastures for cattle. We have two rainy seasons, which helps our farmers plant two crops in a year. For that, we are thankful; there are no shortages of food. We are free to worship in our own way, and we have lots of synagogues, although not as many as you have here."

"That sounds like a good place to live," Pascal said, tapping on his rock. "If Herod has his way, we'll be sucked into the Roman Empire. Either way, there will be more wars to come." Pascal paused for a minute, then he asked, "Is Axum a peaceful place, or are there conflicts between the people?"

"My family migrated from Saba after the flood because of conflicts with the Himyarites. For the most part, there has been peace in Axum. The king supports a strong military to defend the country, and with all the money and goods exchanged there, no one wants to cause problems."

"What about your family?"

"We have no complaints," Myron said. "Why so many questions? Are you considering a move out of Jerusalem?"

Pascal smiled. "Not for myself. I'm too old to change, but I want something better for my daughter. When the war comes, I don't want her to be hurt. The Romans treat women like dogs." He paused again and said, "Darrah is a beautiful girl, isn't she?"

Myron nodded. "Yes, sir, she's very beautiful."

"She would make an excellent wife for a Levite man."

"I'm sure she would," Myron said awkwardly.

"The only price is her happiness."

Myron didn't want to be rude or insulting. Not knowing how to respond, he stayed quiet.

"Stay with us while you are visiting here," Pascal said, putting down his chisel. "I believe we have much more to discuss."

Unsure of what his host had in mind, Myron figured it would be best to politely decline the invitation. "Thank you, sir, but I don't know how long I'll be here."

"It doesn't matter," Pascal said, getting up to go into the house. "There will be a mat for you inside the door where you can sleep."

Myron looked up into the sky. It was a clear night, but the bright star he and the others had followed was gone. Now that he had seen the "anointed one," he didn't know what he was doing there. Certainly, he would visit the Temple and make a sacrifice, but what other reason did he have to extend his stay? He had come in search of the Messiah, not a wife.

***

It was just after daybreak, and the farmers were carrying their perishable goods to the market. Myron had gotten an early start, relieved that he didn't have to speak with his host before he left. From a distance, he could see the Hippodrome, the immense amphitheater that Herod built to showcase horse and chariot races. When he got closer, he saw the huge theatre where Greek and Roman dramas were performed for the rich citizens. Pascal was correct. The city was more like the descriptions of Rome than those he had heard of the city of David.

The streets widened as Myron continued through the Upper City. The homes were large mansions where the wealthy and prominent citizens, including the priests, resided. The palace of the high priest, Joshua Ben Sie, was as luxurious as any king's palace. He felt a tinge of shame for the way the priests, not only here in Jerusalem but in his home of Axum, separated themselves from the people while becoming rich from their sacrifices. He wondered if any of them loved God for God's sake, not as a deliverer or a provider. It seemed that if their needs were met, they didn't need God.

Roman soldiers were surveying the forum where the merchants were discussing business. Myron pulled his robe over his head to pass without notice. He saw Herod's three towers to his left as he approached another market. The goods there were much more expensive. Finally, he stood at the steps of the Temple Mount.

The Temple Mount, surrounded by soldiers and limestone walls, was more splendid than anything Myron had ever seen, and he had laid eyes on many grand structures. There were so many gates and entrances overlaid with gold and silver and tall magnificent columns of marble on the different levels of the temple. There was also a place to check the animals.

Myron climbed the impressive three-storied staircase to the entrance, where non-Jews could enter the Court of Gentiles. It did not feel like a hallowed space, more like a bustling marketplace. He stood in line for one of the moneychangers to exchange his currency so he could buy food and mementos from vendors and an animal for his peace offering.

Next, Myron went to the area where Jews could buy animals for sacrifice before heading to the Huldah gates and bought a lamb. It was there that they directed him to the pools, which were baths with flowing water from underground tunnels for cleansing and purification. When he was cleansed, the attendants gave him clean garments to wear.

Leading the lamb, Myron climbed the 14 steps through the wide Beautiful Gate to the Court of Women, the place of morning and evening worship during the sacrifices. There were chests to deposit sacrifices of money. Women could not go beyond this point. Going higher on a spectacular winding staircase, Myron entered the Court of the Israelites, where laymen gathered to watch the service. There was an altar in the center for the burnt offerings. Two more steps led to the Court of Priests, which was reserved for Levites. In front of the large embroidered curtain veiling the Holy of Holies was a platform where the priests pronounced the blessings and the Levites sang and played their instruments. Only the high priest could go beyond the veil.

Myron had never seen so many priests dressed in white linen and turbans at one time. There seemed to be thousands of them. He didn't tell them who he was, a bona fide direct descendant of Aaron, who had traveled far to make a peace offering. He could smell the stench of slaughter as he moved closer to the front. Those at the altar disappeared within the thick smoke. Animals screeched and bellowed in fear and pain. Myron watched as the priest sliced the neck of the lamb and the scarlet blood gushed out, staining the white wool. He watched as the priest poured the blood around the edges of the giant altar and burned the entrails. An attendant wrapped the other half of the carcass in cloth and handed it to Myron. It was still warm when he tucked it under his arm.

Back in the clothes he wore in, Myron walked back down the stairs to the Court of Gentiles, where he bought souvenirs for his family. Then he walked out of the Temple. At the market, he bought dried fish and vegetables for his hosts. He thought of Darrah when he passed a tent selling jewelry. He saw a pair of earrings made with glass beads and a necklace with the same design. He didn't know why, but he had an impulse to buy them for her.

When he arrived at his hosts' home, Darrah was bringing fresh loaves of bread from the baker.

"I bought you something," Myron said, putting his packages on the ground. He reached into his satchel and handed her the necklace and earrings wrapped in a small piece of cloth. "I hope you like them."

Darrah opened the cloth, and her brow furrowed. "You don't have to give me gifts," she said, handing them back to him. "You don't owe me anything."

"I know that," Myron said, a bit confused. "I thought they were very pretty, and I wanted you to have them, that's all."

"I heard my father talking to you, and I don't want your pity."

Even more confused, he asked, "Why would I pity you?"

Darrah's eyes watered as she spoke, "For not having any better prospects for a husband than a stranger who passed by the well."

"I'm sure your father didn't mean it in that way," Myron said, understanding that she felt humiliated. "I'm sure there is much competition for your hand."

Darrah shook her head hopelessly. "If you were a rich Levite priest, would you come to the Lower City to look for a wife?"

Before he answered, Myron looked at her, really seeing her for the first time, and considered the question. She was beautiful, devoted to her family, and obviously proud.

"Is that what he wants for you?" he asked.

"Yes, he wants me protected from the evils he sees in this world."

"And what do you want for yourself?"

"I'd like to see something of this world outside of this small circle I live in."

Myron smiled at Darrah and said, "If you were my wife, I could show you that."

"I'm not going to play games with you," Darrah said, rushing into the house.

***

"The lamb is roasting, and we will have a delicious meal tomorrow," Beth said as they sat down to eat the skimpy portions she brought to the table.

"If you approve, I would like to contribute to the celebration," Myron said, dropping a handful of Egyptian gold coins on the table. "Accept this as a gift, a mohar, if you'll consent to Darrah becoming my wife."

They were all stunned for a moment, and then Pascal happily exclaimed, "Bring us some wine! This is cause for a big celebration!"

Beth ran to get the wine. "I am so happy! This is a joyful day!" she exclaimed, clasping her hands together. Then she looked at her daughter, who didn't seem as elated. "Aren't you happy, Darrah?"

"If my parents are happy, then I am happy," Darrah said.

"Then you must accept the gift I bought for you," Myron said, pushing the cloth-enclosed jewelry across the table to her. When Darrah didn't move, Beth reached for the folded cloth and opened it. "It's lovely!" she said, admiring the jewelry. Then she placed the necklace around Darrah's neck and the earrings in her ears. Beth put her hands to her chest to hold in the fullness. "So beautiful!"

"When I saw you, I knew you were destined to come here," Pascal told Myron, raising his cup of wine. "I saw the husband of my daughter. May God's blessing be on you both."

Myron left his glass on the table. "Before you give us your blessing, I must remind you that I will be returning to Axum," he said warily. "As my wife, Darrah will come home with me."

"That is as it should be," Pascal said, raising his cup again.

***

All the people in the Lower City celebrated the wedding. Myron was dressed handsomely in white linen and wore a crown of flowers. He walked along a path where musicians played and virgins held oil lamps to guide him to Pascal's house. There waiting for him, Darrah had been pampered and clothed in a fine white dress and fancy jewelry. When the entourage reached the door, someone cried out, "Behold, the bridegroom cometh! Go ye out to meet him!" Darrah, with her face covered by a veil, was carried out to the courtyard. A crown of flowers was placed on her head. Family and friends danced and sang around them, throwing more flowers. After the ceremony, Myron and Darrah returned to the house, and Darrah removed her veil.

"You can still escape if you want," she said, still unsure of Myron's reasons for marrying her.

Myron kissed her and said, "I intend to, but I'll be taking my wife with me."

She smiled. "I am my beloved's, and my beloved is mine."

The marriage feast and the celebration lasted a week.

***

When the heavy rainfall of winter ended, Myron was anxious to make the journey back to Axum. Travel was dangerous for a man outside of a caravan; for a woman, it was treacherous. Myron decided to disguise Darrah as a young man for her safety. After an emotional goodbye, the couple hiked back to Bethlehem, where Myron traded his horse for two donkeys. He and Darrah rode the donkeys to Gaza and then to the port of Alexandria in Egypt.

Myron glanced at Darrah's expression at the sight of the large ships and the amount of goods there to be traded. Her eyes widened to take in all the sights, and her ears peaked at the unfamiliar sounds and languages. There, Myron bought passage on a Roman trade ship sailing down the Red Sea to Adulis. He claimed to be a merchant traveling with his assistant, Davin. When they reached Adulis, they joined a caravan, riding camels to get to Axum.

***

"You didn't tell me you were a king," Darrah said as Myron led her through the courtyard of the family home. "This is a house for royalty."

"I'm not a king. I'm a priest," Myron said, uncomfortable with her assumption. "My father is the chief priest here in Axum. We are direct descendants of Aaron who migrated here after the Exile. My family has benefited from the wealth in Saba and now here in Axum."

"From what I see, you are as prosperous as the high priest in Jerusalem. Why didn't you tell that to my father?"

"What does it matter? We are servants of God," he answered, making light of it.

"It doesn't matter to me, but it does to a lot of people," she said, awestruck.

Myron waved to Gabby, who was out digging in the dirt on the plateau behind the house. She dropped her spade and started toward the courtyard to meet them.

"That is my sister, Gabby," Myron said. "She's an artist when it comes to making pottery. She gets most of her clay from up there."

"I'm not fancy," Darrah said, looking around the grounds of the house. "You know my parents are poor. You should not have married me."

Myron smiled at her. "You are rich in beauty and have a wealth of kindness in your heart. So in you I have found great treasure."

"I can see you are a priest now," Darrah said, laughing at his response. "You insist I feel that which my eyes can't see and ignore things that stand in my way."

"And, not to forget, you are very smart, too," Myron joked.

"Welcome home! I'm glad you're back, brother!" Gabby said, catching her breath from running. "We've missed your good sense around here."

"It's good to be home," Myron said, kissing his sister's forehead. "I have so much to tell you, but first I have someone I want you to meet."

Gabby pulled Darrah close in an embrace and kissed her cheek. "You don't have to introduce me to your wife. I saw her in a dream long before you met her. Your wedding present is inside." Darrah's mouth fell open in amazement.

"We can talk about that later," Gabby said. "Right now, you better come into the house and speak to mother. She's been halfway out of her mind with worry."

Gabby took her brother and sister-in-law by the hands and hurried them to the front entrance.

"Mother, I'm back home!" Myron shouted once they were inside the house.

They didn't hear a response, only footsteps rushing down the stairs.

"Thanks be to Jehovah, my child! I feared that you were dead!" Joelle said when she reached her son. She wrapped him up in a tight embrace and then stood back to look at him. "It's been more than a year's time since I've laid eyes on you. Why did it take so long for you to come back?" Then she turned her attention to the scraggly person standing next to him. "And who is this you've brought with you?"

"This is Darrah, my wife," Myron answered proudly.

"Your wife?" Joelle asked stunned. She stared into Darrah's dirty face and then down at the tattered man's robe she was wearing. "You left here to search for the 'anointed one,' and you come home to say you are married?"

"Come with me, Darrah," Gabby said, grabbing her hand. "I'm sure you're exhausted. I'll show you where you can get refreshed before the rest of the family arrives to look you over."

Joelle watched the two women leave the room, trying to process it all. Then she yelled out to the head house servant. "Leah! Leah! come quickly!"

"Yes, madam?" Leah said. "Is something wrong?"

"No, something is right for a change around here! Go and tell Abbott and my sons to come home, and fetch Aliza, too. We need to prepare a feast to welcome Myron back home!"

After Leah was on her way, Joelle sat down on a stool to gather herself. "Come, son, sit beside me. We must talk for a minute. Where did you meet this girl?"

"Is that all you want to know about my trip?" Myron asked, dropping down on the floor near her.

"Of course not," Joelle said, slightly flustered. "But we can begin there."

"I stayed with her family when I got to Jerusalem, and, yes, she is a Levite."

"Why didn't you come back with the magi you were traveling with?"

"Spies were watching us, so we had to separate. Anyway, I couldn't have gone all that way and not visited the Temple Mount."

"You never said you were ready to take a wife before you left," Joelle said, still shocked. "Your father and I could have found you a very nice girl here in Axum."

"It doesn't matter now, Mother. I have my wife, and I am happy with her."

"This is a lot for me to digest in one day, son. Go clean yourself up before your father gets here. You smell like a passel of pigs."

Joelle had the servants prepare a large spread of food on the table to celebrate Myron's safe return. She resisted the urge to invite friends until she knew more about this young woman her son had brought back with him.

***

Aliza, her husband, and their newborn daughter lived a mile away and were downstairs chatting with Myron. Zachary was hunting, but he would probably be home before dark. The table was already set when Gabby looked through her window and saw her father and Yusef coming in the distance.

"It's time to meet the rest of your family," Gabby said to Darrah, putting a little more oil on her hair. "You look much more presentable than you did when I first saw you."

"Thanks for the clothes. I feel much better."

"Don't be nervous. They'll pick at you in the beginning, but they're harmless once you get to know them."

Darrah followed Gabby downstairs to the dining room. Every eye was fixed on her as she sat down next to Myron.

"Welcome to the family and to our home," Abbott said to Darrah. "It is plain to see why my son could not leave Jerusalem without you."

"Thank you, sir," Darrah replied, bowing her head. "I bring warm regards from my family back in Jerusalem."

Then Zachary burst through the door. "What is all the fuss about?"

"Your brother is back! He was married in Jerusalem, and this is his wife, Darrah," Joelle replied, praying that Zachary would maintain some civility.

Zachary stopped in his tracks, the petty jealousy he felt toward Myron swelled and crashed onto him like a giant wave. He was the one who wanted to go to Jerusalem. Not only did Myron get to have the experience he wanted, but he got a beautiful wife as a bonus.

"Shouldn't we as the older brothers have been consulted before this marriage?" Zachary asked, addressing his father. "What about our approval? Are all the traditions meaningless now?"

"I can't believe this is how we celebrate our brother coming home!" Aliza said. "From this behavior, you would think he had brought a prisoner of war home for dinner."

"I agree, sister," Gabby said to stop the interrogation. "Let's concentrate on our food and let Darrah eat in peace. You taught us better than this, didn't you, Mother."

Myron and Darrah were given a short reprieve while they ate; but when the meal was over, Abbott continued his questioning. He was not concerned about his son taking a bride, though. He was concerned about this Messiah and the message Myron would bring back to the people.

"The point of your journey was to see this so-called anointed one," Abbott said sarcastically. "Did you find Him or not?"

"Yes, we did find the child, as the prophecy said we would!" Myron answered excitedly. "I believe He is the one foretold, the Messiah. There were people from all over to see the child, from kings of foreign lands to farmers and shepherds from the fields. It was the greatest experience of my life!"

Yusef didn't want to hear about his useless waste of money. He interrupted Myron. "I have heard from several traders that Herod issued an order that all male children in Bethlehem under two years old be killed. It is possible that this Messiah is already dead!"

"The child is safe," Gabby said, cutting him off. "His parents were warned, and the prophecy will be fulfilled."

Zachary hit the table in frustration. "Why are we getting all undone because of a child? It will be a while before we have anything to worry about from Him anyway."

Myron ignored Zachary, stood up, and leaned toward his father. "Jeremiah said that there would be a new covenant with Israel and Judah. The Law, once written on stones, would be written on the hearts of all people."

Abbot roared back, "I have not raised you to belittle the mighty word of the Lord given to Moses! My father and his fathers have carried the ark over a thousand miles to protect that word. Now because you have your head filled with the stupidity of star worshipers, you don't see that anymore!"

"It is not on them that I base my beliefs, Father," Myron said, not backing down. "Jeremiah was a prophet chosen by

God. Even you cannot question that. God's words to him were clear, 'And no longer shall each one teach his neighbor and each his brother, saying "Know the Lord," for they shall all know me, from the least of them to the greatest, declares the Lord. For I will forgive their iniquity, and I will remember their sin no more.' This child, the coming of this Messiah, is a wonderful gift to us."

Abbott's impatience turned to anger. "Have you forgotten what the Lord told Moses during the Exodus, 'And thou shall appoint Aaron and his sons, and they shall wait on their priest's office: and the stranger that cometh nigh shall be put to death.'"

"The Messiah is no stranger, Father," Gabby added. "Jeremiah said he would be a descendant of David. We are not in danger from an enemy. The child's name is Jesus. He will be the King of kings, and His kingdom will not be destroyed. It will be established for all eternity. We are to be blessed!"

"That goes against everything that was commanded in the word given to Moses!" Abbott said.

"I respect that covenant," Myron said, "but the word shows that our Lord has changed His mind in several instances."

Abbott shook his head and said, "There's no reason for me to entertain all this newfound foolishness! When Phinehas slayed the sinners, God told Moses, 'And he shall have it, and his seed after him, even the covenant of an everlasting priesthood; because he was zealous for his God, and made and an atonement for the children of Israel.' Until God tells me different, I will carry on with the responsibilities that He designated for my forefathers."

"Why do you wrestle with the thought of a new covenant?" Myron asked, perplexed.

"There is only one covenant!" Abbott said stubbornly.

"We have to teach the people the word of God, and in that word are the words He gave to His prophets," Myron said, trying to reason with his father.

"I cannot in good conscience allow you to fill our peoples' heads with speculations of the truth. You will be restricted from teaching at the synagogue and from leading Sabbath services until you can see the error of your ways!" Abbott declared.

"Father, no!" Aliza cried. "Myron is the most beloved teacher at the school."

Joelle spoke up, too, cautioning him, "Don't act in haste, Abbott!"

"So you intend to keep the knowledge of the prophecy from the people?" Myron asked in disbelief. "You are acting like the emperor of Rome, trying to suppress any discussions that don't support the government."

Gabby held her hand up to quiet Myron. "Father, unless you plan to live forever, you cannot stop the word of God from coming to the people. I can tell you without a doubt that the word of the child will come to Axum, and we will have to choose our fate."

"So be it!" Abbott roared, leaving the table. "It makes me no difference. I'll be lying in my grave before his beard is grown in."

***

Zachary took over Myron's post at the synagogue, not because he wanted to teach God's word and minister to the congregation. It was out of jealousy of his brother. Zachary was soon married and had a family, three daughters but no sons. Yusef never fulfilled his priestly duties, and he never married. He pursued his true love, money, until the day he died. Myron moved away from Axum, south of the city, where he found happiness and contentment raising sheep with Darrah and their son, Cohen.

Abbott tried his best to live forever; he buried his wife and three of his children. He also did his best to shield the people from the controversies that arose from the man named Jesus. If they heard about Jesus clearing out the Temple, it wasn't from him. He did not speak on Jesus' dealings with a Samaritan. When he heard that Jesus was preaching and telling the people about His Father in heaven, that is when Abbott began to talk against Him.

Abbott's congregation had become fascinated with the stories they heard about this Messiah from afar, stories about Him raising dead, healing the sick, feeding multitudes from meager scraps, calling out demons, and turning water to wine. Abbott did his best to dissuade them, saying that the stories were huge exaggerations that grew bigger as they traveled down across the desert. He heard the news of the 12 disciples that followed Jesus, the fact that they were all Israelites and drawing larger and larger numbers to hear Him speak. For two years, Abbott heard of the travels, miracles, and sermons where Jesus gave new laws.

However, Myron reveled in the stories and longed to be part of the new ministry he heard about. He decided to go on a pilgrimage to see the man who he once saw as a child. He wanted to hear Jesus preach and worship at His feet again.

Darrah and Cohen wanted to go with him, but Cohen's wife, Edna, was pregnant with their second child. Myron convinced them that their place was with her. He left, riding on a horse as he had done 30 years earlier. His family never saw or heard from him again.

***

Abbott, though old and feeble, demanded that his congregation reject this Jesus and His teachings. During sleepless nights, Abbott searched for words to keep the people loyal with all they had heard. He knew there were many who wanted the Messiah dead. When Abbott received word of the Crucifixion, it was welcomed news. He was relieved and relaxed in a peace he had not felt in years—only it was not to last. The damage had been done. His congregation was divided on what they should believe, and it caused a permanent split. Abbott gave up the fight and let death have its way.

When Zachary died, the people urged Cohen, as their only direct descendant of Aaron, to come back to the city of Axum to serve as chief priest. Cohen consented and moved his family back into the family home. He ended the animal sacrifices without much friction from the elder priests. Most of them believed that the sacrifices should never have been done at any temple outside of Jerusalem. He taught the Torah to his students at the synagogue, but he also taught them the prophecies of Jeremiah and Daniel. He read from the scrolls the laws given to them by Moses, but he reminded them of the new covenant.

Cohen never stopped wondering what happened to his father, Myron, even after Darrah died. He always thought that one day he would make a pilgrimage to Jerusalem. Maybe there was someone there who knew of his father and why he never returned home.

Cohen stopped wondering in AD 70, the year the Romans attacked Jerusalem and the Temple was burned down again. Whatever hope he had of discovering anything about his father or dwelling in the city where his mother was born was gone. The Romans had slaughtered, enslaved, and imprisoned thousands of his people.

Unable to make sense of the endless suffering of his people, Cohen felt his faith had weakened. He no longer gave sermons on the Sabbath or taught at the study house. When Abner, his son, came of age, he succeeded Cohen as priest at the temple and teacher at the synagogue.

Abner did his best to keep the people united, but it was a constant struggle. The same predicament that caused the Israelites so much trouble throughout their history, intermingling and intermarriage, continued to divide and separate them from Jehovah with the influx of Egyptians, Kushites, Arabians, Middle Easterners, and Asians with varying cultures and beliefs into Axum.

***

Regardless of those who continued to deny that Jesus was Messiah, His birth, life, crucifixion, and resurrection changed the entire world in many ways. Of course, there were the political changes where the spread of Christianity divided empires, first and foremost in Rome and then in Egypt. Widespread civil conflicts made it too dangerous for merchants to travel and trade. The economic changes to the import and export markets had the most impact; the Roman Empire was in decline. Continual internal and external wars were costly, and tax collections were down. The trade of slaves had taken work away from the common people.

Frankincense and myrrh, which had been valued as much or more than gold and traded all over the world, were no longer in demand. Christians stopped burning the incense in religious rituals. For the rest, having food to eat became a higher priority. So the market for products on which Saba and Axum had traditionally grown their wealth for hundreds of years was drastically reduced.

However, Axum was ideally located for trade between the Roman Empire and India at the end of the first century and richly profited while the rest of the world suffered financial challenges. While other Empires were challenged with the lack of food, Axum became one of the largest exporters of grain, in addition to fruits, figs, and beans.

Ivory also became a coveted and quite lucrative item for trade, and the kingdom of Kush was the primary exporter of ivory. Undermined by the lack of food from depleted soil and meager crops and raids by nomads from the east and the south, the Kushites were vulnerable. Hungry men are not the best workers, nor do hungry soldiers make the best fighters. The Axum king seized on the weakness of his trade competitor and crossed into Kushite territory. Axum hunters collected the ivory and exported it out of Adulis instead of Meroe.

The Israelites were like most of the other people in Axum, busy making money. Less time was reserved for worship. The younger people, having never lived in Jerusalem, had not experienced centralized or communal worship and didn't feel it was important. There hadn't been any animal sacrifices in the Axum temple that Deron built in nearly 100 years. Years ago, when Myron left the city to farm on the countryside, half of the congregation left with him. And even though Abner had stayed in the city, most of the people still worshiped in synagogues outside of town. The large temple was seldom used, except for annual festivals.

The division spiked by the fervor over the Messiah had quieted down, but it wasn't completely silenced. Abner treaded the fine line between both sides, avoiding messages about the prophecy and the new covenant. At the end of the first century, his son, Ismael, succeeded him as chief priest in Axum.

Chapter Seventeen
Ismael

Ismael was as wealthy as any of the noblemen in Axum. The inheritance that was kept from Myron had been reclaimed and multiplied. Although his congregation was smaller, the tithes were bigger. Times were good, except it's usually the challenging times that develop and enhance the man, just as rainstorms enrich the earth and a rough stone hones the knife. Ismael had become complacent. The Temple was in disrepair, and his messages were repetitive and far from rousing. Teaching the Torah to young boys bored him, and he passed the leadership responsibility for that to his son, Enoch, as soon as he was of age.

Ismael was more political than his father. He was more like his great-grandfather Abbott. He enjoyed going to the palace to attend council meetings and seeing the exhibitions of the standing army. It wasn't that he advocated aggressive military action to dominate their neighbors, but he did believe in having a capable defense. Ismael sat in a conference with King Zoskales to discuss the additional Jewish migrants that were fleeing Jerusalem after their defeat in the Third Jewish Revolt.

"Axum is an open nation. We have people here from all over the world," the king said, addressing Ismael. "We live together peacefully in respect of our differences and in solidarity for our common purpose, which has been the continued elevation of this empire. My concern today is the motives of the Jews who are seeking refuge among your people."

"There is no reason for concern, my king," Ismael responded confidently. "The insurgents have been crushed. The Second Temple has been razed to the ground. The word we received says that 580,000 Jews are dead, and who knows how many are enslaved. Fifty towns and nearly 1,000 villages were destroyed in this war. These immigrants only seek a place where they can prosper and be free to worship in their own way."

"If only it were that simple, Ismael," the king added. "Your people are in conflict with one another over religious beliefs. How can I trust that those conflicts will not lead to civil war here? It is my understanding that Rome gave the Jews the freedom to worship."

"That freedom came with a tax, sire. The famine added to their misery, and they were starving. It was a decision between rebellion or surrendering to death. The people tried to rise up under the protection of the commander, Simon bar Kokhba."

King Zoskales rubbed his chin as he spoke. "Some say this commander is the messiah your people have been waiting for, the heroic and strong military leader who will win battles for Israel," he said, glaring back at Ismael to judge his reaction.

Ismael saw the trap and dodged it. "That presumption speaks for itself, being that after two years of intense fighting, he suffered a massive defeat."

The king wasn't satisfied. He wondered that if the numbers of the Israelites grew too large that they may get ideas that could endanger the sovereignty of Axum.

"What you say is true, but the fight may still rage in the hearts of your people. Now that they are barred from living in Jerusalem, are they in search of another land?"

"For many, they hope that this banishment will be temporary and that they will ultimately be able to return to their homeland at some point," Ismael said.

The king shifted in his seat and cleared his throat. "Since you are the chief priest of the Israelites, I am going to hold you responsible for the supervision of the Jews who wish to live in Axum. They will be restricted to your city. If there is any dissension among them or disruptions in the business conducted by your merchants, all of the Jews will be driven out of this kingdom permanently."

Ismael was stunned and alarmed. Everything his people had built and accomplished was in question.

"Sire, Israelites have lived here in Axum for hundreds of years. This is the only home many of us have ever known."

The king responded firmly. "Then you have much incentive to see that there are no uprisings within the Jewish community."

The discussion moved on to other subjects, but Ismael wasn't listening. It was the warning from the king that screamed inside his head. He wanted to welcome his people, to offer them refuge at this time, but opening the door to them could put them all in jeopardy.

***

Enoch and his cousin, Seth, who was also an instructor at the school, sat listening in the open-air room as a group of teenage boys took turns reciting the Torah. Ismael waved his hand in a signal for them to dismiss the class. The furrow between Enoch's brows tightened. It was odd that his father would even come by the school, so he knew something important was going on.

"What is it, Father?" he asked as soon as he got the students cleared out.

"I've just come from the palace," Ismael said. "The king has made it clear that if there are any tensions or clashes between our people here in Axum, we will all be driven out."

"We don't have a need to fight one another," Enoch said calmly. "We are all Israelites."

"You can't be that stupid, boy!" Ismael yelled. "I've seen men fight to the death over a larger piece of bread. There are going to be clashes like you've never seen before. Some of our people won't want to make way for the migrants. There will be competition for land and work. The worse will be the contradictions in beliefs. We have to come up with a plan to contain them, or we'll all suffer the consequences."

"What do you think we need to do, teacher?" Seth asked. "Do you want us to watch out for agitators?"

"By the time you hear about a problem, it will be too late," Ismael answered. "We must get ahead of the discord that is sure to arise and settle it in advance. We must call the people together for a great meeting."

"What do you want us to deliver in the message, Father?" Enoch asked.

Ismael chuckled and said, "Be serious, son. I will deliver this sermon myself. It's too important to chance."

***

Ismael shook his head in disbelief when he got home. His wife, Selima, was on her hands and knees, digging in the dirt. He never understood why she insisted on embarrassing him. She was always baking bread, spinning and weaving, or working on her garden. He married her, and in doing so, gave her his status as chief priest and servants at her beck and call, but she continued to work like a slave woman. When they were first married, he thought it was charming, evidence of her innocence. Twenty years later, it was simply annoying. Any other woman would have gladly enjoyed the leisure and pampering that she was entitled to as his wife, but not Selima. She was obviously ungrateful.

"I don't have time for this, Selima," he said, rushing by her. "Come into the house. I have to prepare a critical sermon for the people."

"You intend to speak?" she said, smirking.

"Yes, I do. I'm the chief priest, aren't I?"

"You absolutely are," she said, laying down her tools. "You have peaked my curiosity."

Selima knew that the last thing her husband wanted to do was stand in front of the people. He had always been insecure about his ability to rally or inspire through his preaching. She couldn't count the number of worship services when he simply recited the words that she had written.

"I'll clean my hands and be with you in a moment," she said, wondering what had gotten him all riled up.

Ismael paced back and forth, trying to calm down so he could gather his thoughts. He needed something powerful to unite the people.

"Finally!" he said when Selima returned. "While you're out playing in the sand, everything we have is at stake."

"What are you talking about?" Selima asked, reaching for a bowl of fruit before she sat down on the lounge. Watching her husband parade across the floor with his head in his hands was quite entertaining.

"I attended a meeting at the palace today, and the king did not mince words. He vowed that he would banish all the Israelites from Axum if they disturbed the peace with clashes over beliefs. You know that uniting our people is practically impossible. If I take one side, then I will raise the ire of the other, and then we all will lose."

"You are being so dramatic," Selima said, sighing. "The Israelites are united, and our differences are few. There is so much common ground in our history, so shroud your message in that history. Don't focus on the disagreements on the Messiah. Remind them of the promise to Abraham, the promise that Moses spent the last years of his life to deliver. We all just want a place we can call our home, a place where we can be free to worship and feed our families. Plant the seed of hope that if we are a faithful people, God will keep His promises."

"What about the prophecies? That's what has them all up in arms."

"Give them the words of the prophet Isaiah, 'And I will wait for the LORD who is hiding His face from the house of Jacob; I will even look eagerly for Him.' God will show His face to us, and then all the doubts will be done."

"That's exactly what I was thinking. We must be as patient as we were in Babylon. The Lord has given me the message for the people."

"God has been faithful in doing that," Selima said, smiling to herself.

***

Enoch and Seth stood on either side of Ismael while he delivered his message.

"Children of Israel, we are again as we were when Moses led us out of Egypt. We were a distressed people in search of the Promised Land, the city where we could live, worship, and prosper in peace. While we have been blessed in Axum for a long time, there are still many of us who are distressed and in search of solace. There are Israelites who have left Jerusalem and more who will come here to find relief.

"I want to remind you all today that although we come from various tribes, we are one people. Whatever differences we have, we are one people. There are no reasons why we can't live in peace amongst ourselves. Axum is a place of peace, and King Zoskales has advised me that it is of utmost importance for him that it remain a place of peace. If there is trouble among our people, we will all suffer for it. We will be banished from our homes.

"There are disagreements between us, disagreements on the covenants of God. There is not one in our midst who doesn't recognize how crucial the freedom of worship is. None of us wants another to tell us how to worship our God. Therefore, we must be tolerant and respect our brother's worship of God's word. Our survival depends on it. David's 133rd Psalm says,

> How good and pleasant it is when God's people live together in unity! It is like precious oil poured on the head, running down on the beard, Running down on Aaron's beard, down on the collar of his robe. It is as if the dew of Hermon were falling on Mount Zion. For there the Lord bestows his blessing, even live forevermore."

Ismael's message was received well by the people, and they were committed to maintaining the peace and their security in Axum. For several years, they worshiped on common ground. Nevertheless, there was a split among the Israelites as they gravitated toward the fraction that shared their beliefs.

Ismael was constantly on edge, looking for any sign of discord among the people. He hired men to spy on the people in each of the villages. He became so paranoid that he barely slept at night. Selima couldn't get him to relax or listen to reason. She woke up one morning to find him staring wide-eyed toward the window, dead, having essentially worried himself to death.

***

Enoch was an optimist, or a passive priest. He never worried much about the consequences of some people believing Jesus was the Messiah. He didn't see what harm it could do. He believed the prophets who spoke of the Messiah were true men of God and that He spoke through them, so he never questioned or denied whether the prophecy was fulfilled. He taught the people the Torah and the word from the holy scrolls. He preached that the laws given to Moses must be adhered to—keeping the Sabbath holy, eating kosher, and continuing their tradition of circumcision.

When Enoch died, he was succeeded by his son, Shilo, who was succeeded by his son, Ebon. Ebon was succeeded by his older son, Lamont, who was succeeded by his son, Omar. Hosea, who succeeded Omar, was the chief priest when the peace, like an old piece of cloth fraying away, was hanging by a thread.

Chapter Eighteen

Malachi

Almost 200 years had gone by since King Zoskales warned chief priest Ismael that if the Jews caused any trouble they would all be expelled from the kingdom of Axum. Fortunately, it hadn't been difficult to maintain peace. The Israelites continued to prosper and provide for their families. As Axum grew in population and wealth, the towns expanded into smaller kingdoms with subleaders and junior kings. Israelites of like minds and beliefs separated themselves from the new migrants in the empire to reduce the consequences of intermarriage.

Moving into the fourth century, Hosea was weary of trying to hold the people together with all the forces working to pull them apart. His principal concern was for his son, Malachi. It would be up to him to maintain the independence of the Israelites once he became chief priest. His doubts stemmed from the close relationship Malachi had with King Ousanas and how he might be able to influence his decisions. It was imperative that Malachi understand that his first allegiance was to the Lord and to the people of Israel. No matter how powerful the king was, he couldn't save them from God's wrath if the people were faithless.

Hosea had seen the punishments for disobedience. Both of his parents died of the plague of Cyprian when he was young. As the son of the chief priest, his father had seen to it that he was educated in the Torah and the Scriptures but had not yet arranged a marriage for him. For decades, his father's responsibilities were heavy on his shoulders with Christianity spreading, and he dreamed about returning to Jerusalem, where life might be easier for him. When Jerusalem became part of the Roman Empire, that dream died. So Hosea immersed himself in God's word, so much so that he was 41 years old when he finally found a wife. He first saw her during a feast at the palace. Her name was Kia, the daughter of an officer in the military, and her sister Sofia was married to the king.

The first seven years of their marriage were happy, and they were blessed with a son. But gradually Kia grew bored with Hosea. During a visit with her sister at the palace, she met a sub-king from India and ran away with him. Hosea felt like a fool. He chided himself that he should not have married such a young woman at his age. Sofia convinced him to let her help raise Malachi. In his heartbroken state, Hosea agreed. For many years, Malachi spent more time at the palace than he did at home with Hosea. He and Ousanas were educated together and bonded like brothers.

Hosea stopped the visits when Malachi was 14 years old so his son could focus on his preparation to be chief priest. The other reason was because the palace was always full of beautiful women from every corner of the world. For the future of the Israelites, Hosea needed to make sure that Malachi married a Levite woman to preserve the priestly lineage. He quickly arranged a marriage with Tirzah, the daughter of Simeon, a Levite singer and musician.

***

"I thank God for his goodness!" Hosea cried out when Malachi's first son, Phineas, was born.

Malachi laughed loudly. "Father, you sound as if you were worried."

"Son, it's our job to worry. Now that you have a son to succeed you, that is some relief. But there are changes coming that will weaken and endanger our people."

"Relax your mind. Ousanas is on the throne," Malachi told him, amused. "I trust him completely. We have nothing to fear as long as he is king."

Hosea looked at the ceiling, asking the heavens, "How can a son of mine be so naïve? I can only hope your son will be more thoughtful."

Malachi laughed and poured wine for them to celebrate.

A year later, they had more to celebrate when Tirzah gave birth to a second son, Herschel. Hosea felt confident enough to give up his post as chief priest to his son, Malachi.

***

Phineas and Herschel, who were now ten and nine years old, enjoyed the privilege of and presence of royalty. From the time they could walk, the boys had been playmates of Ezana and Sayzana, the twin sons of Ousanas, the friend of their father and the king of Axum. Upon the advice of Hosea, Malachi decided that Phineas and Herschel had reached the age where their education of the Torah and the Scriptures had become a priority and were given less time to spend at the palace enjoying themselves.

An unusual circumstance brought another set of brothers into the circle of friends. These two brothers were Syrians who were sailing aboard a ship with their uncle, traveling down the Red Sea from Lebanon. While they were docked at one of the harbors, pirates attacked and plundered the ship. The two youths, Frumentius and Edesius, were the only ones not savagely murdered. They were captured and given as gifts to King Ousanas as slaves.

The youths found favor with the king; and he admired their strength, intelligence, and tenacity. He appointed Frumentius, the older brother, royal treasurer and secretary, and he made Edesius the royal cupbearer. Ousanas was aware that his sons had been coddled, and he believed that they could benefit from the guidance of Frumentius and Edesius. He gave the brothers the job of supervising the princes and their playmates, Phineas and Herschel.

A few years later, Ousanas became ill with malaria. Before he succumbed, he freed Frumentius and Edesius. At that time, Ezana and Sayzana were too young to ascend to the throne. The widowed queen, Sofia, requested that the young men stay on at the palace to assist her in the administration of the kingdom and to teach and mentor her sons until they became of age. In return for the kindness and trust they received from Ousanas, they obliged.

Frumentius and Edesius, who had been raised as Christians in Tyre, Lebanon, used their power and influence with the queen to spread the teachings of Christianity throughout the kingdom. This was troublesome to Malachi and his elder assistant priest, Elias. They were worried that the teachings would cause problems among the Israelites and disrupt the peace they had worked so hard to maintain.

"There's going to be conflict," Elias warned Malachi after the students had gone home for the day. "Ousanas is dead; the

Prince Ezana is too young to lead. There are many junior kings who will try to exercise their influence and gain power. Our freedom to worship is at stake."

Malachi was concerned but thought Elias was overstating the danger. "Ezana is a thoughtful child," he said to reassure him. "I don't think we have anything to fear when he takes the throne. He is much like his father."

"How can you believe that?" Elias protested. "The boy is already being taught by foreigners. Your sons should not be there with them. We must protect our faith from outside influences."

"Having my sons there in the palace regularly is the only way for us to know firsthand what is going on and what Frumentious's plans are," Malachi said in his defense.

Elias's temper bordered on rage. Malachi was letting his personal feelings blind him. "I'll tell you what their plans are!" Elias shouted, "They're encouraging the merchants who are Christian to practice their faith openly and renovating pagan temples into churches and monasteries for them to worship in."

Malachi could not deny that, but he didn't feel that was cause enough to panic. "Settle down, Elias. They haven't infringed on our cities."

"Not yet, but they are converting many of the natives."

"We as a people have always rebelled against any power or authority that attempted to dictate the way we worship," Malachi said, attempting to reason with him. "We must extend that acceptance to anyone who wishes to worship in their own way."

"This is very serious," Elias said, pointing his finger in Malachi's face. "This is going to disrupt the peace between our people."

Elias had managed to sow seeds of concern in Malachi's head. Malachi thought that perhaps he had lost his objectivity. He planned to discuss it with Hosea and Tirzah during supper.

***

Malachi stared down at the platter in front of him. He didn't want to appear uncertain or weak in front of Hosea.

"Is something wrong with your food?" Tirzah asked, seeing he hadn't taken a bite.

"No, dear, it smells wonderful. A discussion I had with Elias is weighing on my mind."

"What is it, son?" Hosea asked.

"Frumentius and Edesius are converting many of the people to Christians, and they're providing them with places to worship. We have kept the peace for our people for a long time, but the differences between them have not gone away. Those who believe in the new covenant will be emboldened by the support from the palace."

"None of that matters, son," Hosea said, getting testy. "We don't have the power to rule Axum. Your job is to preach and teach the word that was given to Moses. You are to be sure your sons are equipped to follow in your shoes."

"How can we continue to accept some prophesies of Jeremiah and ignore others as fallacy?" Malachi asked distressed. "Is that being truthful with the people?"

"Our purpose is to teach God's laws to our people. They must be obedient to those laws, or we will suffer for it. That's how it has been for over a thousand years. God has not changed."

"Still, His word has told us of the new covenant, Father. What if we are wrong?"

"God's promise to us was that His word would stand forever." Hosea said. "There's no more I can tell you."

"Do you believe that Jesus is the Messiah the new covenant speaks of?" Tirzah asked quietly.

"How can you ask that?" Hosea bellowed. "This new thing they talk about says that we priests are not needed. That is impossible! God gave the Levites the responsibility of worship and the teaching of His laws. We are the shepherds to His people."

"I can't discount the word of God given to his prophets," Malachi answered carefully. "Still we have to lead and counsel the Israelites if we are to survive."

"There is no way you can walk on both sides of the street, Malachi. If you don't teach that to your sons, there is no hope for us."

"Time will tell," Malachi said. "Jehovah will have the last word."

***

Malachi's younger son, Herschel, and Ezana were close friends. They were both physical young men who liked to compete in sports, and they had similar interests. Both liked to hunt lions and elephants, not for money but for the game, the thrill of conquering. Whenever Herschel came home from one of their escapades, Malachi questioned him about Ezana, asking about their conversations and if they had discussed what he planned to do when Ezana became king. Herschel never had much to say.

Phineas preferred activities that were more mundane and spent his spare time inside the palace with Sayzana, playing complex board games for mental exercise. Malachi questioned him about Frumentius and Edesius. He wanted to know what they talked about and what they learned. Most of the time, the answers Phineas gave Malachi were inconsequential. Then one evening, Phineas came home and repeated a story Frumentius had told them over their evening meal.

"The Torah tells us about the Red Sea parting for Moses to lead the children of Israel out of Egypt and how the Jordan River rose up for Joshua to lead them into the land of Canaan. But Frumentius told us about Jesus walking on the Sea of Galilee. That was just one of the miracles that He performed. He also fed 5,000 people with five loaves of bread and two fish and made a blind man see again."

Malachi had seen how so many others were taken in by the words of Jesus and the wonderful promises He made. But Malachi couldn't take a chance that his sons might be mesmerized by those words.

"What do you think about the things Frumentius was saying?" Malachi asked.

"I don't know. They're just stories, I guess," Phineas replied, shrugging his shoulders.

"Does Frumentius say anything else to the prince about the Messiah?"

"He tells him the prophecy was fulfilled, how Jesus was crucified, and how the tomb was empty because He rose from the dead. They talk about Jesus being the Savior and that those who believe in Him shall have eternal life. He says because of Jesus, any man can go to God on his own."

"Both of you need to listen to me very carefully," Malachi said to his sons. "The belief in the divinity of a mortal man is contrary to our teachings. Worshiping a mortal man is another form of idolatry. There is only one God, and we worship Him solely. Since Frumentius is speaking against God's word, I don't want you two going to the palace anymore. We have to be an example for the people."

Herschel sprang up from the table like an antelope running from danger. "Why are you trying to control me, Father? Ezana is my friend! He is like a brother to me. Why do you want to stop me from going where I want to go and doing what I want to do?"

"As my sons, you have been preordained to protect God's word and to lead the people," Malachi said sternly. "It is our job to keep the people in right relationship with God."

"You don't need me," Herschel said, still standing. "Phineas is the one to lead the people. He will be the chief priest. Let me live my life!"

Malachi stood up to look Herschel in the eye and said, "Your life belongs to God. The responsibility for the people was given to you by God."

"It doesn't matter now. I've joined the military," Herschel said defiantly. "You don't need me. Phineas will be the chief priest."

Malachi sank to his seat. "Things are changing. You both are needed," he said with a sigh. "And you will have plenty opportunities to fight."

***

Less than a year later, in AD 325, Ezana was crowned emperor of Axum. Having been converted and baptized by Frumentius, he immediately declared Christianity as the religion of the state and had the image of the cross struck on their gold and silver coins. Through his declaration, Axum became the first Christian state in the world.

Then out of the blue, Hosea began to tremble and shake. They weren't sure if it was from fear or fever. Tirzah nursed him night and day, and Malachi had him wrapped in healing scrolls to purge any evil spirits, but he was dead before the year ended. Malachi thought his father's death was some kind of sign that he needed to focus on the laws handed down to Moses or they were all doomed. He promptly consecrated Phineas and Herschel to serve as priests in the Sabbath worship services.

Phineas had long been waiting for the day he would stand before the people and deliver a message. He was anxious for them to see how superior he was to the others. They seemed to hang on his every word, hungering for answers to their problems. For him, nothing felt better than receiving the respect he deserved. He had been ignored for too long. It made him yearn for the day his father would finally yield the chief priest position to him, except that would only be the beginning. Every fiber of his being told him he was destined for something greater. After all, he was the only one competent enough to lead.

Herschel held more political and military power than religious. He wasn't motivated by any infringements on his freedom to worship. In his opinion, the importance of formal ceremonies was overstated. He preferred to commune with nature, running through the forests until his lungs nearly burst rather than sitting in a synagogue compiling Scriptures until his eyes ached.

***

Empowered by his newfound religion, Ezana was ready to take advantage of the decline in the kingdom of Kush. Ivory had become a key and coveted item for trade, and the kingdom of Kush was the primary exporter of ivory. He seized on the weakness of his trade competitor and crossed into Kushite territory. As a warrior in the military, Herschel fought with the troops of Axum in Kush. He rode beside his comrade Ezana, with their horses galloping neck and neck.

The Kush warriors were powerful spear-throwers. The Axum warriors faced them with broad-blade, flat-ended swords and round shields made from buffalo hide. In battle, the Kushites were worthy opponents. Even their women were armed and fought in combat, wielding bows as tall as they were. Nonetheless, undermined by the lack of food, the Kush people were vulnerable. Despite the valiant effort of the Kush army, they were defeated.

The people of Kush and their culture interested Herschel. They embraced nature, living in homes interwoven with wood and bricks or made only of straw. How they dressed intrigued him as well. They wore few clothes, but what they wore was made of sheepskin, as opposed to Herschel's people, who draped themselves in robes. He admired the Kushites' courage and fierceness. He respected the fact that they were a proud people living in a country that they had not had to share with other cultures. It was the way he wanted to live.

The Axum army captured the capital of Meroe and burned it to ashes. Herschel, along with other Axum soldiers, collected the ivory to export it out of Adulis instead of Meroe. Hundreds of Kushites who were not killed in the war, who had not escaped, or who hadn't drowned themselves in the sea were brought back to work as slaves. Herschel brought back a woman who was as tall as he was and who was completely fearless. He did not intend to make her his slave. He was more assured that she would be his wife.

She told him her name was Chaka. She wore sheepskin around her waist and a copper ring in her lip. Her strong erotic body and dark skin stimulated him, but her lack of shame fascinated him. He told her he wanted to learn from her and build a nation with her as his queen. But she was not impressed or attracted to the man who helped decimate her motherland and her countrymen. It was a long time before she would even talk to him. More than love or survival, Chaka engaged him for her plan of revenge.

***

Emperor Ezana was gratified that his prayers to Christ the Lord were answered in the victory over the Kushites. From that time, evangelists were invited to the empire to convert its citizens to Christianity. To demonstrate his thanks to the Israelites who fought under Hershel's command in the Axum army, King Ezana gave them the option to move to the southern territory of Axum in a gesture of good will. This would mean they would have their own territory and rulers.

For most, it seemed fitting that Herschel would be their leader. Without a doubt he would be a strong protector as the chief officer of their military. They joined together with Malachi and Tirzah to celebrate their sovereignty and Herschel's wedding.

Phineas could not be more pleased about his brother's marriage. Chaka was not a Levite woman, so that meant that any competition from his brother had been eliminated. The celebration was barely over when Phineas broke up an evening meal to state his case to Malachi.

"Father, as you know, Herschel has married a Kushite woman," Phineas said, speaking as if the couple were not seated across from him. "The law states that a Levite who marries a woman who is not a Levite cannot be chief priest. If he cannot be the spiritual leader for the Israelites, he cannot be the legitimate leader for the people. Not only that, his wife is not fit to be a queen. Her people were not educated. They still live like wild animals. What do they know how to do except hunt?"

To their surprise, Chaka spoke up. "You don't know much about Kush or my people," she said, glaring at Phineas. "We are experts at molding gold. My people have built palaces and temples you can only dream about. We built over 200 pyramids in Meroe, more than Egypt."

Phineas was startled that she as a woman would dispute him. He glared back at her. "It's obvious that the women don't know how to conduct themselves in the presence of men, either."

"Only men who live like wild animals have no respect for women," Chaka countered.

Sneering at her, Phineas spoke to Malachi. "As you can see, Father, she would not be a fitting wife for a priest. She has no reverence for the man of God."

Chaka wasn't intimidated by Phineas. She had stood up to far superior men since she was a young girl. She spoke up again before Malachi or Herschel could respond. "I've heard you preach that your people are loyal to Jehovah, that they will never exalt a mortal man; but you sound like a man who thinks he should be worshiped. Maybe you aren't suitable to be chief priest for the Israelites, either."

"Quiet!" Malachi said, ending the spat between Phineas and Chaka. "Why are you all fighting each other when we are being pushed out of the land where we have lived for centuries? We have been blessed here because of our faithfulness to God. If the people are disobedient, we will be punished severely. The survival of our people is at stake."

"All of Jeremiah's and Daniel's prophesies were given to our people," Herschel said. "How can you accept some parts and reject the others?"

Malachi recognized those words as the same he had asked his father, but things had changed just as Hosea had said they would. They had to choose the covenant given to Moses, or they would disappear and fade in the nation around them. God had ordered them to separate themselves.

"Your brother is right," Malachi said to Herschel, afraid of the divisions that his thinking would foster. "You cannot be chief priest, not because of your wife but because you fail to protect God's word."

"It doesn't matter to me," Herschel said. "The new faith doesn't care about priests."

Malachi was furious. "I will not allow the words of false prophets to poison our people!" he shouted at Herschel. "We will never convert to this Christianity! If you refuse to remain faithful to our teaching, you are not welcome in my village."

"I won't fight you, Father," Herschel replied. "But I ask, what kind of religion would divide a father from his son and a brother from his brother?"

Malachi shook a bony, crooked finger at him. "We Israelites have had to fight to worship Jehovah. It is an honor. We will never surrender to the worship of a man!"

Chaka's feelings softened toward Herschel. Hearing everything he had just said made it clear to her that her enemy was not her husband. He was a decent man. Though he had killed many of her people, she knew from her own experience that war sometimes pits good people against each other, soldiers being loyal to their commanders. Her true enemy was Phineas.

***

The expansion of Christianity was a hostile invasion to many of the Israelites and their beliefs. Isolated skirmishes broke out between those who refused to convert and the Christians in Axum. It was not long before the violence erupted into civil war. Faithful families were divided, despite the single difference between them being the acceptance of Jesus as the Messiah. Even Malachi's household was affected when his sons fought on opposite sides. Phineas fought for the freedom of the Israelites to worship in their own way. Herschel fought for the empire, the country that was his home, but never against his own people.

The civil war soon turned into an internal war between the Jews who practiced Judaism and the Jewish Christians. Ezana referred to the faction of Israelites in the rebellion who rejected Christianity as Beta Israel. Still on opposite sides, Phineas fought for Beta Israel, and Herschel for Axum. Neither brother was fixed on his faith to God as much as Phineas's loyalty to his father and Herschel's loyalty to his friend and emperor, Ezana.

Worn down by years of conflict and brutal clashes between his people and his sons, Malachi stepped down as leader of the Israelites in Axum. His legs had become too weak to stand, and his voice was too weak to rally the people. After Phineas married a Levite woman named Zelah, Malachi had no choice but to consecrate his son as chief priest over Beta Israel.

"It is time for us to leave Axum," Phineas told the congregation while Malachi listened and monitored the peoples' reaction. "This kingdom is for Christians. We must establish our own kingdom. The Lord said to Isaiah, 'You are to seek the place the LORD your God will choose from among all your tribes to put His name there for his dwelling. To that place you must go.' We have been banned from Jerusalem before. It's only temporary. We will return and build an even greater temple and then block the Romans from coming in."

The crowd stood on its feet and cheered. Some were moved to tears. Phineas beamed as he soaked in the adoration. Suddenly, Malachi felt uneasy. While he had been worried about Frumentius filling his sons' heads with ideas about becoming Christian, they had been groomed to become rulers. He was bewildered and disillusioned as he looked at his arrogant son behaving more like a king than a priest.

Chapter Nineteen
Phineas and Herschel

erschel had first considered staying in Axum, but his desire to have a kingdom of his own spurred him to leave. On behalf of the Israelites, he accepted Emperor Ezana's offer of the southern territory of Axum. The Israelites packed up the ark of the covenant and the religious vessels of the temple and migrated west and then south out of the kingdom of Axum to the mountain highlands near Lake Tana. Now called Beta Israel, there they established their own kingdom among 500 villages. They went from living in stone houses to thatched huts. It was no surprise to anyone when Phineas was crowned king of the Jewish kingdom of Beta Israel.

When the conflicts between the people ebbed, Herschel moved further out from the city to the lower elevations of the mountain where he could hunt daily. There the temperature was warmer, with grasslands full of zebras, gazelles, lions, hyenas, and leopards. He wasn't envious of Phineas or his status. Bringing down elephants and black rhinos and trading the ivory was more rewarding than extending his hand for sacrifices from the congregation.

When Malachi died, Phineas was released from the pull of the priesthood. He thought it was too time consuming and kept him from ruling with a strong hand. As king, he created more rules for the people that were not found in the words of Moses. The people's first allegiance would be to him and not God. He demanded that all families have one son committed to the army that would defend his throne.

Phineas feasted on the power that he had craved for so long, but the unchecked power made him paranoid. He laid awake at night, imagining plots of an unknown enemy that would someday come to snatch it all away. He rarely prayed to God. When he did take time to pray, he prayed that his children would be daughters, fearful that a son would look forward to taking his throne. Despite his unfaithfulness, his prayers were answered when Zelah gave birth to five daughters.

As the years passed, Chaka grew to genuinely love Herschel. Their first child was a son they named Ephrem. Two years later, they had a daughter, Maaza; and three years after that they had another daughter named Abena. Herschel wasn't sure if he would raise Ephrem to be chief priest, being that Phineas had no son. Not because of any misgivings he had about his faith but more so because of the hostilities festering among the people. Sometimes it wasn't clear if the people were fighting over religion or using religion as a reason to fight.

The lines between Phineas and Herschel also grew deeper and wider as time went on. Phineas no longer viewed Herschel as his brother. He saw him merely as another threat to his authority. Already, some of the people who thought Phineas's rules were too stringent had begun to move into the villages within Herschel's district. In retaliation, Phineas refused to allow his townspeople to buy food from the farmers on Herschel's lands.

To smooth things over, Herschel went to reason with his brother. He bore him no ill will. It made no sense for them to be enemies. He resisted a snide remark when he was ushered into his chambers. Dressed in a white linen robe embroidered with gold and a red cloak with a bejeweled headdress, Phineas was obviously relishing his role as king.

"Why are you behaving this way?" Herschel asked frankly as they sat inside Phineas's makeshift palace. "Father isn't here to impress, and you have everything you want. What do you gain taking food from the mouths of our own people?"

Phineas smiled slyly. "It is no offense to you or the unfaithful few who gravitate to your village. I'm sure you know that we cannot eat the food of non-Jews."

"I didn't know you were so picky, brother," Herschel replied, his words drenched in sarcasm, "You've never cared where your food came from as long as you didn't have to labor for it."

Phineas's smile straightened. "If you would have studied more than you played, you would know there are restrictions on the food of Levite priests. Our food must be clean and holy."

"How would you know about the food for priests?" Herschel replied sharply. "You are afraid of blood. You've never even slaughtered the meat you eat."

Phineas curled his lip in disdain and said, "None of that matters anymore. I'm the king now."

"Yes, that is true," Herschel said, bowing and mocking him. He turned to leave and then stopped. "Lest you forget, brother, the people walked away from Ezana, and they may walk away from you as well."

Staring at his brother's back, Phineas vowed that he would do whatever he had to do to protect his people from outside influences.

***

Tired of imploring Phineas to be reasonable, Herschel decided that it was time to establish his own empire where he would be king and Chaka would be queen. He wanted to offer more to Ephrem, Mazaa, and Abena. He expanded his small kingdom further south and east from Phineas, and gradually even more Jewish Christians who were pushed out of Phineas's territory came over to Herschel's domain. Closer to the coast, they prospered through increased trade with foreign merchants.

Although Herschel spent a great amount of his time hunting elephants and panthers, more of his attention was required to unite the people on their beliefs to keep the peace. He formed a council of Levite priests, and they established the rules of worship. All Jewish laws and customs would be strictly adhered to, the Sabbath would be observed, and the people would come to worship at the synagogue. Food restrictions would remain unchanged according to the laws of the Torah. All male children had to be circumcised, and intermarriage among the tribes would be limited, particularly among Levites. Herschel assured the council that as a direct descendant of Aaron, Zadok, and Jozadak, his children would only marry Levites to preserve the priestly lineage. The critical change was the acceptance of Jesus as the Messiah.

It went against his father's teachings, but Herschel couldn't deny the prophecies of Jeremiah, Daniel, and Isaiah. In his youth, studying the Torah and the Holy Scriptures wasn't a priority. As a leader, he couldn't ignore the importance or the impact that religion had had on politics. Because of it, wars erupted, lives were lost, and empires were brought down. With a new zeal, Herschel spent hours reading God's word. It would be the strong foundation on which he would build his empire.

Herschel's assistant priest, Linus, who was more orthodox, questioned him as they studied the Holy Scriptures. "My priest, I read and understand the new Scriptures, but how can we give up everything that we were taught? How can we worship a man who is flesh?"

"The new Scriptures say He is no longer flesh," Herschel explained. "He was the Son of God who came to live among us in the flesh, the Son who was sacrificed for all our sins. He is our salvation. Those who believe in Him shall be blessed and have eternal life."

Linus was still unconvinced. "It is inconsistent with all the word given to Moses by God."

"Jehovah has always been consistent," Herschel replied. "There had to be a price paid for our sins. His Son, Jesus, came and asked us to repent of our sins. That is that same petition that the word given to Moses said. Instead of the blood of animals to remove our sins, Jesus was the ultimate sacrifice to pay for our sins. It was His blood that removed our sins."

"That would be good news, sire, reason for us to rejoice. How can you explain why so many people reject Him?"

Herschel closed the book he was reading and rested his hand upon the New Testament. "Our people have suffered terribly for their unfaithfulness. In their desire to be steadfast, they deny the new covenant. Still, we are one people. We all must have a place of worship."

✳✳✳

Continually, more Bantu-Kushite migrants moved into the villages under Herschel's leadership. The word *Bantu* simply means "human beings." They referred to Herschel as

Lemba because of the turban he and the other priests wore on the Sabbath. Chaka encouraged Herschel to welcome them into their community, convincing him of the knowledge and strength they would bring. She understood that their advanced skills in metalworking to forge tools and weapons would be invaluable in the defense of their territory. The Israelites shared with them the knowledge of agriculture and how to breed and care for farm animals. The combined skills of the people enabled them to cultivate areas of land that had at one time seemed inhabitable.

Herschel's villages flourished from their openness and attracted more citizens from Phineas's kingdom. The people of Herschel's villages adopted hunter-gatherer communities that assimilated into the more advanced Bantu culture. They became known as the Lemba people.

Within his closed mind, Phineas reasoned that Herschel had become a menace to Beta Israel. His brother showed no loyalty to their heritage or discipline to the people. He believed that it was Herschel's fault that so many people had been influenced by Christianity. He would have to bring his brother back into the fold, or it would be the demise of their people; but first he would have to reestablish trust between them. Phineas sent for his council to discuss options.

"As you all know, my brother has established his own kingdom," Phineas began. "Within a stone's throw of us, he is besmirching our religion and our faithfulness to God. It is our obligation to protect Beta Israel from degradation and the wrath that will surely befall us."

His assistant priest, Abel, who for all practical purposes was the chief priest, spoke up. "Herschel is your brother,

Phineas. I'm sure you already have an idea of how we should handle this problem. Why don't you tell us what is on your mind?"

Phineas eyed Abel and flashed him a knowing grin. "We attempted to pressure him and his 'Lemba' people financially. We have rejected any trade with them, but they are resourceful. They have gone around us, and they trade with the Arabs. They are very adept in producing metal, which is in high demand for trade. Their production in agriculture is beyond us. At their present rate, they will surpass Beta Israel in numbers, resources, and wealth. We only have two options. Either we unite with Herschel and his Lemba, or they must be eliminated."

"Are you talking of a war against Herschel?" Abel asked, needing clarity of Phineas's intentions. He paused and waited for a response, but Phineas didn't answer, so Abel continued. "If what you say is true, what are our chances for victory? Herschel has many Kushites living on his territory, and they are mighty warriors. Remember that it took the entire Axum army to defeat them. The Lemba people have the advantage with their iron shields and weapons."

Phineas was quiet, appearing to be deep in thought. "We can't initiate an attack if we can't annihilate them. Cutting the tail of the serpent only prompts it to seek revenge. The head must be cut off to kill it. There is no question that Herschel must be removed."

"That will be your determination on how he is to be removed," Abel said cautiously. "I can't encourage you to go against your blood. No one else in this room can make that decision."

***

When Phineas invited Herschel to a special meeting, Chaka insisted on traveling with him and his entourage. Riding astride her horse on the trip to Phineas's region, the earth gave her signs that something was wrong. The wind blew counterclockwise as if a storm were brewing, but the skies were clear. Across a field, she saw wild goats skittishly watching as two larger goats rammed their heads together. Then there was the grey parrot in the tree, biting its toenails. She glanced over at Herschel, who flashed her a confident grin. She nodded back at him with a half-smile while she ran her hand along the side of her robe and felt the sharp blade through the cloth of her pocket.

The entrance into Phineas's palace of stone was guarded by four men. Before Herschel and Chaka were off their horses, Abel had stepped out to greet them.

"Welcome!" Abel said with open arms, walking between the guards and Herschel's escorts. He embraced Herschel and ushered him and Chaka inside.

"There are refreshments for you here," he said to Chaka, directing her to the outer room where two servants were waiting. "I'm sure you will be comfortable here while Herschel speaks with his brother in private."

Chaka smiled pleasantly at him and sat down. One servant girl offered her a glass of wine, but her eyes were focused on Abel as he led Herschel down the hallway and through a door on the left. A few moments later, Abel came out of the room and eased into the door on the right. All her senses were on alert. She broke her necklace and gave each of the servant girls a handful of the colored beads and asked them to leave her. Then she waited for half a minute and tip-toed toward the door Herschel had entered. There was a veil of curtains around the walls of the room. She stayed hidden behind them while creeping closer to the front of the room where Herschel and Phineas were talking.

Suddenly, two of the men who had been standing outside the palace stormed in the door. They snatched Herschel up from his chair and held him defenseless. Then one of them handed Phineas his spear.

Phineas stood up and stepped closer to his brother. "Herschel, you have given me no choice. I must kill you before you destroy our people!" he growled, staring at his brother in disdain. "You are worse than any plague, sickness, or terror. You must be stopped!"

Chaka reached for the blade in her skirt pocket. She knew there was no way she could overpower the two guards and Phineas before the spear did its damage. Quickly, she leapt from behind the curtain in one swift motion, raised her arm, and sliced deep into Phineas's hand with the broad-blade sword.

Shocked, Phineas dropped the spear and shrieked like a wounded baboon. He grabbed his maimed hand as he fell to his knees in pain. "I see my brother needs a woman to fight his battles," he said sneering at Chaka.

The two men held tightly to Herschel, unsure of what to do.

"Only a coward would bind a man's hands before he killed him," Chaka spat at Phineas.

"You are more evil than Jezebel!" Phineas hissed, as his spurting blood stained his white robe. "I knew it the first time I laid eyes on you! You are the one I should have killed a long time ago."

"I promise you, it would have ended the same," Chaka said, picking up the spear lying beside him and jabbing it into his heart. She turned and faced the men, questioning their desire to fight.

With lowered eyes, the two guards released Herschel and darted from the room, nearly knocking Abel over as he came in. In one glance, he realized what had happened and bowed before them. Chaka eyed him cautiously while Herschel stood there in a daze, staring at Phineas's body. It was unbelievable to him that his brother wanted to kill him. More than that, he couldn't conceive that his wife had killed his brother.

"Why did this have to happen?" Herschel asked Abel. "I never begrudged my brother's power or position. I only wanted peace and protection for all our people. Why shouldn't the Christian Jews have a place where they can freely worship?"

Abel held his arms up in surrender. "You must understand, my king, that the rules must be clearly defined, or there will be chaos. We can't be one people with two beliefs. It is what our enemies will use to divide us. When we have to defend ourselves from the Arabs—and believe me, that time will come—we must be united in what we are fighting for."

Herschel walked out of the room, leaving Abel there with his arms in the air. Chaka followed her husband with her blade in one hand and the bloody spear in the other. Their entourage stood waiting, unaware of all that had transpired within the palace. They rode back to their territory in silence. The winds had calmed, the goats were peaceably grazing, and the bird had flown away.

"Lay down and rest," Chaka said to Herschel once they were in their private quarters. Gently, she rubbed his temple to calm the vein that throbbed at his hairline. "Abel was right," she said serenely. "There can be no confusion in ruling."

"What are you suggesting?" Herschel asked, his eyes closed tightly, as if he were deep in thought.

"Your designation from God, from your father and his father and for many generations has been to minister to the people and to protect His word. There is no higher calling. Let that be your focus. If you can keep the people close to God, then that is the strongest foundation on which this growing empire can be built. Your ancestors came here to build a temple that would be the greatest to God's glory. You can even build two temples."

"There is no time for that. With Phineas dead, I must hold the reins of power, or we're vulnerable to insurrection. I can't be all things to the people."

"That's why you have a queen, my king. There is no other who will be as loyal to you as I am. Have I not shown you that I'm capable of leading beside you? You can depend on me. While you oversee the salvation of our people, I will preside over the survival of our people."

Herschel was humbled and perplexed by the responsibility he bore to his people. He went back to the Holy Scriptures for guidance. He read the Torah and the new Gospels. He taught the people to accept the word and the prophecies. On the Day of Atonement, they had animal sacrifices, and he encouraged them all to pray.

"We are more than Beta Israel and Christians. We're one people. The laws God handed down to Moses were to direct us how to live together. Those laws have not changed. We must obey them in order to live together. We can live as one and respect one another."

***

Many objected to Chaka's authority, and there were a few small rebellions against her, which she squashed. After her victories, she sold the rebels as slaves. She proved herself a great queen. She strengthened the military and expanded foreign trade. The society had become a matriarchal one, with the men responsible for the more important religious structure.

Prosperity helped keep the peace among the people. They had bumper crops, increased their cattle numbers, and traded countless elephant tusks and leopard skins; but the source of the great wealth they accumulated was from a gold mine discovered on the hill where Chaka constructed the palace. She built a courtyard around the shaft and kept it hidden from the Lemba people. Although the people benefited from the treasure, she only trusted men from her tribe of Kush with the location of the gold and as miners.

Herschel was 80 years old when he died in AD 380. His son, Ephrem, who was more orthodox, succeeded him as chief priest. After Chaka's death ten years later, their daughter Abena ruled as queen. Ephrem had two sons. His eldest, Simeon, was crowned king in 425 after Abena died. Ephrem's second son, Yonas, became chief priest.

***

Chapter Twenty

The Stranger and Priscilla

The stranger paused in his story. "And so, dear
Priscilla, from the beginning, when God designated
Aaron to proclaim, protect, and preach His Word,
there was uncertainty, mistakes, and bad judgments from his
priests. Aaron was overwhelmed by the needs and demands
of 600,000 people he was called to lead. He struggled with
the task of satisfying the Israelites and pleasing Jehovah. He
experienced the wrath of God, and from then on, he preached a
message of fear of the Lord. He wasn't able to move past it."

"I feel his pain," I said, taking a sip of wine.

"Then there was his son Eleazar," the stranger said,
ignoring my comment. "He began with enthusiasm, but like
you, he felt he was passed over. He had aspirations of greatness
but had to concede that his son was a better man and braver
priest than he was. Phineas who was fearless in his service to
the Lord, had to bear the responsibility of thousands of lives
lost because of the words that came from his mouth. His was
an awesome burden. The privilege of serving has its pitfalls.
Accept your weaknesses as they did and move on with who
you are."

"My words and actions led to the death of my family and
members of my choir. Believe me; I've suffered for my pride.
I have accepted my weaknesses, and I know that the weight
of that responsibility is too heavy for me to carry. I cannot

compare myself to Aaron, Eleazar, or Phineas; they were all greater leaders than I could ever be. My battle to serve the Lord was not a noble one. Although I was desperate to answer God's calling and preach His word, I must admit, it wasn't my congregation that I wanted to please. It was my father. Maybe I should have worried if God was disappointed with my actions; I might have made some different decisions."

The stranger walked and stood closer at the side of the chaise where he could look me in the face. "The next seven priests were the latter half of the 14 generations from Abraham until the time of King David, the time when the 12 tribes were last reunited. The high priest, Zodak, found himself in the midst of much conflict during the wars. He and his son Azariah had the challenge of serving two masters, both God and their king. There were other temptations that you know well, ambition: wealth, and pride."

"Not much has changed then. Maybe none of us is worthy," I remarked, unenthused.

"In Romans 3:23, Paul wrote, 'For all have sinned and fall short of the glory of God.' Still that doesn't give us the justification to abandon our faith."

"That's not what I'm doing," I replied. "My faith has not wavered. It's my will that has given way. There is no fight left in me."

"Haven't you learned from your story that the fight never ends, it's passed from generation to generation."

The stranger kept staring at me, waiting for me to say something. I had no interest in responding if that's what he was waiting for. Yet his penetrating eyes weakened my resolve.

Finally, I relented. "I ask you again, what does this have to do with me?"

"There is much more to tell," the stranger said, clearing his throat.

"Would you like a glass?" I asked, raising mine in the air. "There seems to be an endless flow of wine in my bottle."

"No, thank you, I'm fine," the mysterious man answered. Then he looked up as if he were thinking intently. When he looked back at me, he said, "As I've told you in the story, Priscilla, the responsibilities for those chosen by God to profess and preach his word has never been minimal. Sometimes the road is paved, but mostly it is rocky."

"I'm so sure," I said, knowing any objection would be a waste of breath.

"So many of those I've spoken about, Shallum and Hilkiah, were tired of fighting against the disobedience, and they, as well as others, became cynical and disillusioned."

"So, I'm not the first to realize when their battle is lost," I said, holding out my glass for more wine.

The stranger poured from the empty bottle and said, "Giving up the fight is not new, Priscilla. Countless others have been discouraged by their lot. Nevertheless, it is God who determines when the battle is ended."

Overwrought, I threw my head back, staring in the night sky. "I ask what Job asked: 'Why give light to those in misery, and life to those who are bitter? They long for death and it won't come. They search for death more eagerly than for hidden treasure. … Why is life given to those with no future?'"

"Job was answered, 'Think how you have instructed many, how you have strengthened feeble hands. Your words have supported those who stumbled; you have strengthened faltering knees. But trouble comes to you and you are discouraged; it strikes you, and you are dismayed.' Job said, 'Though he slay me, yet I will hope in him.'"

I took a large gulp of wine. "I suppose I lack the righteousness of Job."

"If you remember, there was another who questioned his adequacy to serve the Lord. Azariah IV was unable to sway the people to repent. Even his wife pulled against him in his leadership and support of his brother Jeremiah. Imagine how he felt as high priest to stand by helplessly while the Temple was plundered. He had to watch people that he loved suffer. It was the same for his son Seraiah, who watched the destruction of the Temple, and then for his wife, Carmela, who lost her husband and then her younger son, she also felt as if her own death would have been easier."

"Now she is someone I can relate to," I noted sarcastically. "My impression when you first began this story was that you intended to change my mindset of hopelessness. I need to let you know that you aren't succeeding. You've only given me more examples of other folks and their despair."

"No, beloved. What I want you to get is that there are circumstances where it doesn't matter how honorable your intentions are. You can't change your fate. God's will be done."

"I don't question God's will or the punishments He exacts. I yield completely to Him. My issue is that I should not be here. I should be dead."

"Our will is not the Lord's will. Remember Isaiah 55:8, 'For my thoughts are not your thoughts, neither are your ways my ways, saith the Lord.' Yet He provides us with fresh mercies and new beginnings in the midst of our sufferings. That was the purpose of the exile of the people of Israel in Babylon, which marked another 14 generations from the time of David."

"Yes, I remember the part of Jozadak, and his question is another one I ask each day, Why is it my lot to lose those I love?"

"The lesson from Jozadak is that we have to accept our lives are but a season. His stepfather reminded him as I remind you, 'You're no different from anyone else in that matter. Truthfully, you have been highly favored.' Because of his pain, he never allowed himself to feel love and never trusted anyone enough to give them his love, not even his wife. He took his first wife for granted as you did with your husband. His strength was in his ability to move forward."

"That was quite an ambitious journey," I said, dodging his reference to me. I uncrossed my legs to stretch. "What was the point?"

"The point is to keep living, right or wrong, and to have faith. Jozadak had enough faith to step out into the unknown," the stranger said.

"The unknown is sometimes an easier choice than struggling in the predicament you are all too familiar with. Unfortunately, for me there is no fresh start."

"There are always uncharted paths for those who want a new beginning."

"I've already made it clear that I don't want a new life," I said indignantly. "I was happy with the old one."

"Most changes in life are not left up to us. Jozadak's decision was not his. It was placed in his spirit. Deuteronomy

4:27 says, 'The Lord will scatter you among the peoples, and you will be left few in number among the nations where the Lord drives you.'

"Yes, but don't forget his son, who traveled with him. He wanted a fresh start, too, but things didn't work out so great for him."

"Rabin made the mistake that many do, beloved. He destroyed his own happiness, refusing to recognize his blessings. Comparing your successes and failures to another will always leave you feeling empty," he said.

"It's the disappointments of life that leave one empty, if you ask me."

"You are more disappointed in yourself than the Lord will ever be."

"I doubt that. But, anyway, I can sympathize with Rabin. Yes, he was blessed; but from his standpoint, everything came easy to his father."

"That was his perception. It wasn't the truth. Allow the Lord to fill your cup, and never focus on the level in someone else's cup."

"Just keep my glass filled, and get on with your story."

"Can't you see the message in the lives of these priests, Priscilla?" the stranger asked.

"It's all father and sons, mister," I answered, yawning. "That was the problem. I wasn't a son. There's nothing there for me."

"Not true, you were like Tobiah. You walked away from a ministry that your father built and the Lord blessed you with one of your own."

My voice cracked as I spoke. "Tobiah's family prospered; mine perished."

"Your life is not over, precious one. You must remain faithful. God will restore to you that which has been stolen from you."

"Will the hands of time be reversed? That's the only way to save me."

"You have the power to save yourself. You have the courage and faith of Deron, who broke away from his father's status quo position in his worship and ministry."

I grunted. "I feel more like Nathan's wife and the guilt she felt for contributing to her husband's death. She wanted to punish herself, and there was nothing any of them could do to change that."

"Jeremiah 3:22 says, 'Because of the LORD's great love we are not consumed, for his compassions never fail.' If he can forgive you for any wrong you may have done, then you must forgive yourself. Next, forgive your father. It's not easy to shift principles on which you have based your entire life."

"My father was a literal preacher, as many of the priests you have told me about. He refused to accept that religion could change with the times. He preferred the Old Testament."

"That argument is as old as mankind, my dear. The division sparked by the fervor over the Messiah has quieted down, but it has not been silenced. Many treaded the fine line between both sides, avoiding messages about the prophecy and the new covenant.

I looked at my wrist, even though I wasn't wearing my watch. "You've asked me for time to hear your story and I have listened. Don't ask me if I can see myself in these priests. I never wanted to take my daddy's place. I only wanted to serve beside him."

"I know that, beloved," the stranger said. "The lesson for you is that even family can break away from one another. We don't have to think alike to be united."

"My father didn't see it that way. Besides, these priests you've spoken about were not on one accord."

"We're all products of our upbringing and the influences we are surrounded by, my dear. We have to go through hard times to see God's mission for our lives. Keep listening."

"Do I really have a choice, mister?"

"Fortunately, you are my captive audience tonight," the stranger said. "What I've told you is just the first part of your story, Priscilla. Your people traveled thousands of miles over 2,000 years. Beginning from Egypt to Canaan, from Jerusalem to Babylon, from Babylon to Saba, and then to Axum. They struggled against enemies, famine, and corrupt kings. They fought and died for their religious independence, and internal conflicts over the new covenant threatened their survival."

I raised my arms in the air out of frustration and yelled toward the sky. "If we can evolve over time and change our thinking, why do men believe that God wouldn't make adjustments or changes in His directions to us?"

The stranger placed his hand on my shoulder. "God has shown us that He is steadfast and faithful. He keeps His promises, but He also hears our pleas and prayers; and from them He shows us mercy and gives us grace. Sometimes we forget those times when He promised to destroy us but then gave us another chance to live."

"That's the problem with this world," I complained, shaking my head in dismay, "So many pick and choose the words of God that suit them and what they choose to believe."

"Yes, my dear, that is truth. After 70 sevens, or 14 generations, after's Christ's death, the children of Israel were furthered scattered. The story continues in Axum, which is now northern Ethiopia, and the battle over the New Covenant rages on."

www.ingramcontent.com/pod-product-compliance
Lightning Source LLC
Chambersburg PA
CBHW070429170726

48291CB00002B/418